SHE CONQUERS

SHE AWAKENS BOOK 3

CAITLIN DENMAN

Copyright © 2022 by Caitlin Denman

All rights reserved.

No part of this book may be reproduced in any form or by any electronic or mechanical means, including information storage and retrieval systems, without written permission from the author, except for the use of brief quotations in a book review.

❊ Created with Vellum

To Ray

For conquering the unimaginable for eighteen years

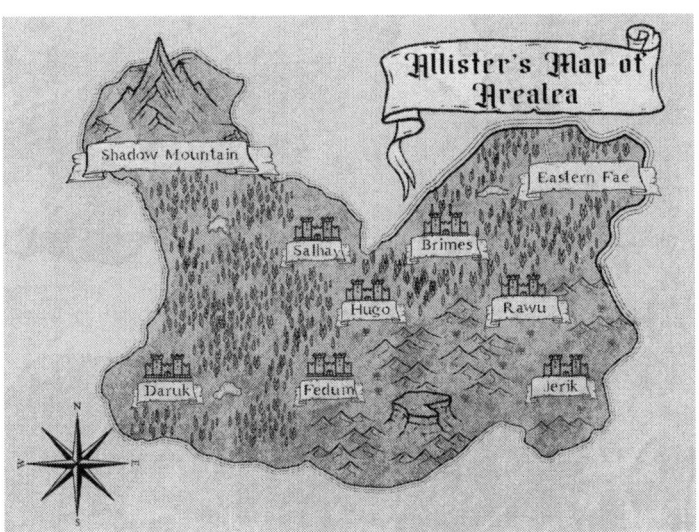

PROLOGUE

I drop my bow and gaze up at the gargantuan owl who calls herself Hazel, lost in the shock and awe her confession brings me.

"You were my grandmother's owl?"

Hazel rolls her amber colored eyes, exactly like a frustrated human would. She curtly says, "I won't repeat myself, Attina." She puffs up her mottled brown feathers on her body, the white throat feathers are striking next to her red mask feathers. Her sharp silver beak gleams in the moonlight with her movement.

I shake my head and walk forward, pushing between Allister and Raven, who've formed a wall in front of me. "I'm confused. You're my grandmother's owl? Why would you want to help me kill Henrik?"

"How do you think your grandmother died?"

"I don't know," I say as I throw my arms up in frustration. "I haven't exactly had the time to contemplate my lineage given what has happened to me lately. I suffered through my Awakening, met my mother for the first time as she killed my father and my mount, I was bitten by not one, but two Solis—"

"I know, I was there. I saw it all."

I turn around and stomp off.

Allister must know where I'm heading because he slides in between me and my bow, his strong arms wrapping around my shoulders. "Attina, stop. You don't want to shoot her."

I glare up at his swirling purple eyes. Red spins around his iris, mixing with blue, and merging into purple. This makes his eyes appear to swirl and dance before me. "Yes, I do." I fling my arm back toward Hazel. "She watched as my mother killed my father and Oak."

Allister pulls me tight to his chest. I fight for a second, but it's half-hearted and we both know it. "She's a bird, Attina. What could she really do?"

I crumble into his sculpted chest; it's firm and yet comforting. His aroma, the smell of a forest right after a rainstorm, fills my nostrils. "I don't know. Maybe she could have scratched her eyes out?" I question meekly.

I hear Hazel in the tree behind me. "Are we done having a meltdown?"

I spin around in Allister's arms. My long brown hair flies around me and I hope the fire and anger I'm feeling can be seen flickering in my aquamarine eyes. "Why would we even want your help? You stood by and idly watched as I went through hell."

"I know things about Henrik no other being in all of Arealea knows."

"Spill it!" I scream.

"No. You're being irrational. You obviously need sleep. Get some rest and I'll be back later." In a flash she spreads her monstrous wings and flies away.

"You should have shot her." Raven turns and locks her piercing gray eyes on mine.

I nod at her. "I might when she returns."

1

ATTINA

I pet Raven's dark blood-like fur and untie my saddlebags, then begin unsaddling her. She's only been my animal companion for a short time, but she's already become my best friend. I don't know how I would have gotten through everything we've been through without her. I pat her neck and as soon as her saddle hits the ground she trots off to a tall green patch of grass and begins happily munching away.

I sit down and start opening up my saddlebags when I hear a voice from behind me. "Don't do that just yet, kitten."

I turn and glance up to Allister's awaiting hand, stretched out toward me. I notice his long black hair framing his face as I answer, "Don't unpack?" I'm confused, but I lift my hand and place it in Allister's anyway. My eyes travel up his arms which are covered in black fighting leathers, to his chiseled jaw, stunning purple eyes, and long black hair. How did I get so lucky to be mated to this gorgeous specimen of a man?

He shakes his head. "I have something to show you."

"Okay..." I say as he lifts my saddle bags and places them

over his shoulder. His black fighting leathers squeak at the movement. My hand still in his, he walks over to the massive tree in the center of the clearing where we've been standing.

Massive isn't the right word for how huge this tree is; it's *gargantuan*. Its trunk is as big as two houses and it reaches up so far I can't see an end to its canopy. As we walk up to the tree, I see its bark. From afar it appeared to be brown like any other generic bark, but up close, it's moving. Grays, browns, and even greens twist through it. I reach my free hand up and tentatively touch the rough surface. My eyes widen as the colors brighten around where my hand makes contact.

From my left Allister says, "Isn't it weird?"

I whirl my head toward Allister. "What is this? I haven't ever seen a tree with such colorful bark and how could it be moving?"

"Honestly, I have no idea. I've never known exactly what this tree is; it's obviously not a normal one." He reaches up and strokes the bark in front of him. "I found this tree as a kid. I've seen other Fae simply walk by it without seeming to notice it. The only other person I've seen here was your mother, Titania. I actually met Titania here, which is how she ended up taking me under her wing. She told me if the tree chose me, then who was she to question it. I still don't know what she meant." He smiles at the tree like he's smiling at the memory. "But anyway, I built a tree house up there." He points up into the canopy. "We'll head up there and make camp, so we don't have to sleep on the hard ground again."

"Awesome! Let me run and tell Raven first!" I shout as I race off to where Raven is still happily munching.

When I get back to Allister he still has a nostalgic smile on his face. "Ready?" he asks.

I nod and we start our ascent. The grooves in the bark are deep enough I can use them as hand holds; my feet even fit in them. It feels like we scale the tree for half an hour before we climb up to a branch. I sit on it and catch my breath. Gazing up, I still don't see a tree house. "How much further?"

Allister looks up, my saddlebags wobbling on his broad shoulder. I don't know how he's lugging those heavy things up here. The only indication he's tiring is his heavy breathing, but he's trying to hide it by taking slow, even breaths. "I haven't been here in at least a decade, I don't remember, but obviously I was in much better shape back then."

I slowly scan him up and down. *I don't think such a thing's possible.*

Allister's head snaps to me, a sly smile creeping up his face.

My face heats. "Ummm, I didn't mean for you to hear that." I almost lose my grip on the tree as my foot falls out of the nook I had it in. Even from where he climbs I can hear Allister take in a sharp breath at my mistake. But I easily right myself. All those years in trees searching for game finally paying off.

"You good?" Allister asks.

"Mmhm," I say, grateful he didn't freak out like James did every time I made a mistake while we were out hunting.

He chuckles. "You'll get used to other people hearing your thoughts. It'll get easier to shield them. I'll teach you like I taught my men."

I nod as we continue up the tree.

It takes us another hour with a few more breaks in between before we make it to the tree house. However, I'm not sure house is the right term. He's built a vast floor between a few equally massive branches, but there are no walls. "You built this all by yourself?"

Allister smiles proudly. "Took me a year to bring up all this lumber."

"Wow," I say as I spin around taking in the meek yet homey surroundings.

A mattress sits in the middle of the floor which is three times the size of the one I grew up sleeping on. Covering it is a mound of plush blankets and two lumps which must be pillows. I don't see a fireplace which makes sense being in a tree. It would be dangerous to light a fire here. The pile of blankets must be for the wintertime. He even built matching nightstands next to the bed. There are no sconces for lights up here, but the nightstands have candle lit lamps on them.

Curiously there is only half a roof covering the area, just enough to protect the bed and keep a small area dry in case of rain. Above, the branches are situated so I can see the moon and stars, making the area feel open and welcoming. To my right is something which appears to be like the elevator in Sanctuary. I walk over to it, then place my hand on the thick branch attached to the floor. It arches up and half of it hangs out over the open air.

"That's the boom," he says from behind me. Allister walks past me on my right and kneels down, caressing the platform which I now realize is attached to the boom by a thick rope.

"It's how I got all this lumber up here." He puts down my saddlebags and strides over to the contraption. "You simply push the boom out." I watch as he does just that, and then a platform slides out and hangs over the open air next to the tree. "See, you just take this rope tied to the floor and ease the platform down." He pulls the rope up and down to show me how it works. "When I was coming here often, I would leave this at the bottom and use it to get in and out of the tree house instead of climbing up and down all the time. We'll need to reinforce this before we use it though, I haven't been here in years, and I don't trust it with our weight. I have a few supplies hidden under a floorboard, and I think I left some extra rope in there."

"Sounds good." I walk over to the bed and sit down.

Hey, you all right?

I peek up at him as he strides over to where I sit. He stands in front of me, and I drop my head. *I'm beyond emotionally exhausted. It's been a hell of a ride so far and I don't see it calming down anytime soon.*

He kneels in front of me, his piercing eyes on me as his hands cover my knees. Seeing him before me like this, so vulnerable, makes my stomach do a flip. "Well, how about I air out these blankets for you. All this dust probably wouldn't be awfully comfortable," he says with a chuckle. "Then we can get some rest. I'll sleep on your bedroll on the floor, and you can have the bed."

I cover his hand with mine and our hands heat where they meet. "Thank you, Allister. I really appreciate every single thing you've done for me, even if your motives weren't the best to begin with. I've been able to count on you without fail."

"Of course, princess." He bows, well as much as one can when already in a sitting position.

Allister stands and I move over to the saddlebags. While he airs out the blankets, I unpack my bedroll.

It's not long until we're both in our respective beds. Neither of us had the energy to change which means I'm still in my last pair of gray sweats I brought from Sanctuary. Allister takes his fighting leathers off, leaving him in only a black tunic. Before long I'm hearing Allister's loud rhythmic snores. I'm always surprised at how soothing the sound is.

I open my eyes. Gazing around in the darkness I see trees with houses sprinkled around me. I know these trees; I would know them anywhere. I grew up in them. I'm back in Daruk.

But this can't be right.

Last I remember I was sleeping in Allister's tree house.

Out of the darkness, James springs on top of me. I fall back hard onto the forest floor, the air leaving my lungs in a huff.

His face is mere inches from mine, his brown eyes sparkling in rage. "You are mine. You will not leave me for that Fae."

"This isn't real," I mumble.

James grabs hard onto my arms. His nails digging into my shoulders, the pain making me wince. "Yes, it is!" He cocks his arm back. I try to bring my hands up to block my face but his knees pin down my arms. He punches me in the face, his knuckles scratching into my skin like razors. "You will acknowledge me!" He pulls back and punches me again and I taste blood in my mouth.

I turn my head and spit blood onto the ground. The warm liquid pours down into my eye and my eyebrow throbs; he must have split it. "No."

James hits me again.

But I don't fight it this time.

Instead I bend my wrist and reach to my side. In an attempt to wake myself from this terrible dream I grab hold of a chunk of skin. I pinch and twist my skin until I cry out in pain.

I sit up in bed. My eyes quickly adjust to the darkness around me. Worried I woke Allister, I clamber to the bottom of the bed and peek over at him. He's peacefully snoring. I sigh. I must not have screamed this time, I guess that's progress.

I crawl out of bed and pad over to where he's sleeping on my bedroll. I kneel down, put my hand on his arm, shake him, and whisper, "Hey. Wake up."

Surprisingly he shakes awake right away and sits up straight, his hand immediately wrapping around his sword lying next to him on the floor.

"It's fine; it's just me."

He turns and blankly gazes at me. "Attina?" He shakes his head and scans the darkness around him, taking the little he can see into view like he's only now waking up from whatever dream he was having. "What's wrong? Are you all right?" His eyes meet mine.

I smile sadly. "I'm fine. I just had a night terror."

He brings his hands up to either side of my face. "You did? You woke up on your own?" His eyebrows lift before he smirks sweetly. "I'm proud of you. Is there anything I can do?"

"You're proud of me?"

"Yes! That's a big deal! It took me years to get to the point where I could wake myself up without help."

"Will you tell me what happened to give you night terrors someday?" I ask.

"Of course. But not tonight." His answer brings a warmth to my chest. I know how scary sharing your deep, dark secrets with someone can be. Then he asks, "Is there anything I can do for you?" His eyes search mine.

I beam. "Can you come to bed with me and cuddle?"

Allister's eyes turn into saucers and his face brightens. "I never thought you'd ask me to hop into bed with you!" He shoots up and around me so fast I have to lean back to get out of his way.

I chuckle and shout behind me. "Just to cuddle!"

"Yeah, yeah, come on. Get in here." I twist around and see he's already in bed, holding up the blankets, waiting for me to join him.

I laugh. "A little eager, are we?"

His eyes narrow and he lifts his chin while he lets the covers drop "Fine. Then I will simply have to cuddle myself." Then he crosses his arms and shifts down on his side.

I roll my eyes. "Oh my goodness, Mister Dramatic." I cross the room and crawl under the blanket, lying flat on my back. "I'm here."

He's quiet.

"Ugh." I roll over on my side and scoot over to him so my front is right up against his back. I wrap my arm around his middle.

We lie there for a minute before he says, "That's better."

"I didn't know you could be this pouty."

He rolls over to face me. "I feel comfortable enough to be my silly self around you." His hand reaches up to caress my cheek. "I can't be like this around anyone else; it's refreshing."

My face heats and I flip over so my back is turned to him. "I'm glad you feel comfortable around me."

Allister sits up slightly, leans over me, and places a soft kiss on my cheek. "Get some rest."

He wraps his arm around me, making me feel completely safe as I breathe in his scent. "Goodnight."

THE NEXT MORNING we wake up as the sun crests the horizon shooting sunlight into the tree house. Allister gets up out of bed, his back muscles pulling tight against his tunic.

I hear in my head, *You can touch me, you don't have to stare.*

I flush. *I don't know what you're talking about.*

He says out loud, "Yeah, okay, sure, pal."

We get up and Allister wrenches up a floorboard. Underneath, I see tools and a cord of rope. He pulls out the rope, and hands me a screwdriver, and a wrench. I help him as he replaces the old rope which brings the platform from his tree house down to the forest floor. It takes us a while, but we get everything replaced, put the tools away, and recover the floorboard.

Allister glances sideways at me. "So, want to be the first one to try out our handiwork?" I merely shake my head and he chuckles. "Don't trust me yet?"

"I do, but I don't trust me," I grumble, annoyed he would think I don't trust him.

Allister swings the boom and platform out past the tree house floor. I draw in a sharp breath as he jumps onto it, but thankfully the platform holds. He grabs one of the four ropes attached to the platform which holds it flat, and he kicks one leg in front of the other, resting his foot on its toe. It makes him seem confident and almost smug. His hands shoot out in an arching motion which encompasses the whole platform, "See! We make a great team." He winks at me.

I shake my head and jump over to the platform. "Anyway, what are we going to do today?"

He snickers. "I figured I'd take it easy on you today."

2

ATTINA

I find out taking it easy on me means we don't work on my magic, instead we work on sparring. How Allister thinks this is easy is beyond me. I'm seriously getting tired of having my ass handed to me continuously. First with my father, then Ned, and now Allister? Will I ever be skilled enough to not have to train like this over and over? I know to become an accomplished warrior you have to train day in and day out, but I thought I'd be further along by now.

"First, we're going to work on how to breathe properly."

"You think I don't know how to breathe?" I scoff.

"I know you know how to breathe, but I can also tell you're not breathing correctly."

I place a hand on my hip. "How does someone," I lift my hands in the air and mimic quotes, "breathe correctly'?"

"You have to breathe from your core. You're shallow breathing in your chest right now. I want you to breathe all the way down into your belly and wait until your lungs completely fill up before you exhale."

I roll my eyes but focus on my breathing and try to do as he says. I'm embarrassed when I understand exactly what he means. We stand there and deep breathe repeatedly until I don't have to focus on my breathing to do it correctly.

"Now we need to work on your balance."

I want to roll my eyes again, but I don't, I nod instead.

Allister cocks his head and raises his eyebrows. "No smart remark?"

I shake my head. "I actually want to tell you I've been riding horses since I was a baby which means I have great balance." I shrug my shoulders. "But you were right about the breathing thing so hey, maybe you're right about this one too."

He grabs his chin. "Huh, maybe there is hope for you yet." I can see a sparkle in his eyes like he's trying to get under my skin, but I don't let him.

I take a step forward and smack his shoulder. "Shut up. Come on. Teach me."

"All right, all right. But only because you begged." My mouth drops open, and it takes me a moment before I start to say something, but he cuts me off. "You are a wonderful rider. You're balanced and agile with four legs under you but when you only have two legs under you—there's a problem."

I can't even argue because I know he's right. I have two left feet when I'm not in the saddle. "So how do I fix it?"

"You need to continue to breathe like I taught you and then I want you to stand with your feet aligned with your shoulders." I align my feet and shoulders. "Okay, now I want you to move your weight back and forth on your feet. Take your weight completely on one foot, balance, and then move to the other foot." I do it until my thighs start to burn. "Do you feel how grounded you are now?"

"Yes, I think so."

"Good. Now I want you to move one foot out in front of

you." I walk forward like I normally would, picking up my feet as I move. "No, I want you to take your foot off the ground as little as possible. Walk in a sweeping motion, gracefully."

"I don't do graceful," I snarl. This is seriously getting annoying.

"I know you don't, but please try."

"Fine, but only because you said please." He brings his hand out in a sweeping gesture signaling for me to go. I barely bring my foot up and sweep it out in front of me.

"Nice. Now with this next step, I want you to take slower." He repeats, "Only move your weight to the foot in front when you've completely put your foot down on the ground. Always have one foot completely grounded. It will stabilize you."

I feel so stupid doing this. It's like I'm learning to walk all over again. But as I move and do as he says, I feel myself become more stable than I've ever felt before. I'm lost in my motions, and I don't realize Allister has walked up to my side until he pushes my shoulder. I waiver but don't fall.

He smirks. "Okay, good. We can work with this. You can take a break."

I turn my head to him, grateful for his words. While I haven't been doing much, my legs are killing me. It's like I'm using muscles I haven't used before.

Raven lies on the ground by the base of the tree, her black mane and tail glistening in the sunlight. She has her side pushed up against the tree which allows her to sit up and watch us. She must have eaten most of the night because her stomach is a little bloated and I've noticed she keeps dozing off as she lies there. I make my way over to where we left our weapons and a bottle of Restore. I take a sip out of the bottle and then walk over to Raven, sit down, and lean back against her midsection.

"So, how's the tree house?"

"It's surprisingly spacious. He did an amazing job. I'm shocked how handy he is." And I mean it. I'm impressed by how well he constructed the tree house. It was definitely a labor of love.

"I was stunned to see you drop down on that contraption today." She angles her head to where the platform sits.

"Me, too." I chuckle. I'm not afraid of heights but getting on the platform today made my stomach do a flip.

She nudges me and almost wiggles her eyebrows as she asks, "What were the sleeping arrangements like?"

"He slept on the floor...most of the night." I feel dumb for having him sleep on the floor in the first place. I know I'm getting better at handling my night terrors but why risk it when Allister was right there on the floor at the foot of the bed. I slept so peacefully after he came to bed, and I seriously needed the sleep.

She flings her head around to gape at me. "*What!*"

Thankfully, Allister waves at me from the other end of the clearing right before I hear him in my head, *Time's up. Get back out here.* I rush out, "Sorry, Raven, that's my cue," as I jump up and trot off.

I hear a snorting noise behind me, and I peek back at Raven. She yells, "You're doing a great job girl!"

I almost trip but the earth under me moves and I'm righted. My eyes bulge. How is this possible? I didn't even think to catch myself. My powers must instinctively be taking care of me still. How cool!

I plaster a huge grin on my face and when I make my way to Allister his hand is on his hip and his eyebrows are pinched. "I saw you. Are you seriously *that* clumsy? Even after all our practice?"

I roll my eyes. "Shut up. I'll get there. Give me a few more days and I'll be floating on air."

He scoffs. "I'll believe it when I see it."

I ignore his smartass remark. "So, what's next?"

We spar for a few hours, and I'm surprised to see I'm pretty much able to keep up with Allister's speed. He's still a smidge faster than me. But when I comment on it, Allister says it's only because he's trained to be a fighter his whole life. I'm still in the awkward learning stage.

Then we work on takedowns. Although I can keep up with Allister he still wants to show me a few things. He says a girl's center of gravity is lower which will make it easier for me to get my opponent on the ground in hand-to-hand combat, which gives me an advantage. As we practice, I see what he means, but I lose each time as soon as I get him on the ground. No matter what I try he still easily outmuscles me.

I drag myself up off the ground and take a fighting stance with one fist next to my chest and another out in front of my face. My feet are perpendicular to my shoulders with my knees bent. I wait patiently for Allister to pull himself off the ground. I'm incredibly frustrated but I don't want to let him see it. I bite my tongue trying to keep the tears back. I hate this about myself. Anytime I get frustrated I start crying. It makes me feel so weak.

Instead of getting up, Allister lies back on the ground, places his hands behind his head, and stretches out. "All right, beating you has lost all its fun now." He turns his head toward me, and I drop my hands to my side. "You truly don't know how to use your body to your advantage do you?"

"I'm not about to grind against you to distract you. That

won't work for everyone." I cross my arms across my chest and jut my hip out.

He blurts out in a belly laugh. "Yes it would, because I would find you and murder your opponent."

"Haha, very funny," I say snottily.

He rubs the palm of his hand across his eyes like he's wiping back a tear from laughing too hard. "Women's strength is in their lower body. Men's is in their upper body. While I'm much stronger than you are," he lifts his head as his eyes drift slowly down to my legs like he's eating up the picture in front of him, "there's no way I can out muscle those legs of yours."

I drop my arms again, frustrated. "Then show me what to do. If you knew I couldn't beat you the way you're teaching me now, why did you waste your time?"

"To *show you*, you couldn't beat me."

I roll my eyes and stalk toward him, closing the distance between us. I stop as soon as I'm standing above him, "Well, then get up and let's—" I don't get to finish my sentence as Allister spins on his back and kicks my feet out from under me. I brace for an impact which doesn't happen.

The earth cradles me as I hit the ground, making it feel like I landed on a pile of pillows.

"Hey! Not fair! The ground caught you." Allister pouts when I sit up and turn to him.

"Jealous much?" I smirk at him and cock my head. I'm not even mad he caught me off guard. I should have been paying more attention.

He rolls his eyes as he scoots over next to me. All too quickly and quietly, he says, "No." I know he's lying by his tone. "Okay now," he says in his regular tone. "I want you to grab my arm with both of yours." He holds his arm up perpendicular to the ground. I do as he says. "Now wrap your legs around my arm and across my chest." I give him an, it isn't funny look by narrowing my eyes at him and crossing my arms over my chest. He shakes his head. "It's not sexual, just do it."

I shrug my shoulders but oblige. I have his arm between my legs and I'm leaning back with my feet over his chest.

"Now lean back and lift your hips."

I do and almost instantly I feel a tap on my leg, the signal we use to tell the other person they give up. I immediately sit up, my eyes wide in shock.

"See how easy that was?"

"You really gave up so quickly? You're not only saying that?"

"Yeah, you don't have to put much pressure on someone's arm like that to break it. Oh, and another small tidbit of information, it barely takes any power to break someone's knee. Simply kick the knee from the front and their leg is useless."

"Hmm, good to know! Show me more please."

He chuckles. "Yes, my princess," he says and bows his head, making me blush.

He spins up into a kneeling position facing me. "Trust me?"

I nod with one eyebrow cocked. I'm confused why he'd ask such a thing. But then he takes his hands and pushes on my shoulders, pushing me down to the ground as he slowly crawls over me.

I take a sharp breath of air and my body tenses. The motion reminding me of a night terror I had where James did the same type of thing.

Allister must notice how stiff I get because he says, "It's okay. I won't hurt you. However, a man might try to pin you down and I want you to know how to get out of it alive." I relax a little as understanding floods me.

My gaze slides over his body hovering over me and it's like a switch flips in me. I'm instantly not scared anymore. A heat burns in my belly as my eyes rove over his muscled body. I slowly bring my gaze up to his face, his hair falling down toward me. He slyly smiles. *Like what you see?*

Yes, I nod my head slowly, entranced by his heated stare. His eyes glaze over as he slowly leans down, and I breathe him in. The smell of a rainstorm permeates the air. I tilt my head to glance down at his lips.

The movement pulls him out of his trance, and he jerks back. "Right, so um—I'm the enemy and I have you pinned." His voice is a little huskier than normal.

I push past the knot in my stomach and say, "Got it." As the words leave my lips I realize my voice is raspy like his. I wonder if our interaction is twisting his emotions up like it's doing to mine. He makes me feel so nervously excited.

"Now, I have total control over you—or I think I do." He takes in a huff of air, like he's steadying himself before he continues. "Now, bring your hands together and take one of them and grab your other wrist."

I do as he says.

"Now, I'm not stabilized on either side so I want you to lift your hips as high as you can and roll me."

I grunt and, using all of my power and concentration, roll him fast and hard. He goes flying over onto his back and the momentum throws me on top of him. Now I'm sitting on top of him with his arms above his head.

"Nice job." His voice is sultry as his eyes roam over me sitting on top of his stomach.

I can feel the embarrassment rising and my cheeks begin to heat. I feel like a fire is igniting in me. But instead of letting him see it, I swoop down and plant a quick kiss on his cheek. I lean back and see his eyes are opened wide in shock.

"Thank you for teaching me all of this, can you teach me some more?" I stand up.

He quietly nods.

"Man, if I knew that was the quiet button on you I would have pecked you on the cheek a lot sooner." I laugh as I feel confidence bursting inside of me. I didn't realize I could affect him this much. I reach out my hand and help him to his feet.

"I'll teach you anything you want, kitten," he says as he wiggles his eyebrows.

3

ATTINA

Allister works with me day in and day out on my breathing, keeping my balance, and spars with me. We work incredibly hard every day. By bedtime I barely have the forethought to take a deep gulp from the Restore bottle to keep myself from being sore the next day. I don't even have the strength to pull my boots off before falling into bed and drifting off to sleep. I don't have any night terrors either. I'm not sure if it's because I'm exhausted or because Allister sleeps next to me every night.

Waking up every day in his arms is peaceful.

I especially enjoy the days when I wake up before him. When I can lay there and take in his masculine form without him making some kind of snarky comment. I'd normally feel weird watching someone while they sleep but I've caught him doing it to me plenty of times. This is just payback.

I've also been working on my magic during breaks. Allister hasn't offered to help me with my magic, and I haven't asked. Honestly, I'm scared to try to figure out fire and water, so I don't even try. I'm scared because what if I can't call to water or fire? If I fail what would it mean? If I try and fail will my powers leak out more? Could I accidently hurt somebody with them?

As the days pass, controlling earth and wind gets easier. As I work, I notice myself becoming more graceful. I hardly fall anymore. Even when Allister and I spar and he knocks me to the ground, the earth cradles me, protecting me from any real damage.

"You know that's not fair, right?" Allister says as I pick myself up off the ground where he wrapped me into a chokehold, and I tapped out.

"What's not?" I answer.

"You don't even have any bruises. Bruises are like a rite of passage when you're learning to fight, and you get them from being thrown on the ground *hard*. The earth just keeps catching you. It's not fair. Even when I throw you off balance the wind pushes you back upright."

I smirk, tilting my head, and lifting my shoulder. "It's not my fault I have powers. You have powers too, remember."

He slowly nods. "Yes, I do." A devilish smile crawls across his face. "I have a proposition for you."

"Oh?"

"You're becoming one helluva fighter. How about we have one more fight for today?"

"Ooookay?" I say skeptically; it's only mid-day. Why would we end training already?

"We can both use our powers, and the winner gets to ask one thing of the other person." I quickly jerk my head and take a step back. He quickly adds, "Nothing sexual."

I deliberate it for a second, but I can't come up with a reason not to agree so I shove my hand at him. "Deal." Even with my previous reaction, I'm surprised to find I'm disappointed he took anything sexual off the table. It almost feels like a hit to my ego. I know I'm being ridiculous, but I can't help it.

He reaches his hand out and shakes mine.

We move back a fair distance from each other, and I lift my hands into fists. *You ready?* I hear his words in my mind, and I wink in reply.

We rush at each other, my speed matching his. He throws a fist toward my face, and I duck at the last moment. I turn and will the earth to pop up under his feet. He goes flying, but of course, he gracefully rolls as he hits the ground.

He gets up and spins back toward me. I run back at him and will the wind to push me from behind so I'm running faster than he is. When I get close, I slide on the ground and throw my leg out, knocking Allister's feet out from under him. He falls forwards but as I continue sliding, I feel cold as I see ice forming under me.

"What the?" I keep sliding and put my feet out and try to get traction to stop but I can't. I reach out for the earth to break up the ice but it's too late. I slam hard into the big tree in the middle of the clearing, hitting the whole right side of my body hard against its magical bark. The bark might be mesmerizing, but it hurts as badly as any regular tree when I make contact. All the air leaves my lungs and I bend over gasping for oxygen.

Before I realize he's walked over to me, Allister is by my side rubbing circles on my back. "You're all right Attina, just breathe."

While I continue to stare at the ground, I lift my hand up and smack his hand away. "*What the hell!*" I yell.

He lifts his hands up and a relaxed smile crosses his face, like he's pleased. "I told you we were using our powers."

I turn my head, my eyes turning to slits. "You didn't tell me you could control water!"

A devilish grin spreads across his face. "You never asked. Remember when you woke up after being bit by the Solis and you were covered in water? I did that."

I sit up and lean my back against the tree. "So, everyone knew except me?" I suddenly feel betrayed. I know it wasn't anyone else's secret to tell but seriously? Ned and Raven didn't bother to tell me either? "I didn't keep it from you intentionally. We've been going through a lot."

I put my finger up and lock eyes with him. "Oh no. You don't get to give me that bullshit answer. You can control water. One of the elements I can't, and you don't bother to tell me? That's not okay and you know it."

His gaze drops to the ground for a second before he bends down, allowing him to lock eyes with me. "You're right and I'm sorry. I shouldn't have kept it from you. I won't keep anything from you again. It was unfair and childish of me." He lifts his hand and places it on my cheek so softly and tenderly. I forget for a split second I'm mad at him. I turn my cheek into his hand and allow him to caress me.

We lock eyes again but this time it feels like lightning arcs between us, pulling us toward each other. I lean into him. I reach my hand up and place my hand on his cheek, mirroring his hand. I turn his head and wrap my hand around his head and pull his face down to my lips, placing a soft kiss on his cheek.

When I pull back I see his eyes are as wide as saucers.

"Well, isn't this charming," I hear from above us.

Allister jumps up and runs over to where our swords are leaning against the tree. He grabs his sword, then pulls it out of its sheath and at the ready. Raven even runs over from where she was taking a nap on the other side of the clearing.

"Hazel?" I question as I use the tree to slowly push myself up off the ground. I gaze up and see her perched on the same branch she was on the first time we met. Apparently later, to Hazel meant not coming back for days.

She cocks her head. "He lies to you about his powers, and you kiss him on the cheek? Maybe I was wrong about you."

"He's her mate, bird," Raven almost growls.

I'm surprised to see Hazel's eyes actually grow as she glances between me and Allister. "*He's* the future king?" Even from this distance I see her roll her eyes. "The Fae are screwed."

"Listen here, you overgrown chicken—" Allister spits out.

I lift my hand and cut him off. "Where have you been?"

"I was letting you cool off and gathering more intel."

"Intel?"

Hazel shakes her head. "We can talk about it later. From what I heard you can't use some of your powers? I saw you move the earth and use wind. You can't control water; is there something else you can't control yet?"

My cheeks heat. I gaze over to Allister and Raven, and they jointly nod their heads at me before their eyes latch back on Hazel. In my head I ask Allister *Do you trust her? She could be a spy.*

I don't think so. I've heard Henrik's late wife had an owl. People said her companion animal was an owl because she was uncommonly wise. When your grandmother died there were rumors Henrik killed his wife because she was incredibly loved by their people, and he was threatened by her. After her death her owl disappeared and was never seen or heard from again. I believe her.

I gaze back up at Hazel. "I can't control fire or water."

She glides down from her perch and lands on the ground in front of me. "What about your magical animal?"

I tell her the story of the serpent attacking my blackbird. "I only felt the bird one other time, when he," I point my thumb over at Allister, "almost died. I felt a flash of panic, but only a flash."

She's quiet for a second. "Well, you're still using your powers which means it must still be alive."

My mouth drops open. "You mean magical animals can die? What happens when they die?" I shout.

"You can't use your powers anymore," she says nonchalantly, like it's no big deal. "You haven't felt your bird lately though?"

I shake my head.

"Have you tried investigating your mother's hideout inside the tree?"

It's only then I remember what Oak told me. This tree would only open for my mother. How had I forgotten such a crucial detail? "Do you know how to get inside?"

Hazel cocks her head and says, "How would I know," right before she flies off. She doesn't say anything else, so who knows when she'll show back up next.

THE REST of the day is spent searching all around the tree and climbing up and down it at various points to try to find an opening. I ask Allister, "You never saw a door?"

He shakes his head. "You didn't seem too shocked when Hazel mentioned the hideout."

I point to Raven who's trotting bigger and bigger circles around the tree. It sounds easy but one pass around the tree takes her what feels like ten minutes to complete. "Her father was my mother's mount before he was mine. He told me this tree used to open up to my mother, but he didn't tell me how. She even got this necklace from the tree." I lift the rose necklace my mother left me. "At the time I simply assumed the tree was magic and chose her. When we got here I'd completely forgotten about the story."

He huffs. "I've been coming here most of my life and I never knew there was a hideout inside it. Why didn't Titania show me?"

I shrug my shoulders and look around. "It's getting dark, maybe we should head up."

"Yeah, you're probably right."

I whistle and Raven trots over to me. "Why don't you get some rest girl? We're gonna head up to bed."

She nods and says, "Goodnight, girl," before trotting off to her spot on the other side of the clearing where she can lie down on top of some thick, luscious grass.

Allister lays his arm over my shoulders. "Between the three of us, we'll figure it out."

I gaze around. "Did you ever see Hazel after we talked?"

His mouth droops and he shakes his head.

"Ugh what is her deal? She shows up, talks to us for five minutes, and disappears? I hope she's not gone for a week this time."

We make it to the spot where we left our swords and Allister grabs for his. I bop him in the hip with mine playfully and he stumbles forward, knocking my sword down. It slides partway out of its sheath and all of a sudden I see a blue glow.

"What the?" My eyes bulge. How is this possible? The runes on my sword are glowing! "Raven, come here!"

She shouts, "What's wrong!" I hear her hooves hitting the ground and almost instantly she's at my side as Allister bends down and picks up my sword, letting the sheath drop to the ground.

The runes on the face of my sword, which used to be black, now pulses with blue light. I stare at the sword for a minute before peering up at Allister. He asks, "Has it ever done this before?"

I shake my head. "No."

He holds his chin. "Moonlight reveals all shadows. Huh. I wonder what that means."

I glance over at Raven. "It must have something to do with this tree. Father told me that's what the runes said, but he didn't know why. It must be some message."

Raven still stares at the sword as she says, "I wish Oak or Ned were here. They might know what it means."

I stare at the sword. I wish they were here too; things would have been a lot easier if they were still around. I walk over and take the sword from Allister. "What if this is some kind of clue?"

I slowly make my way around the tree, intending to pace and think, but as I move, I notice the pulsing of the blue glow on the runes intensifies. I stop and back up. Immediately the pulsing lessens. *Huh. Interesting.*

How did you know it would react like that?

I turn around and lock eyes with Allister, *I didn't.*

I turn back around and continue making my way around the tree. I make it halfway around the tree before the glow stops pulsating and it turns into a solid buzz. I face the tree and scan its bark. All the colors dancing around on it almost makes me miss the small glowing blue circle, about chest level to me.

"Do you guys see this?" I point to the small spot in front of me. Then press my fingers into the indentation in the bark.

"It's about the same size as your necklace," Raven says from behind me.

"What?" I spin around and grab onto the rose in bloom necklace my mother left to me.

"I've stared at your necklace our whole lives. Remember, I didn't used to think much of you, and I never thought you deserved to wear something which used to be your mother's. I've stared at it enough to know how big it is. I think it might fit in the indentation."

My mouth drops open, "You're right! Oak told me Titania got this necklace from this tree." I reach behind my neck and carefully unlatch my necklace. I hate taking it off, what if I drop it and can't find it until morning or I lose it all together? I can't think of a time I ever took my necklace off outside of my room back in Daruk.

I quickly glance at Allister, but he seems to be in quiet shock. My breathing becomes labored as I carefully and gently push the face of my necklace into the indentation in the tree's bark.

To my right, a door quickly swings open, and light pours out of the doorway.

4

ATTINA

I want to run into the room, but I can't leave my necklace, so I yank it out of the tree's bark first. Allister reaches over and takes it from my hands. I lift my hair and turn my back to him so he can hook it back on.

We move as a unit over to the door. It's big enough even Raven can fit through.

My skin tingles and my gut drops as I take in the space in front of me. My mother's space. The room is as massive as the tree itself. Sconces dot the circular room but they're not like any sconces I've seen before. There are no candles in them, but a fire still bounces inside them. Have these been lit since the last time my mother was in here? I mean that's not possible; it must have been decades since my mother was here, but maybe with magic it could be? My eyes take in the edges of the room, where more books than I could read in my lifetime, line the walls all the way up the tree further than I can see. A huge rolling ladder leans against one side of the room.

I walk into the middle of the room where a massive bed sits, the purple bedding rumpled and dusty. At the end of the bed sits a desk with papers piled high on top of it. I sit down at the desk and the bed has a permanent indent in it, like my mother sat on the bed at the desk, for what must have been hours on end. I pick up a pile of the dust covered papers and blow the dust off of them which causes Raven, who's made her way over to me, to sneeze.

I absentmindedly say, "Bless you" before staring down at the paper. I'm disappointed to see all her writings are in Fae runes. I know it's her writings because Father still had a love note she wrote to him framed in his room. Even though the alphabet is different, the flow of the runes is the same as her letter to Father and the letter she left to me before she let our family forever.

"You read the runes on my sword, can you read this?" I turn and fix my eyes on Allister.

He steps forward and I hand him the paper. "This one has to do with the costs of having my family stay in Shadow Mountain." He hands me back the paper.

"So, she would come here and do work?"

"Seems like it."

I sit and stare at the papers. "Why would she bring her work all the way out here instead of simply working in Shadow Mountain?" Then a yawn escapes my mouth I hadn't realized was coming.

"I don't know but why don't we get you to bed? You're exhausted." Allister says as he walks over and rubs my back.

"I can't go to sleep now. Look at everything we just found. There has to be some kind of answers here!" I want answers more than anything right now, any sort of answer to anything. It would be better than stumbling around blindly like we have been.

Raven says, "He's right, girl. You have dark circles under your eyes. This room sat here for decades; it'll last a few more hours and you're no good to anyone when you're overtired."

"We can sleep here tonight if you'd rather," Allister offers.

I shake my head. "No, this is all a little overwhelming anyway. I'd rather sleep at our place tonight." There's too much of my mother in here.

A sweet smile crosses his features and his eyes sparkle as he bows his head. "As you wish."

We all walk out of the room, and I pat Raven on the neck. "I'll see you in the morning, girl."

She pushes me with her baby doll head. "Get some rest."

"I won't keep her up too late," Allister says from behind me.

Raven's head jerks toward him, her eyes turning to slits as she cocks her head at him. "You're smarter than you look, I'll give you that. If you weren't standing behind her right now I'd kick you."

Allister wraps his arms around me, and I can hear the smirk in his words. "Goodnight, Raven."

I seductively run my hand down the arm wrapped across my chest, throwing him off guard. I hear him take a rough breath and I quickly latch onto his arm with both my hands and fling myself forward, throwing my butt out, and flipping him over top of me. He hits the ground with a loud thud and Raven's foot is instantly on top of him, squashing him in place.

He gapes up to me. "Well, that was rude."

I shrug my shoulders as I glare down at him. "You might be my mate, but she's my mount and you wanted to play dumb games. If you want to play dumb games then you get to suffer the consequences."

He then gawks up at Raven. "I feel like we've done this before." I shake my head; he never learns.

"And you obviously didn't learn the first time." She pushes down with her foot.

Allister lifts his hands and wheezes out, "Okay. Okay. I'll try to stop messing around as much."

Raven removes her hoof and lifts her chin in a superior gesture. "That's all I want."

She steps over to me and rubs her head on my chest. I wrap my arms around it and say, "Goodnight girl."

She takes a step back, says, "Nighty night," and trots off into the darkness.

Allister pushes himself up off the ground and stares down at me. The intensity in his eyes pins me to the spot and heat pools in my gut. His voice has a husky tone to it as he says, "Well I guess I know where I stand when it comes to the three of us."

I shrug, trying to act like his stare doesn't affect me in the least. "Well she is my mount."

He takes a step forward, forcing me to lift my head to peer into his eyes and our breaths mingle. "And I am your mate. You were made for me, and I was made for you. I can feel you even when we're not together. You are my forever." His voice turns sweetly dark.

My stomach plummets with his confession as nervousness spreads through me. "Ye... yes you are," I stumble out, not sure what else to say. I'm surprised he can feel me even when we're not together. Why I can't feel him? What must such a thing be like?

He reaches forward and gently grabs my hand. "Come on, let's get going." I silently nod, a heat pooling in my stomach. I grab up my sword and we walk hand and hand, around the tree, to the platform. Allister pulls down on the pulley and the platform speedily climbs the tree.

By the time we make it back to the tree house, Allister has a slight glisten covering his brow from the exertion of pulling us up. He ties off the rope and we move into the room. The air around us is charged. We've been sleeping next to each other for over a week now, but something feels different now.

I grab one of Allister's old shirts I found in the nightstand, off the bed and walk behind a curtain I hung this morning in the corner of the room to give me some privacy to change. I quickly change out of my sweats and by the time I get out, Allister has changed into a clean gray tunic. I hurry across the floor and slip under the covers. I quickly reach my hand under the pillow and feel the dagger Ned gave me, still where I left it. I know I probably don't need it up here, but it's comforting to have a weapon by my side at all times.

I prefer to sleep on my side, so I turn away from Allister's side of the bed. I feel the bed move from the weight of him sitting on it. He blows out the candle in the lamp and darkness fills the room. The bed moves again as he lies down. My body goes loose and taut at the same time. Heat rises to my cheeks, and my breathing hitches expectantly in apprehension.

I hear Allister's husky voice behind me. "Can we cuddle?"

I don't answer him. I just wiggle my body back over to his side of the bed and he wraps his thick, corded arm around my stomach, pulling me the rest of the way over. He sits up a little and threads his arm under my head so I can use him as a pillow.

My back hits his hard, warm, chiseled chest and my

body loosens automatically. As I try to get comfortable my butt inches back an inch and I accidentally move his considerable, hard length against my backside. I shoot forward as I suck in a breath, and I hear Allister do the same. I feel myself break into a sweat in embarrassment. I meekly get out, "Sorry," and throw my hands up over my face.

Allister's arm tightens over me. He answers, "I'm not," as he leans over me and kisses my cheek. I turn to face him, not realizing he's leaning in for another kiss on my cheek and our lips touch. It's just like the time we kissed after he almost died. The fire is still there but it burns hotter this time. I feel as if a bolt of lightning burns throughout my body; first my face, then my chest, all the way to my core.

I turn further and wrap my arm around the back of his head, pulling him harder into me. I hear and feel him moan into my lips and his body goes limp onto mine. His tongue moves against my lips, begging for an invite inside. I open my mouth and when our tongues touch it feels like a flame igniting in my mouth.

I pull back in shock and put my hand over my mouth.

"What's wrong?" Allister says into the darkness. I hear the shock in his voice. "Did I do something wrong?"

I take my hand off of my mouth and place it on his cheek. "No you did nothing, it's—" I'm cut off before I can finish though as the moonlight illuminates a big puff of smoke as it rises from my mouth. I see Allister's head as it moves following the puff.

"What was that?" he asks in awe.

"I don't know. It felt like a flame ignited when our tongues touched. That's why I pulled back."

In the moonlight I can see his eyes widen into saucers. "Last time I was in the throne room with Henrik he spit out this lava flame stuff and it melted the ground in front of me.

I wonder if you can do it too!" He's obviously excited about this turn of events but I'm not. I feel like a freak all over again.

"I'm sorry; I'm so embarrassed." I cover my face again and push my forehead into his chest.

Allister hooks my chin and lifts my face to his as he pulls my hands down from my face, locking eyes with me. "Hey, you don't have to be sorry or embarrassed."

"Yes I do. We were kissing and I turned into a human chimney. It's embarrassing."

He holds my hands in his and squeezes them. "No it's not. It's really freaking cool!"

I chuckle. "You're just being nice."

"No I'm not. My mate is so turned on by me her body literally started a fire! You know how many people can say the same thing?"

"I don't know."

"I'm willing to guess zero because Henrik is the only person I've seen able to spit fire. He shakes my hands. "And hey, we will figure this out together. For how worthless Hazel's been thus far I have a feeling the stupid bird will be able to help us. And tomorrow I will search through all of your mother's papers, maybe there's something in there which can help us figure all of this out."

"All right." I whimper as I stare down at his chest. I hate myself for how sad the words come out.

He cups my face with one of his hands and pushes my face up so he can lock eyes with me. "And until then, I can wait. I can keep my hands to myself until we can figure out your powers and you're comfortable with this."

I smile. "I am comfortable with you though, I hope you know that."

"I do now. But the smoke obviously spooked you and I

want our first time together to be perfect. I don't want you worried about what could happen if you lose control of your powers if something did happen between us."

I nervously grab at my mother's necklace. "Thank you for understanding. I honestly didn't think about that, but I could never forgive myself if I hurt you; even on accident."

Allister brings his hand down and turns until he's flat on his back, dragging me with him so my head lays where his chest and shoulder meet. "Of course, kitten. I'll always have your best interest at heart. Forever."

The word scares me. Forever is an awfully long time, but it doesn't scare me in the way I thought it would. It frightens me in the sense of what if my lifespan isn't as long as his lifespan? What if he outlives me? I try to push it from my mind though, no sense in worrying about something we may not figure out until we live it.

But then it feels like a bucket of cold water is thrown over me as my mind races to my parents. My mother fell in love with my father knowing she wouldn't get a forever with him. A human life must feel insanely insignificant compared to a Fae life. I decide I need to talk to Allister about something.

I ask into the night because I don't think I can look Allister in the face while we talk about this. "Allister. Can I talk to you about something?"

He tugs me in closer to him. "Yes of course, always."

"Just please let me get this out before you say anything. Can you do that?" I feel his chin nodding against my head, urging me to continue. "It's about my mother. I know you and her had a great relationship," I place my hand on his chest, "and I'm truly happy you did. *But* I didn't have the same relationship with her. She gave birth to me and then disappeared. My father was both my father and my mother.

I didn't meet Titania until my Awakening when she was killing my father and Oak. I hate her. I know you won't like hearing it but it's true. She took all the people I adored from me. I know you want to tell me more about her but in my mind I killed a crazy monster, not a person. If you start telling me things about her, then she becomes a person. I don't think I could handle it if the crazy woman from before became my mother in my mind. Does that make sense?"

His hand reaches over and cups my chin, pulling my face up to meet his intense gaze. When our eyes meet, tears instantly fill my eyes. His gaze always lays me bare, it's truly loving and I can almost *see* the hurt he feels for me there. "I understand completely. We don't have to talk about her until you're ready. But when you are ready I'd absolutely love to tell you all about her. She was like a mother to me growing up and it would make me incredibly happy to share my memories of her with you." He brings his lips down and lightly kisses my lips before bringing his forehead down to mine. "Whatever you need, I'm here for you."

Tears run down my face as I settle back onto his chest I whisper, "Thank you" into the night. I take in a deep, calming breath. "Goodnight, Allister."

"Goodnight, Attina."

5

NED

THANK THE GODS I WAS ABLE TO MAKE IT BACK TO SANCTUARY long before James. Mylo is a much bigger and faster horse than the one James brought along. Besides, from what I saw when he rode away, he didn't appear to be a particularly adept rider. From the little I've gleaned from Attina, he's a much better hunter than rider.

I took a more direct route than the one we took to search for supplies. I bet James only knew the route on which he followed us, and I was right. After unsaddling and feeding Mylo, I head over to Commander Demarco's office. I stride past his young secretary, Sarah's desk.

Her short, cropped hair bobs against her gray sweats. She stands up and walks right along with me as she hurriedly asks, "Um, do you have an appointment with Commander Demarco?" She tries to stop me, but my steps are too long for her to keep up even a short distance.

I make it to the door with a silver plaque in the middle which says, "Commander John Demarco." Waving her away with my hand, I throw a glance at her dull brown eyes. "No but this can't wait." I put my hand on the doorknob before she has a chance to grab it and push my way past her.

John is sitting hunched over at his enormous desk reading some papers. I notice although he wears the same gray ensemble everyone here wears, his massive shoulders pull the fabric of his sweatshirt tight. Behind me, I hear Sarah's meek voice. "I'm sorry, Commander. He barged right past me."

He finally gazes up from his papers and pulls the reading glasses he wears down off of his face. "It's fine, Sarah. I doubt you would have been able to stop him anyway. When he's determined he's damn near impossible to reason with." His gaze shifts to me and turns to a glare. It's so slight that unless I knew him as well as I do I wouldn't have caught it. His eyes shift back to Sarah. "You're dismissed."

She bows and backs out the door, closing it behind her.

I gaze down at the glasses in his hands. We really are getting older; he didn't need glasses to read before. John folds them up and quickly puts them in the drawer to his right, obviously embarrassed by them. He clears his throat and focuses on straightening his papers as he says, "Well, where is that girl of yours?"

"*Attina,*" I emphasize, "is still out searching for supplies."

His fierce green eyes dart up to meet mine and his face scrunches up in confusion, "What do you mean? Why are you here then?"

I take in a deep steadying breath. I need to tip toe over this the right way. I need to get him on my side before James gets here and throws a wrench into our plans. "It's a long story, John, but the gist of it is there's something mentally wrong with James. He's obsessed and seeing things."

John shakes his head and says, "What? Start from the

beginning." I do as he asks and start with the night before we left on our mission. When I'm done telling him how he assaulted Attina, John's face has become a little ashen. "And I sent him after you guys. I played right into his hands."

"Don't blame yourself you didn't know what happened and you were told there was a sighting of a Fae around us. I understand why you did what you did." I make my way over to one of the chairs in front of his desk, taking a seat. Then I tell him how he caught up to us and tried to forcibly drag Attina back to Sanctuary.

I leave out Allister and how she used her magic to defend herself and instead say, "Thank goodness I taught her to fight. By the time we got too far on our journey she had become such a skilled warrior she was able to fend him off. When he gets here you'll see a big shiner on his face, Attina put it there." So I bent the truth a little, she was the one to kick his ass, Allister only helped a bit.

His mouth falls open and he sits up a little straighter. "Good for her."

I continue. "When he left he said he would come back here and tell you we were consorting with the Fae. He wants you to start a war with the Fae, all to get Attina back."

His eyes narrow, "Well, why didn't you bring Attina back here where she would be safe? Why did you leave her out there? Didn't you realize he could have simply turned around and gone back to her after you left?" His hand goes up to grab his chin between his fingers. "Besides, why would you leave her out there on her own?"

"She's perfectly capable of being out on her own. If you remember, she made it all the way from Daruk here on her own."

His brow furrows and his hands clench. "Still, something doesn't seem right."

Fuck.

We talk for hours in circles but eventually I get him to see things my way. He's a lot more likely to believe James is crazy than to believe I could be disloyal him. I hate to betray him, but this is the only way to bring peace to the world. John is too quick to start a fight, and the humans would be massacred by the Fae if they went to war against each other —whether he can see it or not.

6

JAMES

When I make it back to Sanctuary, Ned already has his claws dug deep Into Commander Demarco. Sarah told me he's twisted the story around. According to him, I came out, attacked them both with no provocation, and then left to bring back some made up story to the Commander. Ned then chased after me, leaving Attina out in the world to continue searching for supplies. She told me he said I was crazily flipping out about some Fae and attacked Attina.

What a crock of shit.

Attina is mine and she ran off with that Fae. She must be brainwashed by him. Their mission to take down the Fae king will get us all killed. I know it. She needs to be *forced* to return and never allowed to leave again.

I'm to have a meeting with Commander Demarco tomorrow to see what he wants to do with me, but I'm not worried about it. I will sway him to my way of thinking. He's a man and all men can be manipulated; you only need to find the right bait.

And I know just the bait to use.

7
ATTINA

THE NEXT MORNING WE DRESS AND HEAD DOWN THE TREE. Raven is already standing next to where the door opens when Allister and I make it around the tree. I don't even unlatch my necklace this time, I simply lean my face up next to the colorful bark and place my rose pendant in the keyhole.

Just like last night, the door opens, and we all walk in.

The rest of the day is spent scouring the gigantic room. Allister sits on the bed and pours over the mountain of papers covering it since he is the only one of the three of us who can read Fae runes. Raven and I search the rest of the room, but pretty much come up empty.

Before I get frustrated I decide to make myself useful. I walk over to Allister and put my hand on his shoulder. He lifts his head for a split second before putting his nose back into the paper he was reading.

"I'm taking Raven to go for a hunt. We'll be back in a few hours."

He waves me off. "Fine, sounds good I'll see you then."

Well that was more abrupt than I expected. I huff and

stomp out the door calling over my shoulder, "Let's head out, Raven."

I get outside and trudge over to the other side of the tree, by the platform, where my bow, sword, and Raven's saddle were left. Raven trots up to my side. "You all right? What happened?"

I shake my head. "It's nothing, I'm probably being overly sensitive."

I throw her saddle on her back and tighten her cinch. Then I buckle my sword to my hips and throw my bow across my back before climbing into the saddle. "You ready to go hunt?"

"Always."

We walk in silence. I'm too lost in thought to talk to Raven. I feel like last night Allister and I really connected, but when Raven and I left, he seemed flippant, like he didn't care.

Raven shakes her body under me, knocking me out of my reverie. "Hey, did you hear me, kid?"

I shake my head, clearing it. "No, what did you say?"

"What's happening between you two? Is everything okay? Do I need to kill him?"

I sigh. "I think so?" I proceed to explain what happened last night. Making sure not to leave out a single detail. "I felt like we had a breakthrough between us last night, but when we left just now, I felt like he blew me off. I'm confused. Maybe I'm making too much of it." I scan the scenery around us. "This is probably a good spot to stop."

Raven stops by a tree and I stand up on top of the saddle. I grab hold of a branch and lift myself up into the tree. Below me I hear a voice say, "So I guess this means we're done talking about it?"

I sit down on the branch and peer down at her. "I don't

even know how I feel or what's happening at the moment, so maybe later? When I've collected my thoughts, if that's all right?"

She nods, "Of course." She scans the area around us. "I'll head out and hide a little deeper into the forest. Yell if you need me."

"I will. Be careful, it's always possible for Solis to be roaming the woods." Raven grunts in affirmation and starts walking off but before she gets out of ear reach I call after her, "Thank you for always being someone I can count on."

Raven turns her head but continues walking. "I'll be by your side forever." She makes her way through some trees, and I lose sight of her.

I continue climbing up the branches until I'm tucked into a spot where I'm hidden between branches and leaves. I get into a comfortable position, wiggling my butt down onto the branch and pulling my bow off of my back. I nock an arrow and lean back on to the tree trunk.

Taking a deep breath, I close my eyes and feel the world around me. I still have to concentrate when I use my powers. I hope one day it'll be second nature for me, and I won't have to think about using them, but that isn't the case yet. I feel the air touching my skin. The wind brushing over the leaves. The roots spidering down deep through the earth's floor around me. All the other tree's roots around me intermingling in places.

I reach my senses out further. I feel what must be rabbits, by how daintily but quickly they move, scuttling around a den. I dig deeper into my powers and feel four split hooves, pushing down on the ground not far off.

A deer.

I push a gust of wind behind the deer which urges it forward while also pulling my scent, which would spook the animal, away from it. The animal takes a tentative step forward and then starts confidently striding toward me.

I pull the string on my bow back, with the arrow between my fingers, and let the string sit on the side of my lip. I freeze in position as I wait for the deer to walk through the tree line close enough that I can loose an arrow into it.

The minutes tick by but eventually the animal pokes its head through the trees. Its head is up and alert. Its ears move back and forth along with its head, constantly on the lookout for a predator. I push another gust behind it, urging it forward a little closer. I take a deep breath in, planning to release the arrow after my next exhale, between breaths.

But I can't.

This isn't hunting; it's shooting fish in a barrel.

I felt the deer when it was impossibly far off. I pushed the deer to me with my magic and I kept the deer from smelling my scent. It didn't have a chance.

I huff out loudly and the deer slices its head up staring into the tree I'm sitting in. I lower my bow and it must see the movement because it gazes directly where I'm sitting, turns and runs off.

Thank goodness.

But as the deer turns and races off between some trees, two pheasants pop out of the brush, flying up, trying to flee the chaos. I quickly re-aim my arrow and shoot one. I see it fall down in my peripherals as I nock another arrow and let it loose. The arrow hits the second bird right before it could fly up into the canopy and away from my line of sight.

"Hey, Raven, get over here!" I shout as I crawl down the tree and stride over to where the pheasants landed.

One has an arrow poking out of its eye and the other has a huge hole ripping right through its chest. The birds would be brilliantly beautiful if it wasn't for the blood staining their feathers. They have blue heads with red masks; both have a white band around their throats which leads into a purple chest. Their wings and back however are brown with speckles dotted throughout, perfect for hunkering down and blending in.

"I thought you wanted to get a deer?" Raven questions beside me.

I turn my head to her. "I did." I bend down, pick up the birds and wrench the arrow out of one's eye. I scan around the immediate area, but my other arrow is nowhere to be found—great. Now I only have one arrow left. I used all my special Fae arrows, which were made out of Fae hawk feathers, and shot faster and truer, on those Fae slayers back in Rawu. And I've lost arrows along our journey off and on, I guess I need to sit down and make some arrows. "I was able to get a deer to come to me with my magic. But it didn't feel fair. The deer didn't have a chance. I didn't know I would care about it having a fighting chance against me, but apparently I do. We're not starving, and I don't have a town full of people to feed, I couldn't bring myself to kill it."

"What about those?" she asks as she peers down at the birds in my hand. "They couldn't have had any more of a chance than the deer did."

"Actually, I didn't even know they were here. I never felt them. I guess I overlooked them. I spooked the deer, and it took off. When it spooked, it also spooked these guys up." I lift the birds, "They had a fighting chance, I didn't feel bad shooting them. It felt like more of an even playing field."

She nods her head and stares me straight in the eyes, no judgment coating her features, only understanding. "Okay, I think I get it." She moves forward, allowing me to put my foot in the stirrup. I lay the bodies on her neck in front of the saddle for a second while I heft myself up and over into the saddle.

We make it back to the clearing and I hop off of Raven, I put the birds on the ground, and unsaddle her. I stride over to the clearing where the fire pit, we use for cooking, sits, and take a seat.

Raven follows me and lies down behind me so I can lean against her. "You're not going to tell Allister we're back?"

I shake my head. "No. First I want to get dinner cooked and then I'll get him."

She doesn't say anything in response. She simply tucks her head down between her legs and I feel her breathes even out as she falls into a deep sleep. I quietly sit and start plucking feathers. Plucking any bird by hand always takes longer than you think it will and by the time I'm done yanking, my arms are sore. I stand up and grab some firewood we collected after our first day here and start a fire.

I truly thought starting a fire was easy when I was a child. When I would camp with Father he always made it seem exceedingly easy—it's not. By the time I finally get the fire started and the birds turning on the spit, the sun is starting to set. I cook the birds until the outside is golden brown.

It's probably horrible etiquette, but I take my dagger from my boot and cut through each bird to make sure they're cooked all the way through. When I see they're cooked through, I remove them from the fire. Leaving them by the fire I make my way over to my mother's secret room where I know Allister still sits, staring at those papers.

"I'm gonna head to bed. After dinner you should too," Raven calls behind me.

I turn around. "I will, goodnight Raven."

"Goodnight," she says and turns and trots off.

I walk inside, Allister is still sitting at the desk, papers in hand. I walk over to him and clear my throat. "I caught some pheasants and cooked them, want to eat?"

He slowly turns his head to me; his eyes are wide in shock and his mouth hangs open. *"What's wrong, are you all right?"* I shout.

"You won't believe what I just read."

"What?" I say with less urgency in my voice.

He says slower, "You won't believe what I just read."

I roll my eyes and cross my arms, putting all my weight on one foot and jutting my hip out in annoyance. "I heard you the first time."

He bursts up out of his sitting position on the bed and rushes over to me, wrapping his arms around me, picking me up, and falling on the bed on top of me. I want to giggle but I train my face into stone. He searches my eyes for a second before laughing out, "You beautiful, frightening thing."

My arms are still crossed in front of my chest and I'm glad for it because if they weren't trapped there, I would wrap my arms around this beautiful man and get lost in the moment. As things are now I can focus, okay that's a lie. How in the world could I focus with such a gorgeous, tightly muscled man on top of me? My eyes stray over as much of his body as they can with how we're situated on top of each other and a sly grin crawls across his face.

I wiggle underneath him. "No, I'm still annoyed with you!"

He pulls back and his eyes bulge in shock, "You're annoyed with me? Why?"

My face sags and I focus on a spot on Allister's chest. "You were short with me when I left to go hunt, like you didn't even care."

His hand leaves my waist and cups my chin, lifting it. His eyes are soft, no playfulness left in them. "I'm sorry, I was engrossed in what I was reading, but it's no excuse for making you feel like I didn't care. I do care. I will always care." He gently leans down and places a soft kiss on my cheek.

My cheeks heat and warmth spreads in my gut. I clear my throat, "Um... what were you so excited about a second ago?" I slowly sit up and he tenderly moves off of me. We sit up facing each other on the bed. He rubs the back of his neck, and I can feel tension in the air between us. "Was it that bad?"

His hands lace through mine, holding them as our eyes lock, "No! No it wasn't bad at all. It's actually wonderful news."

I prod. "Well then?"

"Titania was doing research on how to take her father down." He smirks, puffs his chest out and you can hear the pride in his voice as he says, "I knew she wasn't only some obedient dog."

My mouth drops open. "Well, did she find anything?"

"She found a prophecy written by our ancestors thousands and thousands of years ago. The prophecy tells of an all powerful king who far surpasses his predecessors. A king who *could* conquer all of Arealea."

"Could?"

Allister smirks. "Could. If he rules from a place of love he will be unrivaled. If he rules out of a thirst for power he can be struck down."

"Well, we know which path he chose."

A sly smile cracks his face. "We do, but there's more."

My eyebrows perk up. "Oh?"

"According to this prophecy, the one to take him down will be a child born of his people and his enemy."

My eyebrows raise in shock and my chest instantly gets tight, making it hard to breath. "Wh...wait it actually says that?" My head spins back and forth between Allister and the desk he'd been sitting at. "You're not bullshitting me are you?"

He chuckles. "Is it so hard to believe?"

I vigorously nod. "Yes!"

"Why? What's so weird about this?"

I grumble. "Have you read any human books...like ever?"

He shakes his head, sarcasm drips from his words as he says "No. I can't say I have. Surprisingly, being ruled and living under the same roof as someone who's mortal enemies with humans didn't give me much time to read their books or become familiar with their ways."

I take my hand from his and push him in the shoulder, knocking him backwards onto the bed. "Fine, good point." He sits up grinning and opens his mouth like he has some retort, but before he can say anything I continue. "This is all like some fairytale. I was just some girl who took care of her hometown by hunting." I stare at the desk, disbelief over what's happening flooding over me. "Then one day I'm told I'm not completely human, I'm part Fae, and a princess of all things!"

But you're pretty I hear in my mind. I turn to him. His face is bright and happiness exudes off of him.

I send him a withering glare. *Not funny.*

Then aloud, I continue. "And now there's some random prophecy saying I'll be the one to take Henrik down?"

He gleefully nods. How can he do this? One minute he's a smart, calculating warrior, and the next he's an over the top goofball.

From behind me I hear a voice say, "That's not all of the prophecy."

I spin in my seat, shocked to see Hazel standing on the ground in the doorway. "What the hell?"

She cocks her head. "Did you think I wasn't coming back?" Her eyes focus on Allister. "I heard what you said, but that isn't all of the prophecy."

8

JAMES

I make my way down to the lowest level of Sanctuary. As I stride past Commander Demarco's secretary, Sarah, I wink at her. My eyes prowl over her body like I'm noticing how well it fills out her sweats. She's proved useful at gathering intel and I might need to use her again; I need to stay in her good graces.

I lift my chin and steel my spine as I push through the door to Commander Demarco's office. I'm surprised to see Ned standing behind Demarco's desk, right next to the wingback chair which holds Demarco's hulking body. But I keep the surprise out of my features and paste on a lazy smile.

"You summoned me, sir?" I say as I place my hands behind my back and quickly bow.

"Yes, we have some things to talk about." He crosses his thick arms over the massive desk in front of him. "I sent you out after Ned and Attina to check on what was transpiring. We had reports there was a Fae in the area and I was concerned for their safety."

Liar, you sent me after them, thinking they were taking off with the Fae. I think this to myself, but I keep my mouth shut.

"And now Ned comes back and tells me you attacked them? What the hell's all this about? Explain yourself."

I take in a deep steadying breath. I want to lunge at Ned, wrap my arm around his throat, and watch as the life drains out of his eyes. But there's time enough for that later. I'll bide my time—for now.

"There *was* a Fae, sir." Demarco's head turns to Ned. "There was a Fae, and Attina is with the Fae right now." I see his eyes widen.

Ned screeches. "Bullshit! You're obsessed with her. You've attacked her twice."

It feels like a slap to the face. Anger rises from the pit of my stomach, but I don't let it overtake me. These men stand between me and Attina. I must get to her and break her free of that Fae's hold. So, for now, I just ignore him and wait for the Commander to say something.

"Is what he says true?"

"I will admit I slapped her, but it was a personal matter between Attina and me. It has no bearing on what I'm saying now. She is with a Fae and Ned knows it. I'm scared she is brainwashed by him. I'm not sure why he," I point to Ned, "thinks this is all right. Maybe he's already told the Fae where Sanctuary is."

"I would never!" Ned shouts as blood rushes to his face.

Commander Demarco slices his head to Ned, anger crossing his features. "I'm honestly not sure who to believe. There are sentries who said they saw a Fae leave with you and Attina." He then turns back to me. "I also know you're obsessed with the girl. But why you're obsessed is beyond me." He throws his massive bear-like hands up in the air. "She's not at all special." Anger floods me but I take deep breaths, calming myself. His hand lifts to his cup his chin. "Hmm, what to do."

We all sit there in silence for a minute before I offer, "I've been thinking about this and I have an idea, if you'd like to hear it, Commander."

His eyes dart to mine and hold my gaze for a beat, "Okay, let's hear it."

"Let's you and I go find her. I'll show you she is with a Fae, and we can kill him together. With the Fae dead, Sanctuary and our people will be safe."

He closes his eyes and sits there unmoving, for what feels like ages before he says, "Fine, we'll head out and take a peek."

Ned stares down at him, throwing his hand out toward me and shouts, "You're not seriously about to believe this boy are you? He's out of his mind!"

Commander Demarco slowly turns his gaze to Ned, his eyes turning to slits. "There's enough truth to his story. I'm inclined to believe him. He's also calm, cool, and collected whereas you're a flustered mess."

"But—" Ned starts but Demarco lifts his hand, cutting him off.

"Besides with your," he looks Ned up and down, "predilection, I wouldn't be surprised if something like this happened."

Ned takes a step back and lifts his hand to his chest as his mouth drops open. His eyes turn to slits. "After all these years? That's how you really feel?"

Commander Demarco sits there, cold as stone, and stares down Ned.

"Fine." Ned continues, "All I ask then is you take me with you." He crosses his arms over his chest, "I think with all the battles we've been in together and all the years we've been, what I thought was friends, earns me the right."

The Commander's eyes soften."Fine, we'll leave tomorrow at dawn."

Good, let Ned come. It'll be easier for me to kill him out in the open. I place my hands back behind my back and bow. My eyes shift back and forth between Ned and Demarco and I calmly state, "I'll see you both in the morning."

I spin on my heel and leave the room, closing the door behind me. I hear arguing as I leave but I don't eavesdrop. I've spread enough doubt between them that whatever Ned says won't change what's about to happen. We're heading out there, we will find Attina, and I will kill that Fae monster and anyone else who dares to get in my way.

As I pass Sarah's desk, I throw her a wink and watch as her cheeks redden.

9
―――
NED

AFTER LEAVING JOHN'S OFFICE, I MAKE MY WAY TO MY ROOM. I decide to check on Mylo one more time before turning in for the night. I veer down the aisle his stall is on and almost run smack into someone.

I rear back. "Oh I'm sorry. I didn't mean to—"

"Where's Attina?" he spouts out. Now I notice his gray hair is tousled like he's been nervously running his hands through it. His eyes stare me down expectantly.

"Nathan right?" I ask because I'm not sure who he is. I know he works for me in the livestock level, and I remember Attina talking to him before she left, but other than those basic things, I really don't know the man in front of me.

He eagerly nods and shoves his hand out for me to shake. "I'm sorry, of course you don't know who I am. I'm Nathan. I was a town leader in Attina's hometown with her father. I've known Attina most of her life. I think of her as a daughter I never had."

My eyes widen at his admission. He must truly care about her to spill this much information this quickly. I reach out and shake his hand. "Hello, Nathan. I'm Ned." I take a step back and put my hands behind my back, assuring he can't see as I fiddle nervously with my fingers. I'm not sure how much to divulge to this man, I need to be careful with what I say. "I'm curious why didn't you ask James? He's also from Daruk and I'm sure you knew he followed us."

Nathan leans on the stall next to him. "Attina told me what happened between the two of them before she left, and I honestly don't want to deal with him. You seemed to be close with her and you left with her, so I figured you were a safer bet to find out what happened to her anyway."

I incline my head. "*Attina,* is fine." I tell him about what happened with James, how he followed us, and what transpired when he found us. Nathan's eyes grow with each word. Although, I don't know if he knows about Attina being half-Fae. I don't want to be the one to break the news to him if he doesn't, so I leave that part out of my story.

When I finish, Nathan stares down at his feet and rubs the back of his head. "I seriously can't believe how obsessed James has become with her. They were childhood friends back in Daruk. They spent every day together. I'd hoped they would end up together one day, but he's completely jumped off the deep end. So, she's still out searching for supplies? Are you sure that was a good idea? She's all alone. What if she stumbles across a Solis?"

I stop myself from chuckling. If he only knew how capable our girl is now. Instead I say, "I taught her self-defense daily while we were out there. I'm sure you know how capable she is with a bow, and she's quickly become equally as capable with a sword." I take a step forward and place a comforting hand on his shoulder. "She can take care of herself. I promise."

Tears fill his eyes, surprising me. "I'm sorry. I'm just incredibly proud of her."

I take a step forward and wrap him in a hug. I don't care that I barely know this man, he obviously cares about Attina, and it seems like he misses her more than I realized. "You and her father did a great job raising her."

"Thank you," he whispers into my shoulder.

When we've finished talking and Nathan leaves I finally make it over to Mylo's stall. He hangs his head out of it and waits for me. He probably heard us talking and wanted to see what the commotion was about.

I lift my hand and as I pet his big head I let out a huff, "Well, seems like James outsmarted me this time. I guess I know what I have to do now, boy."

10

ATTINA

Allister shoots up to his feet. "Then what is all of the prophecy? It sounds like you know already."

She shakes her brown, speckled head. "I've only heard it spoken of once in my life. When it was read to your grandmother I was there, but neither of us took it particularly seriously. Henrik was a different man back then. He wasn't always this tyrant, you know."

Allister throws up his arms. "Great!" He steps back to the desk, sitting back down. "Looks like more searching for me then."

I stand up and cross the small space over to Allister. I lay my hand across his shoulders. "It's late. Why don't we leave the rest of this for tomorrow?" I gesture with my hand to encompass the table and its pile of papers. "I killed us a couple of pheasants for dinner," I remind him. "Let's eat and head to bed." At first I think he's ignoring me again, but then he reaches his hand up to my arm and brings it around to his front. His hand slides down my arm and he kisses the back of my hand.

"Yes, my queen." He turns to me. His eyes are sultry. And I can see fire dancing in them.

I turn back to Hazel as she says, "I'd like to talk to you privately."

I shake my head. "No, it's been a long day. We can talk in the morning. Right now all I want is some food and a nice warm bed."

Her eyes dart from me to Allister and she scoffs before flying off into the night.

"Well, she's rude," Allister says next to me.

I turn, grab his hand, and lead him out the door. "Who cares, I'm going to try to not let that bird get to me." The door closes silently behind us.

Right before we make it to the fire, and our dinner, Allister spins me around. My body flies into his awaiting arms. He picks me up and walks us to a log we've placed by the fire and sits down with me in his lap, "You're amazing you know that?" My eyes dart away from him, and I nervously shake my head, all off the sudden feeling extreme self-doubt. "Well, you are, and I will tell you how amazing you are over and over until you see it for yourself."

I dip my head in embarrassment, staring at his chest, and meekly squeak out, "Thank you."

He reaches between us and cups my chin, pulling my face up so he can lock his gaze on me. "I mean it. You truly amaze me. You're astoundingly tough and self reliant. Sometimes I forget how unsure of yourself you are. But I will be here every single day for the rest of our lives to remind you constantly how amazing you are." My eyes tear up. I'm not sure what I did to deserve someone so supportive and sweet. "Also, it helps being as gorgeous as you are." His hand gently caresses my face and I lean my head down into his touch.

When he pulls his hand away I find I don't want to lose contact with him.

I wrap my arms around his neck and pull him to me, pressing his head into my chest. The light of the fire dances off of his dark silken hair as I run one of my hands through it. He almost melts into me as I whisper, "Thank you." He leans back and peers into my eyes, the shadow of my body making the blue in his eyes pop, and stares at me like he's staring at the most precious thing in the world.

I lean forward and gently place my lips against his and the electricity which always runs through us tickles my lips, making me moan. The sound of my moan makes Allister grab his hands tightly around me, pulling me into his hardened body. I move my arms from around his neck to cup his face as he picks me up and we're moving. I'm not sure where he's taking me, but I don't really care. I would follow this man to the end of the world.

Our lips move over each other's, and I feel each step as his body scrapes against mine. Everywhere our bodies touch is like fire being breathed into life. I open my eyes for a split second and see my arms are turning red from the fire dancing under my skin.

He pushes me up against the tree, the abrasive bark scratches down my back, making me hiss. Allister ignores my sounds though as he runs one of his hands from my butt, up my torso, and cups my breast. I lean back against the tree pushing my chest forward, further into his hand. He kisses down my neck, but I can't help myself as I release a yawn. Allister stops moving and gazes up at me with hooded eyes. I don't think he's going to say anything for a moment, but then he breaks out in a chuckle. He drops his head down to my chest and takes a heavy sigh.

"You must be exhausted. I should get you to bed. You've had one helluva day."

I grab either side of his head and pull him away slightly. I feel a drop in my gut and my chest tightens. He's over me already? What did I do wrong? I'm sure the hurt is plain on my features. "You don't want me?"

He lets me slip down the tree a bit and thrusts his hips forward into me allowing me to feel his arousal against my hip. "You seriously think I don't want you, kitten?" He drops his forehead down on mine. "I do, more than you obviously know. But I want to take the best care of you I possibly can, which right now means I need to get you some dinner and get you to bed."

I drop my head and purse my lips, but in the same moment a louder yawn leaves them. I sheepishly peek up at him and he's got his head cocked and his eyebrow lifted, the look he's giving me makes his face seem like it's saying I told you so. I find it extremely unflattering.

"Fine. Let's head to bed." I move my legs down out of his grasp, plop down on the ground. After he adjusts his pants a little, he grabs my hand and I allow him to guide me to the platform which will take us to our tree house and our warm bed. Before he pulls up though, he races over to the fire where our dinner waits. He douses the fire with his magic and grabs up the pheasants. I guess we'll be eating in bed tonight.

THE NEXT MORNING Allister and I are sparring while Raven sunbathes when Hazel finally shows up.

"Let's go for a walk." She spreads her enormous wings and circles above me.

"Okay. Let me get my sword. Will you grab Raven?"

I lock eyes with Allister as I hear him in my head. *If you need me just tell me here.*

How far away can you hear me?

His eyes become hooded and sultry. *Kitten, I could hear you from across the entire continent.*

My eyes go wide, and I gasp. "Really?"

Before he has a chance to answer I hear Raven walking up behind me, then from above us I hear Hazel. "Are you two done?"

He answers out loud. "Yes, I'll head in to decipher some more of your mother's papers." But Allister's eyes move up to where she's flying and turn to slits. *I still think she'd make a tasty dinner.*

I laugh out loud and turn on my heel. I know Allister watches after me and I make sure to swing my hips a little extra as I stride over to Raven.

"What's so funny?" Hazel asks, but I ignore her.

I walk over to the tree where Allister and my weapons are leaning. Allister yanks me into him and plants a swift kiss on my lips that leaves me reeling. I collect myself, lean down, and grab my sword. In preparation for whatever we're about to do I decide to down the last bit of Restore I have left from Sanctuary. I then walk over to Raven. "Wanna head out on a walk with us?"

She turns her side to me. "Hop on. Let's go."

Growing up I would ride Oak without a saddle all the time, but it's been a while since I've ridden bareback, this will be fun. I grab onto her mane and throw my leg up. But instead of landing on her back like I thought I would, I end up on the other side of her.

I hear Allister snigger right before Hazel snips above me, "For god's sake." I can hear the exasperation in her voice.

Raven chuckles. "Not used to your Fae strength yet are you?"

"I thought I was." I try again and this time I end up with my butt on Raven's back and my sword hanging down my side. I lean down and pet her neck. "Thanks for being patient." She bows her head, and we turn and ride off. Before we make it to the tree line I remember something and turn around. "Hey Allister!" I shout.

He turns from where he was walking around the tree and faces me. I pull my necklace over my head, "You might need this!" I chuck the necklace harder than I mean to and it flies *way* over his head. Luckily it hits the tree, or I probably would have lost the necklace forever. When it hits, it smacks almost all the way up to the first branch of the gargantuan tree. "Shit! Sorry!" I yell. He throws his hand up and races over to where my necklace fell. He picks it up and raises it over his head, showing me he found it.

I turn around and as we breach the first row of trees I tilt my head up to where Hazel's flying above us. "So, what did you want to talk about? Allister can be a part of whatever you have to say you know. Did you forget he's my mate?"

I hear her snort above me. "No, I definitely remember. He just annoys me. How he could be destined to be the future king is beyond me."

I roll my eyes. I want to argue but it's not worth it, instead I simply say, "Well?"

"We need to figure out what's happening with your powers. He's too much of a distraction for you and it's more helpful for him to continue deciphering those papers anyway."

I shrug my shoulders. "Fine, I get your point. What do you suggest we do?"

"I've been searching around these woods and I found the

perfect spot for us to work through what's brewing inside you."

WE WALK for what seems like hours before the forest opens up and we come across a lake. It's not a huge lake, barely big enough for a couple of people to swim comfortably. What's surprising though is I can't see the bottom. I jump off of Raven and inch my way to the edge of the lake. Peeking down into the water, I see a black void.

"How is *this* the perfect spot?" I glance into the tree closest to me, where Hazel perches on a branch.

"The powers you can't handle are fire and water right?" She cocks her head and her brows knit, like the answer should be obvious.

"Yes..." I roll my hand, encouraging her to continue.

She fluffs her feathers up and shakes herself. "Ugh. Isn't it obvious? You can stand in the water and work on controlling fire without burning the forest down. And hopefully being around this much water will help you figure out your water power."

I face the lake, plop down on the ground, and pull off my shoes before standing up and taking off my shirt and pants.

"What are you doing?" Hazel asks.

I gesture with my hand out towards the lake. "Did you even actually look into the lake? Do you see how deep it is? There's no way I'll be able to stand up in it."

"How could you possibly focus on your powers while you're treading water?"

I turn to face her and throw my hands up into the air "This was your plan!"

I start putting my clothes back on. "We're going back. I'll figure it out on my own somehow. Thanks for nothing."

She flies down and lands in front of me, throwing her wings out dramatically as I'm pulling my boots back on. "Just put your fucking feet in the water and stop acting like such an asshole."

I glare at her. "You first."

She puffs her feathers out again. "What do you mean? You're the one acting like a dramatic child, not me."

"No, you're acting like a know-it-all asshole," I snap.

She pulls back and her beak drops open. "I've done nothing but try to help you if you'll recall!"

Heat rises in my body as I start shouting. *"What exactly have you helped me with? Opening the tree? I would have figured it out on my own."* I probably wouldn't have, but she doesn't need to know that. "Fighting with everyone around me, being shitty to Allister, and disappearing when you feel like it for god's knows how long isn't helpful!"

She takes a step back away from me and flies into the air. I throw my hands up. "Surprise, surprise! You're leaving again!"

I notice Raven takes a couple of tentative steps back away from me. "Umm kid..." I slice my head over her way "What!' I snap and it's only then I see the fire radiating off of the skin on both of my arms. The fire coating my arms burns the gray sweatshirt I brought from Sanctuary, the last shirt I have left in my possession. My mouth dries and I take in sharp, quick breaths. The fire rises up my arms and almost instantly burns to my shoulders.

"Water now!" Hazel shouts above me.

I don't even take a second to think before I dive into the water in front of me. The cool liquid instantly putting out the fire on my arms and calms my temper along with it. I swim back up and gasp in a lungful of air.

Did that really just happen?

Hazel lands on the water's edge, her head cocked, and Raven stands next to her with her eyes wide.

"Huh, interesting."

I shake the water from my face. "What now?"

"You got angry, and your fire came out. The other times you've lost control of fire were you angry? What's happened when your water came out, was it like this?"

I continue treading water as I speak, my cheeks heating. This is going to be embarrassing. "Most of the time my fire came out from anger, but it's also came out when I was kissing Allister. It felt like electricity was in my mouth and then smoke came out of my mouth." Hazel stares blankly at me so I continue. "I can only think of one time I lost control of water when I was remembering the time Allister almost died."

Hazel angles her head and closes her eyes. I swim over to the edge of the lake and find out there's a small ledge. It's barely big enough so I can sit on it while my legs hang into the water. I turn, and beside me Hazel's chest rises deeply as she takes in a deep breath and opens her eyes. "So, fire and water seep out of you when your emotions are high."

"I can't replicate it on my own though. And I can't have you around pissing me off every time I need to use fire."

"No, but I can do it until you can figure out how to call on your power on your own."

My shoulders slump and I put my face in my hands. "Isn't there some other easier way to do this?"

"You haven't found one, so I doubt it. Magic comes from self-control. If you can manage to control your emotions a bit, you'll be able to control your powers." I open my mouth, but she cuts me off, "Let's get back to camp. I think this was enough for today. Tomorrow we'll at least have a starting off point."

I get up, but instead of getting back on Raven I take off the rest of my clothes. "What are you doing?" Hazel asks. "We need to get back."

I dive into the lake, sinking down into the cool, silky water. Instantly I feel cleaner, happier. With a swipe of my hands I'm popping my head out of the water and gasping for air. I run my hand back and down my long brown hair before I answer. "Do you know how long it's been since I've had a bath?" I can almost hear Hazel huff from where I tread water. But I ignore her as I feel the water washing away all the dirt and grime from the past weeks.

When I'm finished and thoroughly clean, I dress, crawl on top of Raven, and we head back to camp.

By the time we make it back to camp and I jump off of Raven, it's almost dusk. Hazel soars past me shouting, "I'll see you tomorrow," as she leaves.

Raven nudges me with her muzzle. "Why don't you search your mother's room. I thought I saw some clothes in there while we were searching through it yesterday."

I turn and wrap my arms around her. "Thank you. I love you."

She says, "I love you too, kid," before heading back to her spot where she beds down for the night.

I move to the cut out in the tree where my mother's room is. As I walk in, Allister turns to me. I watch as his eyebrows raise, and his mouth drops in shock while he takes in my appearance.

"I'm assuming things didn't go well."

I cross and rub my bare arms. "You could say that." I clear my throat and drop my arms as I walk across the room to a dresser I saw clothes in yesterday. I didn't bother looking through it because all I saw was clothes and I figured there wasn't much of a point searching through them. I'd completely forgotten they were here until Raven mentioned searching for them. "But Hazel thinks we figured out what triggers my fire and water powers, so I guess that's a plus."

I open a drawer and reach down into it pulling out a dark blue tunic. I hold it up to my body, noticing how the color shimmers in the light and I can tell it will reach down to my shins, covering all my private bits.

"That's pretty," Allister says behind me.

I glance over my shoulder at him. "Turn away so I can change."

"What if I don't want to?" he says as he smirks and wiggles his eyebrows in a playful gesture. I turn around to face him, my eyes turning to slits, a scowl on my face. He holds up his hands. "Wait. It was a joke, I'll turn around."

I chuckle under my breath and get changed as soon as he's fully turned around. I keep my eyes on him though, I don't want him peeking.

When I'm done getting dressed I walk over and lace my hand through his. He jumps in surprise when our hands meet. He must not have heard me coming up behind him. When he turns to me, I say, "Why don't we eat something and head to bed?" A soft smile cracks his features as he silently nods to me.

11

JAMES

We're on our way finally.

It took the old commander half the morning to get ready to leave. I can already tell it's been too long since he's been out on a mission. I'm second guessing if this was a good idea or not.

He's too slow, and we won't ever catch back up to Attina at this rate.

Ned simply sits there smirking at me like he knows something I don't. I hate him with everything I am.

I'm going to cut his throat open as soon as he falls asleep tonight.

12

ATTINA

The next day, Allister and I head down from the tree house to the ground below and put our swords against the tree in our usual spots. Raven saunters over, says hi to us, and I start off for our normal training area. I walk a few steps before I feel two bulking arms wrap around me.

"Hey, I thought we were sparring?"

"We are," Allister says with a little giggle.

"No. You're just hugging me." As the words tumble out of my mouth I feel his arms wrap around me tight like a serpent suffocating its prey. "Hey, knock it off."

I feel his head shake against my head. "No. I taught you how to get out of this yesterday. Now show me what you learned."

I turn my head. "Are you sure?"

He vigorously nods against my back and constricts his arms down tighter across my chest. I take in a sharp breath; the last one I can get in through his tight grasp. *Okay you want to play like that?*

With that thought I pick my foot up and slam my heel down onto his foot hard, not holding anything back. His grasp loosens enough for me to take a small step sideways. I ball my fist and bring it up to my chest before slamming it down between his legs. He huffs out as he doubles over. I turn on my heel and lift my elbow like he showed me to deliver the kill shot, right where his head meets his neck, as his hand shoots up in between us.

He grunts out, "I yield! I yield!"

Surprisingly, Raven races over to him and puts her head under his chest, helping him to stand up straighter. "What the hell, girl! He's your mate! How could you hit him so hard!"

I freeze momentarily before taking a step back. "Did you see how hard he was crushing me? I asked him if he was sure."

Her voice becomes solemn. "It was too much, Attina."

Allister coughs but speaks up, "No, Raven, it's all right. I deserved it. It's what I get for playing too rough."

Raven's head slices back and forth between me and Allister. A second later I hear Hazel's curt voice above us. "Attina. Let's head out."

I throw my hands up and my voice is clearly exasperated when I say, "Now you're giving me shit too?" It sucks getting ganged up on like this.

She flies down and smacks me in the head with her wing. It surprises me how much it hurts. "Fuck! Let's go then!" I thought a bird wing would be soft, but it feels like a rough bone hit me instead of a wing. I lift my hand to my head, checking if there's any blood there but not finding any.

I walk over to Allister and put my hand on his shoulder, tilting my head down, trying to meet his eyes. "Are you okay? Really?"

He lifts his head and quickly throws his arms around

me. I gasp in shock. "Yes. I'm fine, I promise. You did great, Attina. Just like I taught you." He pulls back and there is a gleam in his eye I didn't notice there before as his eyes lock on mine. "I don't care what they say, if *anyone* grabs you like I just did, don't hold back. You fight with every single thing you have." I nod to him.

Raven huffs behind him, pulling my attention to her. "Whatever, let's get going, girl," she snarls out.

I hop on her bareback and off we go into the forest.

Hazel doesn't say anything for the first half of our trek to the lake where we'll practice my powers again. "You have more of him in you than I thought."

I glance up to where I can sense her wings slicing through the air. "What?"

She peeks down at me. "You have more of Henrik in you than I thought you did."

I lean back in my seat. "What are you talking about?"

"I was watching you. I saw when the power from beating him settled on you. You enjoyed it. You wanted to bathe in it."

I gulp. She's more right than I want to admit. It did feel amazing. I've felt powerless more times than I care to admit, but when James hit me it changed something in me. Now there's a need for power stirring inside of me. I don't know how to answer her, so I don't.

We're all quiet until we make it to the lake. I hop off of Raven, walk in front of her, sit down, take my boots off, and put my feet in the chilly water. Hazel drifts down to me and plants herself by my side. I knew she was big, but I didn't truly realize how large she is. With her standing and me sitting on the ground next to her, our heads almost come up to the same height. "What happened to make you crave power? You're nowhere near as bad as Henrik, but I can see it there, growing behind your eyes."

I sit there quietly for a bit, thinking. I stare into the water as it sparkles where the sun touches it. I let my mind wander through what I've been through.

My mother killing my father, being bit by two Solis, everything going on with my powers, and the confusion it's brought. Finally, I think of James hitting me. I know that's when I started craving power. After James hit me, when Allister was helping me with my powers, I can remember staring into our campfire and wishing I was as powerful as the fire. I can almost understand how easy it would be to fall into using my vicious fire and burn down anything or anyone opposing me.

Raven nudges me, pulling me out of my reverie. I shake my head and clear my thoughts. I turn my head back to Hazel next to me. "I know you watched me grow up. You probably saw a lot of what I went through, but I know you couldn't see what happened in that underground prison." She bows her head, urging me to continue. "You saw me with the boy I grew up with and hunted with?"

"Yes. I believe you used to call him James. You two seemed like quite close friends," she says, and I stare down at my feet immersed in the lake and nod.

"We became something more than just friends. To this day I still don't actually know what it was, and maybe it's part of why he was furious." I shrug my shoulders. "But it doesn't excuse what he did."

"What did he do?" she prods.

"He hit me. He couldn't deal with me leaving to come out here and he slapped me across the face. I crumpled to the floor in a pathetic pile. My powers came out to protect me, I burned him, and almost took down all of Sanctuary with an earthquake I created."

She turns her head out to the lake, her far away eyes making her seem lost in thought until she says, "I remember the earthquake. I didn't realize your powers protected you so much. You're lucky."

Tears well in my eyes it's hard to talk about this with myself, let alone other people. But I'm willing to do almost anything if it means I'll get somewhere when it comes to controlling my powers. "When he hit me," I stumble out, "something broke inside of me."

She flaps her wings, calling my attention back to her. "Something may have broken in you, but you have people who love you. We will put you back together," she says matter of factly like it's simply how life will be.

I feel Raven place her head lightly on my shoulder, comforting me. I tilt my head and rub my head into hers as tears flow down my face. I'm not even upset really, I'm just sad for what happened to me. It shouldn't have happened, and I will make sure I'm strong enough it never happens again. I need to start building that strength now, so I wipe the tears from my face, straighten my back, and take in a deep breath of air.

Then something hits me, "We? As in you love me too?" I throw my arm over Hazel's wings and gently pull her to my side. She wiggles and fights as I say, "It was inevitable." I chuckle and release her struggling form.

Her feathers puff up and she shakes her whole body as she huffs, "I didn't say that."

I chuckle. "Oh but you will," I say as I wiggle my eyebrows at her.

Raven lifts her head and scoffs. "Now you're sounding like Allister."

I gasp and place my hand over my mouth. "Oh gods you're right!

"It was bound to happen, they *are* mates. Two sides of one coin. It'll happen more and more the longer they're together."

"Great," Raven says in such a tone I know she doesn't mean it in a nice way.

I throw my hands up. "Hey! Can we please get back to what we came here to do? You remember? Work on my powers?"

"Yes, yes let's get back to your powers," Hazel says. "I think you can keep only your feet in the water for now. Then, if you need to, you can jump into the water like you did last time."

"Okay," I say as I shift in my seat. I'm nervous this time. I'm not sure if I trust Hazel yet and I'm not sure what she has planned.

"I know you've felt for your magical animal before and it was in distress, so I want you to connect with it again when we're done practicing. Yesterday, you lit on fire when you were angry. Can you replicate it? Remember what you felt and try to feel it again?"

"I can try."

"I'll walk you through it. Close your eyes and listen to my voice."

I do as she says.

"This will be unpleasant, but I want you to think back to when James hit you. How it felt. I want you to remember the pain it caused. How helpless and worthless you felt."

"Hey! I didn't say I felt worthless!" I snap without opening my eyes, even though I know she's right.

"Shh and do what I say. Feel it flow over you like it's happening all over again." I think back and let those feelings wash over me like water cascading down my face. I take a deep breath in as I remember the crazy look in James' eyes the second before his hand connected with my face, the burning pain of when his hard hand met my soft cheek. When my knees collided with the hard rocky ground. My room door slamming into my back as Ned came rushing in. His soft hand cupping my burning cheek.

From somewhere in the distance a tiny, whispering voice breaks into my thoughts. "Perfect. Now focus on your hands as you remember." I do as the voice says. I hold my hands up and I'm right back into my memory of James hitting me.

He grabs onto Ned with his claw-like grip and rips Ned's hand away from my face. The force of the action slices along my cheek as his hand leaves it. I remember the anger pooling in my gut. The fire which raised in me as I grabbed onto James' arm. His squeal of pain and the satisfaction it immediately brought me. I remember walking across my room, grabbing for my sword and my willingness to strike him down where he stood.

"Open your eyes!"

The shouted words surprise me, and my eyes shoot open.

Fire dances in my hands.

My hands aren't covered in fire. No, in my palms are two balls of fire, no bigger than an apple. I gasp and my hands instantly start shaking.

"It's all right. Don't freak out." I hear Hazel say beside me as I feel Raven's legs inching up behind my back. I lean against them, her presence grounding me. I take in a deep breath trying to calm my vibrating nerves. "Do you notice anything different within yourself? A pull anywhere?"

I stare into the dual fire orbs in my outstretched hands and try to think logically and feel around within myself, checking for anything which seems out of place. After a second of searching I answer, "There's a dropping feeling in my gut. It's the same sensation I had after James slapped me. Come to think of it, I had this same sensation when Raven made me mad, and I burned a hole through my father's sparring gloves." I close one hand and the fire disappears from it. I reach back and pat Raven's leg.

Hazel says, "Now, zero in on the sensation. I want you to push that feeling to grow." I do but nothing happens. "Focus harder, Attina."

I close my eyes and focus on that sense of dropping. I feel it get bigger and spread into my chest. I open my eyes and watch as the fireball grows, along with my awareness of the drop in my gut. I cover my mouth with the hand not holding a fireball in it.

"Good." I glance over to Hazel and a whimpering noise tumbles out of me.

Her head slices over to me. "Don't turn into a big baby now. Suck it up. You're doing this. You're doing great!"

I drop my hand and steel my spine. She's right. I've wanted this since this journey started. I should be proud of this, not scared of it. This fire comes from me. I shouldn't be scared of something from me. I feel the heat of the fire on my face but not on my hands. I lift my chin and a toothy grin cracks my face.

I notice Hazel fidgeting beside me. "Great job, Attina. Now see if you can make it disappear. Ignore the drop in your gut. Make it disappear and I bet the fire will disappear."

I close my eyes and do as she says once more. I breathe slowly and deeply, in and out. Opening my eyes I see the ball of fire shrinking before me. When I relax and roll my shoulders the fireball disappears completely.

"Hell yes, kid!" Raven shouts behind me, making me

jump. She'd been so quiet it's jarring to have her shout right above me. She moves from behind me to as much in front of me as she can manage while I'm facing the lake. "You did it! I'm so proud of you! You've been working incredibly hard. Silas and Oak would be proud of you too!"

I glance up to her and notice tears in her eyes which brings a tear to mine. She drops her head and I wrap my arms around it and squeeze her massive head before standing up and wrapping my arms around her neck.

"They would be proud of *both* of us. I couldn't have made it here without you." I pat her on the shoulder and turn back to Hazel. Bowing my head I say, "Thank you for your help. I truly mean it, thank you."

"You're not done, Attina. You need to check on your magical animal now. We need to figure out what's happening with her."

I peer between the canopy above us and see somehow the day got away from us, the sun is already starting to set. "I agree. I need to do that, but we also need to get back to camp, it's going to take us a few hours, why don't I do it while we make our way back to camp."

Raven stiffens beside me. "Um, last time you connected with your magical animal you freaked out and turned into a human fireball. Your magic can't hurt you, but it can definitely hurt me!"

I chuckle as I jump onto her bareback with such ease it's still a little shocking to me. "Raven, if I do that again you have my full permission to toss my ass on the ground."

"Oh okay," she says happily as I feel her shoulder shrug underneath me and she happily trots off.

"Hey! I didn't give you permission to toss me whenever you want you know!"

She puts her head down and throws her head around

like horses do when they're about ready to buck. I lock my legs down on her and clamp down on her mane, ready to hold on. Then, as quickly as she started, she stops. "Just kidding."

I glare down at her. "You know I could probably use your hide as a coat or something."

"Probably, but then you would miss all this fun!" she says happily.

"Now who's sounding like Allister?"

I hear her make a gagging noise but before she can say anything Hazel talks above us. "What is with you three? It's constant prattling with all of you. Can we please get to it?"

I wave my hand in the air like I'm dismissing her comment. "Yeah, yeah sure hang on."

I roll my shoulders, close my eyes, and search inside myself like Allister taught me to do. I take a few calming breaths and then I see my beautiful black bird. Its wings seem to gobble up all the light surrounding it. Its orange beak is like a shining beacon.

The bird's head is turning, searching. I can feel panic radiating off of it. I try thinking, *Shh, it's all right* and the bird sharply turns to me and throws its wings out. I see the moment it realizes who was talking to it, trying to calm it. The bird's posture visibly relaxes as its body slumps. I try again, *Shh,* I coo. *Are you okay?* It violently shakes its head and then I see and somehow feel its pain lace through me. Blood flies from the bird's head as it shakes its head.

When I last saw the bird, a serpent came out of the shadows and attacked it. That's why I freaked out and turned into a fireball, I felt its panic and pain. The serpent must have bit it. It's the only thing I can think of which makes sense.

You all right? I ask and it must understand me because it

tentatively nods its head. *You're stronger than that icky serpent. Do you understand me?* The bird stands up straighter and vigorously nods its head, puffing out its chest like it is proud. *I'll be back to check on you sometime soon I promise.*

I pull myself out of the vision and slump over Raven's neck, only now realizing how exhausted I am from using so much magic. Raven wiggles under me. "Hey! You okay up there? Not turning into a fireball are you?"

I shake my head against her neck. "No. I'm fine, just tired."

From above I hear, "So? What's happening?"

I slowly ease myself back to an upright position. "It's not good. She's bleeding. Well, I say she, but I don't actually know if it's a she or not."

"Stop rambling. Magical animals are always the same gender as the person they're attached to. You say she's bleeding? How bad is it?"

"The serpent I saw last time must have bit her in the head. I was able to speak to her this time." I explain to Hazel and Raven what happened.

When I'm finished Hazel says, "This isn't good."

"What's happening?" Panic is clear in my voice.

"I haven't ever heard of something like this in the entire history of the Fae. If I were to guess, there are a few things which could happen. Your bird could kill the serpent, but honestly I don't see such a thing happening especially when it's already injured. The serpent could kill your bird and you along with it."

"What!" Raven and I shout simultaneously.

Raven shouts, "You didn't mention that little tidbit earlier!"

Hazels says louder, *"Or* it might be possible for the two animals to merge."

"What would happen then?" Raven asks as I'm in too much in shock to say much of anything.

"Then she would have some sort of amalgamation of the two animals. Who knows what it would become though? And I have no clue what it would do to Attina. The strain of the two animals melding into one could kill her or she could become more powerful than she already is."

13

ATTINA

I sit quietly in shock for the rest of the ride back. No one else says anything until we make it to the tree break at the edge of the clearing. As we head into the clearing, Hazel states, "Get Allister I have something I want to talk to everyone about and I'd rather not have to repeat myself."

I silently jump off of Raven and do as she says.

When I get to my mother's room Allister is sitting at the desk reading more papers. He doesn't lift his head as I stride over to him. I make it to his side and lay my arm over his toned shoulders. He turns in his seat and wraps his arms around my hips. He pulls me into him as he finally looks up at me. When his eyes lock with my face he pulls back, and his mouth drops open.

He shoots up and is on his feet, holding my shoulders with both of his hands. His eyes are locked on mine in an instant."Your face is white! Are you all right? Did it all go well?" His eyes rove over me as he spins me by my waist sideways to examine me better. "You don't appear to be hurt. What's going on?"

"I'm fine. I was able to master fire today. I didn't even

freak out. But I got some bad news too. Hazel or Raven can tell you more about what happened. I don't have it in me to talk about it. I'm exhausted from using my magic today and broken about what we found out."

His hands reach up and cup my face "Whatever it is we'll get through it together. I'm here for you until our dying days."

I shake out of his hold and grab his hand, pulling him out of the room. "That day might come sooner than we thought."

"What?" he shouts but I ignore him as I pull on him harder, toward our fire pit, where Raven and Hazel are already waiting. "What happened today? Attina doesn't want to say anything."

Surprisingly, Hazel, who's perched on one of the two logs we drug over by the fire pit, says, "I don't blame her." Then she proceeds to explain what we talked about on the ride back. By the time she's finished, Allister is left speechless with a gaping mouth and Raven's head is drooping so low it almost touches the ground.

It takes Allister a minute to pull himself together, but he eventually does. He sits on the other log next to me, close enough for our legs to touch. He reaches out and wraps his arm protectively over me as he shakes his head before screeching, "Well what do we do? There must be something we can do!" His arm latches down on my shoulders.

Hazel shakes her head and solemnly says, "Not that I know of. We just have to let nature run its course."

Allister glances over to me and I can see the pain behind his eyes. We'll *figure this out. You are not dying and leaving me here alone for the rest of my life. I can't live without you.*

He wraps his arms around me, and I lean into him. I breathe him in, the smell like a forest right after a rain, so fresh and inviting. His smell makes me think of new life and growth, things I might never get.

His hot breath on my ear pulls me back to the here and now, and I realize I don't believe him. I know in my heart, there's nothing he or anyone can do to stop this. Whatever's going to happen is going to happen. All I can do is sit around and wait for the outcome.

I pull out of his arms and turn to Hazel. "Okay, now since we're past that, what else did you want to talk to everyone about?"

"We all need to watch Attina." Everyone's head turns to me, the fire dancing across their features. I instantly feel self conscious.

It feels like a rock drops into the pit of my stomach. "What do you mean? Why?"

"What we talked about today, about you craving power. Remember how I said Henrik wasn't always evil?"

Allister nods, but I just sit there waiting for her to get to the point.

"Your grandmother Lillian's family was close with Henrik's family. Before she was even born, she was promised to Henrik. Growing up, Henrik and Lillian were playmates and by the time their respective Awakenings came to pass they were in love."

I glower at her. "What a heartwarming story. Can we please get to the point?"

Hazel's wings shoot out and she extends her legs. *"Cut out the attitude Attina!"* She shouts and then ruffles her feathers she wiggles back down. "Anyway, when Henrik came into his Awakening, things changed. He wasn't the warm, happy kid he used to be. He became cold, calculating. He lost interest in Lillian almost overnight and when he did show interest in her it was to torment her; he seemed to take pleasure in it. Their relationship deteriorated and she fell out of love with him, but it was too late, she was already promised to him. She pled with her parents to let her be free of him, but no one defies the Fae royalty. So she married him."

"Poor thing," drops out of my mouth without me realizing it.

Hazel turns to me but continues. "She had your mother not long after. She was extremely happy to be a mother. And once Henrik had an heir out of her, he pretty much left her alone, unless he got bored. When that would happen," her eyes grow dark, "he would lock her up in the dungeon, burn her gowns off of her, and other more devious things."

I take in a sharp gulp of air.

"They lived like that for years until she told me one night he stumbled into her chambers, drunk on Fae wine. He was back to the boy she grew up with. He cried and plead with her to forgive him. Told her how he had been acting wasn't who he truly was. He explained to her that during and after his Awakening, his father tortured him. His father told him it was to remind him he was not king. He wanted to show Henrik he couldn't overthrow him, and it would be pointless trying. He said being tortured during his Awakening broke something in his head. He wasn't himself anymore. Like he's lost a piece of his soul."

Allister cuts in, his eyes wide in shock. "So, that's what happened." His head swivels between me and Raven. "Since the beginning of the Fae kingdoms each king has become king by overthrowing the previous one. Your great-grandfather wanted to head Henrik off at the pass. Show him he couldn't take the throne from him."

"Each king?" I'm shocked. How could such a thing be possible?

Allister shrugs his shoulders, the corner of his mouth quirking up, "What can I say? Your family is ruthless." He opens his mouth like he's about to say more but Hazel cuts in.

"The next day she told me all of this. She was unusually happy and hopeful he would turn back into the man she grew up with."

My head droops. I know he never did.

"But the next night she disappeared and wasn't ever heard from again. No one in the palace ever looked for her. I searched for years but never found her. I know he killed her and turned her to ash."

"Why?" I ask.

"Because she had sensitive information on him. Information which made him seem weak and vulnerable and he couldn't handle it. She was better to him dead than alive. So he killed her and not too long afterward he killed his father."

"It's a heart wrenching story, but I don't see what it has to do with me besides me being related to them."

Hazel's head shifts back and forth between Allister and Raven. She ignores me completely. "He was tortured by his father, and it broke him. When Attina beat you up today Allister, I saw the same crazy gleam in her eyes. I used to see the same gleam in Henrik's eyes. Today I only saw a spark of it, but it was there. This James person hitting her did something to her. It changed something in her. We need to make sure she doesn't lose control like Henrik and follow in his footsteps."

"*I would never!*" I shout but everyone ignores me.

Hazel continues. "I know in my feathers she's good. She will be an exceptional queen, one of the greatest. But she needs us to keep an eye out for her. She needs us to have her back, to love her, and to keep her on the right path." Allister and Raven quietly nod as she talks. Do they seriously think I could ever be like Henrik? I feel anger pooling in my stomach.

Allister leans forward and cups his chin in thought. "I didn't think there was a reason behind him being downright evil. Now more things make sense. The last time I was home he slapped my mother, and he was incredibly disheveled and—" he struggles for the word for a second. He opens and closes his hand like he's physically trying to grab for the word. "Insane is the only word I can think of to describe how he was acting."

"I couldn't ever become a monster like Henrik," I repeat but I'm so angry it comes out calm.

"He must be stressing that Attina is still alive. I wonder if all the stress is getting to his already broken mind?" Raven answers him.

Everyone ignoring me is *seriously* pissing me off. I feel the dropping in the pit of my gut again as I shout, *"I will never become that bastard!"* As the words leave my lips the fire pit in the center of us flairs up. The flames burst into the sky, sending sparks fluttering down to the ground all around us. The heat of the flame makes everyone turn their faces from the fire.

All eyes glue onto me, pinning me to the spot. No one says anything for a second. It's not until I see Raven bow her head and glare at me that I see how much trouble I'm in.

"What the hell! You scream and throw a fit? Is that supposed to be you showing us you won't be like Henrik? Cuz it does nothing but prove Hazel's point! Obviously we *do* need to watch you and your tantrums! I will *not* let this eat you away." She snorts. "You *will* get through this, even if I

have to drag you by your hair through whatever you're dealing with, I will."

When she's done she immediately stands up and quietly walks off. We all watch her walk and when she gets to the other side of the clearing and lies down. We all turn back to the glowing fire. I stare into it; how did I lose control so easily? Is there something wrong with me? Maybe I am a danger?

Hazel glares at Allister. I know she's glaring because of me and says, "I'll be sticking around for awhile. I want to be able to keep an eye on her," and I watch as she flies off into the pitch back night.

I slide my gaze to Allister "You must be pissed at me too. Maybe," I pause for a second, "maybe, I am crazy." I turn back to the glowing fire.

He doesn't say anything, he simply wraps his arm around me and pulls me into him. He lifts me and before I know it I'm sitting in his lap with his arm wrapped around behind my back. I stare down at my hands which ended up in my lap and pick at my nails nervously. He lifts his free hand to my chin and turns my face toward his, locking eyes with me.

"You're not crazy, Attina. I would tell you if you were crazy and we would somehow fix it. *You're not crazy.*" He repeats the words, emphasizing them. "You've been through an immense number of terrible things in such a short period of time. If I'd gone through what you've been through I'd be a mess in a pile on the floor." His hand drops from my face, and he wraps it around my torso, holding me tight. "I've known a lot of warriors in my time, but you know what?"

I shake my head.

"None of them are, or ever could be, as strong as you.

You're my hero for traversing through what you've been through and holding your head high every single day. You still put one foot in front of the other and keep fighting your hardest to, one day, make this world a better place." He places his hand behind my head and pulls my head down to his lips, planting a gentle kiss on my forehead.

Tears form in my eyes. I know he means what he says, I can see it in his eyes and the weight of his words. I lift my head up. Allister draws his head back as he notices the tears in my eyes. I bring my lips down to his with force. Maybe if I kiss him hard enough he can squish back all the broken pieces of me. My lips tingle as they make contact with his. I rub my tongue along his lips asking for an invitation which he gladly gives. Every time I kiss this man I forget everything else. It feels like it's only the two of us out in these woods. Nothing but us and the stars.

Our kissing ratchets up as I rub my hand down his rock hard chest, feeling the peaks and valleys of his muscles as I roam. His hand drifts down my thigh and even with the fire only smoldering behind us the air becomes too hot. My skin is slick with sweat as I turn in his lap, straddling him. He steadies me as I move, his hands ending up holding my back. They then slide down my back to my hips and he lifts me off of our log.

As soon as I'm in the air though, the fire behind us shoots to life. Where there was only a smolder before, now is a newly lit rolling fire. We both turn and peek at it as our heads droop. Allister turns back to our log and sets me down on it. I groan inwardly, *Great, Attina, good job at killing the mood.*

Then Allister is in front of me. He smirks and there is a gleam in his eyes. *Definitely not a mood killer. My mate just made fire because I got her so worked up. Do you realize how amazing you are?*

I shake my head, embarrassment rolling over me again. I don't know how to take it when he tells me all these sweet things. I believe him but it makes me feel weird, like I'm unworthy.

He brings his forehead down to mine. *You are the most amazing creature I've ever laid eyes on.*

I stare down at my hands and start to nervously pick my fingernails again.

He notices and lays his hand on mine, stopping me. He cocks his head. "How about I put this fire out and we head to bed? I'm teaching you about water tomorrow. That chicken doesn't get to teach you everything."

"You've taught me an awful lot," I say under my breath but loud enough so he can still hear it.

He chuckles. "Not enough, kitten." With a wave of his hand, water fills the fire pit and douses out the flames. A plume of smoke fills the air. Then he holds his hand out to me. I take it and he helps me off of the log.

My head swivels behind me to the wet pile of ashes as we leave for the elevator platform. "Hey, shouldn't I have put the fire out with my powers? You know, practice?"

Allister walks in front of me, pulling me along. "You don't have to always do it all. I know you're exhausted and I want to get you to bed." He turns around and wiggles his eyebrows at me. I pull my hand away and cross my arms over my chest, making him turn back to me and I glare at him when he does. He throws his hands up and shouts, "I'm kidding!"

I shake my head and we head up to the tree house.

14

ATTINA

THE NEXT MORNING WE GET DRESSED AND HEAD DOWN TO ground level. Hazel is already there waiting impatiently for us, tapping her claws annoyedly against the log she had been sitting on last night.

She locks her gaze on me. "Are you ready to work on water today?"

I open my mouth to answer but Allister cuts in. "I'll be teaching her water today." He lifts his chin and strides past me. He walks over and sits down on the adjoining log and pulls out the saddle bags we leave there, which holds the jerky I made from the meat of those pheasants I killed the other day.

Hazel simply shrugs her shoulders and says," I have better things to do anyway," before taking off into the sky.

I sit down next to him, and he hands me a piece. "Here, this is the last of the meat. We'll have to go hunting again today."

I silently bow my head and begin eating my breakfast. I figured we would have much more to eat out here in the forest, but it hasn't been the case. We've done some gathering. Dug up some late season mushrooms and similar things, but I haven't had the time to hunt. Then there was the disaster the last time I went. I'm not sure how to overcome the feeling of hunting becoming just plain killing now.

When we finish eating, Allister stands up and I follow him to a spot in the clearing. He sits on the ground and pats the space next to him. I sit facing him cross legged.

"Okay, I know your water powers haven't come out much. Only the one time you were telling Raven the story about when I almost died right?"

"Yes."

He cradles his chin with his hand, thinking for a second, before he continues, "We can try this one of two ways. You tell me which way you want to try, deal?"

"Deal," I answer. I know I'm being short with him, I don't mean to be, I'm simply nervous. I'm not sure why I'm nervous. I've never hurt anyone with water, but it's incredibly elusive. What if I can't conquer it?

He takes a deep breath in before beginning, "All right, for me I feel the water all around me. Water is literally *everywhere*." He throws his hands out in emphasis. "You just need to know where to look for it."

I cock my head, my brows drawing together. "What do you mean?"

He puts his hand to the earth again, splaying out his long dexterous fingers. "There's water in the ground beneath our feet." He fingers the grass. "It runs through each blade of grass around us." He lifts his arm and angles his hand, palm up, to the trees around us. "There is water running through every tree around us." Then he leans forward and brings his hand to me, bringing his pointer finger and placing it on my chest. "There is even water racing around inside of you."

Well I feel stupid. I knew all those things; I simply didn't think about it.

He lifts his shoulder. "Most people know all of that but never really think about it. I heard humans have died from lack of water and I can't fathom it."

I cross my arms over my chest, annoyed. "We told you we didn't have enough water to share with you on our journey and you didn't say a word."

He glances away almost embarrassed. "Well Ned annoyed me at the time. But I never would have let you or Raven go without water."

"And what about Ned and Mylo?"

He straightens his back and passes over my question completely as he says, "So, I was thinking."

I uncross my arms and lean back on my hands and flatly say, "A mistake really."

Allister immediately cackles with laughter, leaning back and forth as he does so. When he's done, he brings his hand to his face like he's wiping away a tear.

"Why do you do that?" I ask.

"Do what?" His face pinches in a questioning look.

"Burst out laughing when I'm snotty to you."

"Oh that." His shoulders sink. "Well back at Shadow Mountain I've made a reputation for myself."

I cock my head.

"A pretty awful reputation. I'm known as the king's most ruthless slayer who will kill without mercy over the smallest slight against me." He takes in a deep steadying breath, obviously this upsets him. "I formed my reputation on purpose. I wanted the respect of the other Fae and I also wanted Henrik to leave me alone. I figured if I was ruthless he wouldn't bother me."

"Did it work?"

"Too well. When I was there last time some kids lost a ball and I picked it up. The kid who came and got it from me was shaking, he was terrified of me." He drops his head. "That's not what I wanted. I don't want regular people afraid of me, only the people who would do me or my people harm. All those people I killed for no real reason? They were all evil Fae who were picking on the weak and the poor in the castle. They were scum and I used some stupid excuse to bolster my reputation and get rid of them all at the same time."

Without thinking I crawl over to him and wrap my arms around him.

We sit in silence for a second before I feel his arms wrap around my middle and his head lay against my shoulder. It's not the first time we've hugged or been sort of intimate, but this moment feels heavier somehow. Like he placed a vulnerable piece of himself on the table and I didn't throw the piece on the ground like he expected, I picked it up and cherished it instead.

I don't release him. I simply sit there and wait for him to end the hug and take whatever comfort he needs from it. It takes much longer than I thought it would, but he eventually releases a big exhale and lets go of me.

I sit my butt back on my ankles and stare into his eyes as I say, "You are such a wonderful person. Everyone will see it someday."

I swear I see a tear well up in his eye but when I blink it's gone. He just shakes his head and drops the topic. "So, how do you want to work today? Either you can sit here and try to feel for the water all around you *or* we can try having you remember when I almost died and see if it will help you figure out your water powers."

I move off of my ankles and sit down fully on the

ground. I stare at the still green grass in front of me. It's weird, this forest is still vibrantly green. Back home the seasons must be changing already. Why is everything unchanging here?

I clear my throat. "Let's do the first one. Can you guide me through it?"

Close your eyes, kitten. I hear in my head.

I do as Allister asks.

Now I want you to reach out and touch the grass under you. Feel the blades run through your finger. The cool sensation it brings to your skin.

All I feel is grass. No water running through it, nothing.

Give it a chance. I want you to sit here and breathe deeply, really ground yourself, and connect with the earth around you. Let the water in the grass, flowers, trees, and air call to you. Open yourself up to it. Take your time, we're not in a rush. If you still haven't figured it out by lunch we'll try the other way.

I notice as Allister quietly stands up and walks off, presumably to my mother's room to scan over more papers. He should have found what he's been searching for already right? I do appreciate him leaving me to work on my own though. Now I don't feel incredibly self conscious.

I sit there and try my best to do as he says but nothing happens. I slow my breathing and sit there reaching my senses out into the world, searching for anything to grab a hold of but there's nothing, only a vast void of emptiness.

Before I know it I sense footsteps coming toward me. "You better not be coming over to bother me Allister."

He walks over and stands over me with his arms crossed over his chest, my bow and quiver strapped to his back. "Still nothing?"

I open my eyes and glare up at him. "I've only been here a little while, give me some time."

He cocks his head. "You've been here for hours. I gave you as much time as I could. It's *well* past lunch and I'm starving. We need to go hunt something."

I take in a sharp breath of air. "Hours? I've been here for hours?"

He lifts his hands in the air and shrugs. "I guess you were trying hard. From over there," he points toward the tree, "it looked like you were sleeping."

I grunt as I get to my feet. Allister pulls my bow and quiver up over his head and hands it to me. "*We? We're* going hunting?" Now it's my turn to cross my arms over my chest, "Have you even actually been hunting? I have a feeling you're the type who has your food caught and prepared for you."

He scoffs and turns his back to me as he walks off. "Follow me, kitten."

I bring my hand up to whistle for Raven but Allister spins around and grabs my arm. "Let's leave her alone I'd like some alone time with you."

My cheeks heat, my breath hitches, and it's all I can do to barely dip my head. Before I know it, he's taking off at a run.

Great, running again.

I won't ever understand the fascination with running. It hurts your knees, makes your legs cramp, and leaves you winded. Not fun at all.

I take off after him and I'm surprised to find out how easily I can keep up with him. It doesn't take long or much effort for me to catch up to him. "Why are we running?"

"Because I want to get there before dark. We're heading to the lake Hazel took you to. It's almost dusk which means the deer will be getting their last drink of water before bedding down for the night."

My eyebrows knit as my head slides to him. "I'm

surprised you know that, Mr. Prince." But at the same time I'm again shocked at how long I sat in the same spot feeling for water and nothing happened. I hate that I failed at calling my water *again.*

His eyes narrow but he doesn't turn to gaze at me. "You seem to keep forgetting I *was* a prince. I haven't been a prince for over a century. I used to come out here and stay in that tree" he points over his shoulder with his thumb, "for weeks at a time. I hunted my own food out here. I learned how to hunt to feed myself. If I ran out of food it meant I had to go back home. Back to Henrik."

"Oh," is all I say as I turn my head back forward and find the road in front of me incredibly interesting.

As we run I realize this isn't too bad. I haven't genuinely ran, unless it was out of necessity, since father died. Along with my Fae speed, I realize my stamina is ten times what it used to be. I barely feel winded when the lake comes into view. When we get close to the lake Allister starts walking around, gazing up into the trees, searching for something. I start to ask him what he's doing but decide to simply stand there and let him do his thing instead.

"This one," he says as he points up into a tree I wouldn't have picked as an ideal one. It's much smaller than the other trees, which won't give us a great vantage point, and I'm not completely sure it will be able to hold our combined weight.

My face pinches, my voice questioning as I ask, "You sure? I bet we can find a bigger, better tree to scope out the lake."

"Bigger isn't always better," he says as he wiggles his eyebrows.

I exaggeratedly roll my eyes and stomp over to the tree, climbing up into its branches. I'm actually surprised to see he was right. It's branches almost cradle your butt. In one spot, two branches are so close together you can sit on one and lean back on the other. The view's the best part though. You can see underneath the canopy of all the other trees, giving you a perfect picture of all around the lake.

I reach my hand down and help pull Allister up onto the branch beside me. It creaks but holds our weight. I turn to him and whisper, so as not to scare off any animals around us, "Fine, I'll admit it, you were right."

He brings his hand up over his chest and grabs onto where his heart would be. I mouth har de har and we both turn back to the lake. I pull out my bow, nock an arrow, pull back on the string, and scan the horizon in front of us.

Just as the sun is falling down past the horizon I release my bow string, ready to give in. As I move, Allister places his hand on mine. I turn and he gestures to the lake with his head and mouth, hang on. I set myself back in my ready position and wait.

Sure enough, right as the sun is descending past some hills on the other side of the lake, a deer pokes its head out from between the trees. How the hell did he know it would show up? He must have hunted here for years and years to be this familiar with the wildlife around the lake.

I see the deer lift its head and sniff the air, checking to see if it's safe. We're lucky the wind is pushing our scents away from the deer and it strides out to the lake. I slowly pull my bowstring taught as it walks. When it reaches the lake I get a perfect side view of the creature. I take in a deep steadying breath.

Coming out here I was more nervous than I've been since my first hunt with James. I was worried we would use our powers to find a deer like I did the other day and I'd chicken out again. I'm happy to realize I don't have the same feeling this time. This doesn't feel like leading a lamb to slaughter. This feels like real hunting again. Allister put in the time, decades probably, with how well he knows these animals' habits, to stalk the deer around this area. This is Allister's kill, I'm simply his executioner.

This kill is honorable, I am okay with this.

I release my breath slowly and release the arrow.

It hits its mark.

15

ATTINA

We don't finish quartering the deer until after nightfall, but when we do, both of our hands are stained red. This was truly the worst part of hunting for me. Staying still for hours and hiking through the nastiest parts of our woods wasn't too bad. I didn't even mind the killing because it provided much needed food to the people of my town. But having the blood stain my hands for days after, always made everyone in town give me a wide berth, like I was something to be afraid of.

While I'm remembering days past, I notice out of the corner of my eye a stream of water floating its way over to Allister's outstretched hands. He starts rubbing his hands in the water. *I hated walking around with blood stained hands so I used my water power to wash them immediately before it could stain.*

When I was hunting with James, water was precious so I couldn't wash my hands until we got home. By then the blood had worked its way down into every nook and cranny of my hands. *Send some of that water my way* I think as I stretch out my hands.

He turns toward me and plops down on the ground. "No."

"What?" I ask, shocked.

"No. You can summon the water on your own if you want to wash your hands so badly."

I huff out, stand up, and walk away from Allister. Ready to walk to the lake to rinse off my hands but then I hear a meek, "Please," behind me.

I spin on my heel.

Allister continues. "I know you can walk over there and wash your hands but please try to use your powers."

"Don't you want to get back to camp? It's already dark."

I can barely see his outline and I notice him shake his head and reach his hand out to me. I step forward and reach my hand out to his. He grabs it and yanks me down into his lap so my back is against his chest. He nuzzles his face down in the back of my hair. "No, I'm perfectly happy here with you. It'll be just as dark in a couple hours. Let's stay here and work on your magic."

I nod and close my eyes. I slow my breathing and with my Fae hearing, I listen to the slight buzz coming off of the lake behind us. I hadn't noticed it before, but I can definitely hear the water shifting in the lake as fishes swim around it. I splay my hands out in the grass around me and sense the water which runs underneath my hands. I call to it. And I hear as it forces its way up through the earth. I move the earth away little by little, making a path for the water to travel up through. It's actually working, and I don't want anything, even the earth below us, stopping the water from getting to me.

Water flows up into my hands. Not much, barely enough for me to rinse my hands off with. When I peer up, Allister's mouth changes from dropped open in shock to a knowing grin. "I knew you could do it; I just didn't think you'd be so upset by being dirty you'd figure it out." His arms squeeze around me tightly, playfully.

I slap the arms wrapped around me. "You know I'm not like that!" He starts chuckling behind me, causing my body to shake. I turn in his arms so I can gaze into his eyes through the shine of the moon. "I think having the lake here helped me. I could hear the fish moving in the lake, it was the strangest thing."

He rolls his eyes and flaps his hand in front of his face close enough to my face I can feel the air fly by me. "You lie. It's because you're in my lap. All this perfection must've rubbed off on you." He snickers.

I don't miss a beat as I lean in. My pointed finger traveling to his chest. Allister pulls back a little and sucks in a tight breath. Perfect, I wanted to shock him. I drag my finger down his chest, watching my finger crawl over the sculpted muscle. "Wh...whhaa..." he stammers out.

The moonlight streaming down gives me a perfect view of him. I glance at his beautiful face through my eyelashes. "I'll give you something to rub on, mister perfect." His eyes grow wide along with something else I can feel under me. I jump up and bend over laughing.

His eyes narrow and he shoots up after me, grabbing me under my butt. He lifts me up in the air and spins me around as we both chuckle. "You beautiful, frightening thing," he says. I lean down and plant a kiss on his forehead.

He flops down on the ground and drags me with him, his hand cupping my face, caressing my cheek. I push my face deeper into his palm. "You know I think I'm falling in love with you."

"You think?" I snigger. "Well, let me know when you know for certain." I wink at him, trying to play it off like it's no big deal, but it is a huge deal. Do I want him to tell me he loves me? I haven't really thought about it. I mean we're mates. I should want him to love me, but right now all I am is confused.

I stand up, reach down, and grab his hand in mine. I intertwine our fingers and start dragging him back to the quartered deer. "Let's start packing this back to camp." When I take my eyes off of him and turn back around to start, I face three Solis.

We must've been so engrossed in our little moment we missed their footsteps coming toward us. We all stand there quietly in shock for a minute. They stand there audibly huffing in and out. The middle one, a girl younger than me with sable hair and unhealed slices, probably claw marks, all down her arms, moves first. She lunges at me and as I take a step back into Allister's firm chest I call to the earth. Slamming it up under all their feet, throwing them backward.

I left my bow and sword on the ground by our kill, I move to grab them, but the Solis are up and moving toward us before I can reach my weapons. Allister pushes past me, drawing his sword, which he left on his back. In one swift motion he unsheathes his sword and slices the Solis closest to us, the girl, in half.

The two on either side of her take a step back, glancing down at their fallen comrade. Taking a closer look I can see now these two must have been related to the girl. I notice the same raven hair and delicate build the girl had in both the men before me. They glance at each other and simultaneously unleash pained roars, like they realize what just happened.

I feel the pull in my gut and instantly fireballs appear in each of my hands. I call to that pull and the fireballs grow as the men's eyes lock on Allister, I unleash my fire onto their rotting bodies. They stop moving and drop to their knees, screeches pouring out of them. By the time they've both fallen on their sides the screeching has stopped and they're both dead.

Allister turns around and playfully swats at my arm. "Impressive!"

I stare at the three in front of me, my mouth hanging open. That was strange. It was like the men knew who the girl was. Like they knew she was important to them, but it can't be right, Solis don't understand those sorts of things. All they understand is their hunger for human flesh. Right?

I feel Allister's lips press against my cheek and it's enough to pull me out of my reverie. "You did wonderfully. I'm stunned by your control of fire already. They must have smelled the blood and come running."

I shake my head and move to the deer. "Yeah, you're probably right. Let's get this back to camp and have dinner. I'm starving and I really don't feel like dealing with any other Solis."

By the time we get the deer back to camp I'm utterly exhausted. Raven is asleep but I wake her and make her move into my mother's room. We will have to hoist up whatever meat we don't use for dinner up in the tree to keep it away from the Solis. I don't want Raven out where any Solis who smells the blood can attack her.

After I get Raven tucked into the floor of my mother's room and I'm sitting on one of the logs around our fire. Allister is diligently cooking our dinner in front of me. He dips and dives, peeking all around the meat, making sure it's cooking perfectly. I don't know for certain, but I think he must be using his water power because somehow he is able to keep the fire at a perfect height for grilling meat, something I've never been able to do.

He must decide it's going well because he stands up, takes the seat next to me and says, "You have dark circles under your eyes again. You must be exhausted. Why don't you lean your head on me and close your eyes? I'll wake you when dinner's ready."

I do as he says and lay my head on his shoulder. I don't know why, but I'm always wonderfully surprised at how comfortable he is. My body melts into the side of his as I let my heavy eyelids close.

16

ATTINA

I'M STARTLED AWAKE BY A SCREECH. "WAKE UP ATTINA!"

I shoot up and pull my dagger out from under my pillow, pointing it to my right, towards where the voice came from. It takes a second for my eyes to focus, but when they do, I see Hazel perched on a branch not far from the end of the tree house's floor.

I huff and put down the dagger as I rub the sleep from my eyes. I gaze around me. I'm in bed, but Allister isn't next to me. The blankets are ruffled like he slept in bed with me, but he must have gotten up early. I don't remember coming up here last night. I had to have fallen asleep last night down by the fire. I guess Allister must have brought me up and put me to bed. I turn, throwing my legs over the edge of the bed, and notice on my nightstand is a hunk of cooked meat. My stomach rumbles and I'm thankful for his thoughtfulness as I pick it up and stuff it into my mouth.

"Get up, Attina. I know you were exhausted, so I let you sleep in, but the sun's been up for hours. You need to get out of bed and start practicing with your powers."

"Where's Allister?" I question as I walk behind my

makeshift changing area to change into the dark blue tunic I found in my mother's room.

"He's down studying those papers again," she says matter of factly.

When I'm changed, I bring the platform back up the tree and I'm surprised how heavy it is. Each time we've left the tree house Allister has been the one to bring the platform up and down for me. He's always made it seem easy. It's definitely not.

I make my way to ground level. When I'm back on solid ground I head over to peek my head in on Allister. Sure enough, he's diligently studying a piece of paper before him, his brow knit, cupping his chin between his thumb and forefinger.

I snicker and move on.

On the air, I feel Hazel swooping down towards me and step out of the way at the last second before she can smack right into me. "Good job," I hear behind me.

I keep quietly walking. I'm not ignoring her, I'm simply weary of what she's up to. I walk over to where we tied up the meat last night and begin slowly dropping it out of the tree. I need to make all of this meat into jerky. Dried meat isn't as tasty as a juicy piece of steak, but it keeps longer and makes traveling with it easier.

As I move, I notice the air behind me shifting. I wait until the shifting gets closer before I call to the earth around me. I build a wall of earth next to me as I continue my work. I hear a screech and feel a slam into the earth right next to me.

I grab one of the quarters and walk towards the fire pit, letting the earth fall away as I go. I turn my head as I walk and see Hazel on the ground, her feathers puffed out and shaking her head.

I bend over and begin chortling, forcing myself to put one foot in front of the other. I make it to the fire pit, sit down on a log, and pull out my dagger. I brought it down here to make cutting the meat into jerky-sized pieces easier.

I haven't been cutting long before Hazel is perched on the log next to me. "You're not bad with your powers."

I shrug my shoulder. "I'm getting better. Although earth and air elements are easier for me."

I notice Hazel puffing next to me again. "Well I'm not letting you light me on fire and I'm not a huge fan of water so that's all the help you're getting from me." She says the words snottily, like I was asking for her help.

"I'm not asking for your help. I'm sure turning all this meat into jerky will be enough practice for me." I calm my thoughts and my breathing. I reach down deep inside of me and tug on the pull I now constantly feel in my stomach. It takes a bit, but I see smoke lift out of the cold fire pit. I relax, letting out a loud sigh. As the sigh leaves my lips the fire bursts to life.

"Not bad." I hear the words from my side. I don't reply though, because honestly, I don't know what to say to Hazel. Our relationship has been exceedingly strained from the get-go, I'm not sure how to talk to her now since the strain is gone.

Silently, I cook the first round of meat, trying to keep the fire as consistent as Allister did last night. I'm not particularly skilled at it at first, a couple of times I light the meat on fire. When I'm done cooking one quarter of the meat, I summon water. I hear a tiny stream of water below us, under the water table, as it winds all around. I focus on the sound and watch as water bubbles up under the fire before me, staunching the flames where they start. I do this over and over until all the meat is cooked.

Surprisingly, by the time I'm done making all the meat into jerky I have pretty good control over my powers. I'm able to quickly call my flames and anytime my flames get a little wild I'm now confident enough with water I can put out the fire by throwing some water from under the fire itself on it.

Allister is still in my mother's room reading over her papers when I finish turning the raw meat into jerky. I decide to leave him to his work and make my way over to Raven. She's in her normal spot. It got cold last night so she's out basking in the sun's warming rays.

"Hey girl," I call as I walk up to her.

"Hey," she says without picking up her head.

"Sorry I didn't let you out this morning," I say bashfully. I'm embarrassed I slept in and wasn't the one to let her out of mother's room.

Now she lifts her head and rolls, getting her feet are under her with her front end up. "It's fine. Allister let me out early this morning. I'm glad you got some rest. You needed it."

I tilt my head. "He was up earlier than usual?"

"He's been up since a little bit before dawn. He opened the door, said good morning, and sat down at the desk. He hasn't taken a break either."

"Hmm... maybe we should give him a break in a minute." But before she can answer I walk over and wrap my arms around her as my knees hit the ground. "I miss you. We haven't had much time together lately."

She wraps her head around mine and leans into me. "I miss you too, girl. I'm getting fat over here eating and sleeping all day."

We chuckle together and I let go of her, sitting back on my heels. "Will you let me try something on you?"

Raven narrows her eyes and huffs out, "Will I like this and is there fire involved?"

I snicker and lift my hands in an I surrender gesture. "No fire involved. I only wanted to try to brush you with my powers. I'll only use air, earth, and maybe a little water, I promise."

Raven lifts her head high in the air in an indignant way. "I suppose that's all right."

I stand up and over exaggeratedly bow to her, my brown hair falling around my face. "Thank you for such a wondrous blessing."

Raven rolls over on her side and belts out a louder laugh than I've ever heard tumble out of her before. She's not very playful so it's rare to see her this carefree and happy. It brings a smile to my face.

It takes her a minute, but her laughter eventually calms down and she pulls herself together. She lets out a big sigh before getting up on her feet. I take a step toward her. I close my eyes and run my hand down her neck, calling the wind to run its way through her blood red hairs.

I open my eyes and watch as her hair ripples through the soft wind blowing through it. I run my hands over the rest of her body and anywhere I feel dirt, I summon it into my hands. I walk all the way down one side of her body and drop the small handful of dirt I retrieve, then I head around her and work on the other side. When her other side's all done I make my way to her dark black mane, it almost appears blue as the sun glistens off it.

The wind I call untangles her mane and tail. I hear the water underneath me, I bid it to wrap around my hands and it does as I ask. Water cascades around my hands, wetting the hairs, forcing them to stay in place as I deftly braid Raven's mane and tail. When I'm done, I tie off all the braids with various pieces of long grass. They won't stay in long, but it works for a moment of beauty.

She shakes her whole body, a few of the grass blades already falling to the ground, as I take a step back to peer at my handiwork. "I must say I've never felt cleaner without taking a bath in my life."

I chuckle. "Good! I'm glad."

As the words leave my mouth I hear, *"Attina!"*

I spin on my heel and see Allister running out of my mother's room, with a piece of paper in his hand. He stops right outside the door and frantically spins around, searching for me. In my head I say, *Calm down.* Out loud I call to him, "Allister, I'm over here!'

He stops spinning and locks his gaze on me before rushing over to me. Stops right in front of me, he blankly stares at me and spits out, "I found it! I can't believe it. I finally found it! It makes total sense. I don't know why I didn't think of it before myself."

I touch him on the shoulder as I hear bird wings flap above and behind us. "Hey, you're not making any sense. What are you talking about?"

The blank cloud lifts from his eyes. "We can defeat Henrik."

"Okay good!" I cry, ecstatic he found the key to conquer the evil tyrant.

Allister shakes his head. "It's not all that simple."

I cock my head in question.

From a tree above us I hear, "Spit it out," come from Hazel.

"The prophecy states, the child born of the evil king's people and his enemy can defeat him by joining the broken clans and shedding blood together." He takes a deep breath before he adds, "I think it means we'll need the human and the Fae to work together to defeat him."

It feels like a rock drops into the pit of my stomach.

Humans and Fae will refuse to work together. We'll never be able to defeat Henrik.

I stand there in quiet shock for a minute before calling out to the air above us. "Hazel, did you know this and simply not tell us?" I'm not sure where she's perching, and I am not about to search for her.

She glides down from wherever she was sitting and plops in front of me. She gazes up at me. "No. As I said before, I didn't remember what the end said but now, hearing Allister say it, the words sound familiar."

I cross my arms over my chest. I'm not sure I believe her, but I push on anyway. I scan around at the four of us. "What do we do from here then?"

Allister takes a step forward and takes my hand in his. I'm so thankful for the gesture, it's grounding and comforting. He turns to me, "Well you remember when you told me we would travel back to the Eastern Fae one day?"

I cock my head and exaggeratedly say, "Yeeeaahhh..."

"Well, I think we need to head there and get them on our side."

"What?" I pull away from him, my hand shooting up to my necklace.

Raven pushes her side up against mine. "He's right, girl. The humans and Eastern Fae are his enemies. Henrik killed their king, and essentially usurped their throne by taking their queen for his own, they must hate him. Getting their help is our best chance at defeating him. We can't do it on our own, and maybe if we have the Eastern Fae army on our side, the humans will understand if we join forces we can take down Henrik together."

"But... how?"

"It was my birthright to become king. I will simply go claim my birthright."

I scoff and narrow my eyes. "You make it sound easy."

"It's a solid plan, Attina. It's the only plan we have." Hazel pipes up.

"What about all the intel you told us you were gathering? None of it helps us take down Henrik. Maybe we can make some other plan with it?"

She shakes her head and flies down, landing on the ground in front of me.

"What was the point in it then?"

"I went to see his mental state."

"What? Why? He's a crazed madman."

She ruffles her feathers and begins pacing in front of me. "He's been perpetually crazy. But it's been a calculated crazy, until recently. Over the past decade, I've noticed him taking some major missteps, more so lately." She stops pacing and faces me, "Like you. What would possess him to allow you to remain alive? He could have easily killed you as a baby."

"My father would have protected me," I counter.

She audibly huffs. "He was human, he couldn't do anything against the Fae king. He wouldn't have stood a chance." I don't argue with her again. I know she's right.

Allister shimmies back over to me, placing his arm around my waist and pulls me to his side. Keeping me grounded. I briefly turn to him, and mouth thank you.

"You're his blood. Even if he didn't think you would have any powers, he had to have known you would come after him, with or without them, and he still let you live. He took every single thing from you and now here you are trying to take him down. He must have seen this coming. Was he so deluded he thought you wouldn't be a threat?

Even after he turned your mother into a monster who killed your family?

I hear Raven gulp in air behind me. Even though her perfect image of my mother was shattered the night of my Awakening I know she still holds a soft spot for her and probably always will.

Hazel shakes her head. "No. Henrik's pride is what made him ignore you, and it will be his downfall. I've been keeping a closer watch on him since your Awakening, and he's been losing his mind. No one is allowed in his chambers or the throne room. You," she says as she pointedly stares at Allister, "seem to be one of the only exceptions to the rule. You saw what he was like when you were there last time. He's only gotten worse. His people weren't fairing well before, now they starve. The only ones not starving are the royal family and his army."

Allister wraps his arm around me and pulls me into his chest. "When I was there last he hit my mother. He's always been a vicious tyrant but, to my knowledge, he hasn't laid a hand on her before. He was unkempt and his behavior was maniacal. Some primal thing seems to have broken in him. We can't let our people starve, Attina."

"I agree they need to be saved, but how am I supposed to do such a thing? I'm only one person!" I shout, suddenly overwhelmed.

"It's already been foretold you will be the one to defeat Henrik," Hazel cuts in.

I throw my hand toward the tree where my mother's desk sits with all those papers piled high. "Why? Because some paper says I will? For all we know my mother made it up!"

All of a sudden I'm shot forward and I fall onto my knees. The earth catches me at the last second so it doesn't hurt when I make contact with the ground. "What the hell!" I shout and spin around, but I'm stopped mid turn by Raven's hulking head.

Her eyes are thin slits as she puffs out, "You are not doing this."

"What?" I snap.

"We have not gotten this far, lost this much, for you to chicken out now. I won't allow it. I will grab your hair in my teeth and drag you to the Eastern Fae if I have to."

I gulp and drop my head. As I stand up I whisper, "I will die, Raven. There's no way we can pull this off. We can't get the Fae and humans to work together. You know how awful humans can be."

"I also know they can be easily manipulated." She almost smirks as she says it and I stroke her muzzle.

Allister steps up to my side. "And if anyone is going to try to kill you, they'll have to get through me first." I grab his hand and pull him into me. He leans down and presses a kiss on my forehead. The gesture takes the overwhelmed feeling I have and turns it into a calm determination.

Hazel says, "Then, we're agreed?"

I turn and peer down at Hazel. I chuckle and shrug my shoulders as I answer, "I guess we are."

17

JAMES

We've made it past the town where I last saw Attina. Ned is in the lead now, showing us where he sent her to search for supplies.

Each night I swear I'll kill him in his sleep, but he's constantly awake.

The man doesn't sleep.

How does he do it?

I know he knows what I'm up to now.

Each night he situates his bed roll right next to the Commander's. And each night I wait until Ned's breathing deepens. I quietly get up and make my way to his side, my hand inching to the dagger on my hip. Figuring I can kill him, drag him off, and make it look like some animal took him off into the night and clawed out his throat.

Then every single time at the last moment his eyes shoot open.

It's like he can hear me somehow but there's no humanly way he can hear me when I reach him. I'm quiet as a mouse.

He doesn't even ask me what I'm doing. He just winks at

me, reaches behind him, and puts his hand on the Commander. Threatening to wake him. He doesn't show an ounce of fear as he stares me down.

I can get rid of Ned without much backlash. But the Commander, while he might be old and slow, I can't harm and still be welcomed at Sanctuary.

So, for now I will wait. It's a long trip, he has to sleep at some point.

I'll get him. One way or the other.

18

NED

I hope Attina and Allister are far away and have figured out some sort of plan. I wish I knew how to contact them and warn them we're coming. I'm not sure how all this will turn out.

If John realizes James is telling the truth, I don't know what it would mean for us all.

19

ATTINA

We make our way up to the tree house, Allister gets the lamps lit, and we both get changed for bed. I pull on one of Allister's shirts he left up here from his time here before and Allister changes into loose pants.

I make my way around my makeshift changing area and my stomach drops when I see Allister. He's sprawled out on our bed, lying on his side, waiting for me. His black hair is flipped around his back cascading down to the bed. His purple eyes are intense as they prowl over every inch of my body. The hungry gaze he gives me makes me want to wrap my arms around my body and hide. But I refuse to show him how nervous he makes me. I realize this is the last night we'll be sharing this bed for who knows how long. I don't know how long it will take us to get to the Eastern Fae stronghold, and until we make it there we will be sleeping next to Raven and Hazel. This is the last night we get some privacy.

I slowly walk over to the bed, hyper aware of each step I take. As I walk, my eyes devour Allister's hard body. I can't deny the attraction between us. He draws me to him like a moth to the flame. The curves of his body make my mouth run dry. I lift the cover and crawl under the blankets.

He cocks his eyebrows at me before he crawls under the blankets along with me. His strong thighs and rock hard abs tighten as he moves under the blankets. I roll on my side, embarrassment getting the better of me. My cheeks become scorching hot, I'm not sure how I'm not on fire.

Allister's arm wraps over the top of me, constricting around my body, his massive muscles flexing as he pulls my body back into his. He inches forward, his breath hot as he whispers in my ear, "Do you realize how gorgeous you are?" His hands move from around my stomach to around my hip, and down my thighs. I try to answer him, but words fail me as I lean back, allowing his hands better access to roam over me. I lean my head back and shake my head in response. He growls in my ear, making my entire body go loose and taut at the same time.

He gingerly runs his hands back up my thigh to my hip. His calloused hand travels up my shirt covering me as he leans over, kissing my neck. His hand reaches up further and further until his calloused hand is cupping my breast. He nibbles my neck at the same time he pinches my nipple, making me moan out in pleasure. "Do you like that kitten?"

"Mhmh," I unintelligibly groan out as I rub my butt into him in emphasis. He groans into my ear in answer.

His fingers continue to move over me, I try to spin around toward him, but he pins me in place. "I want to see how your body reacts, if you're comfortable with this?"

I say, "I am, but I want to touch you." It comes out as more of a whine.

He chuckles. "You will, kitten. Just give me tonight. I did win our fight the other day. Remember you owe me one request." I want to argue. He said it wouldn't be sexual, but I really want this man. I guess I can let him have this one.

His hands search my body, finding all of my pleasurable spots, and claiming them for his own. As his hand moves between my legs I begin panting as I feel myself coming closer and closer to a precipice. I move into his hand, intensifying the pleasure. Closing my eyes, I cry out in pleasure as I find my release.

I instantly smell smoke and when I open my eyes I see the smoke hanging in the air around us. I lift my hand to my mouth, embarrassment coursing through me as I roll over to face Allister and see a wolfish grin covering his features. My cheeks instantly heat. "Well, I guess you're not too scared of your fire now?"

I shove my head into his chest. "I honestly didn't even think about it until it was all over."

His finger sneaks under my chin and he lifts my gaze to his. "I'm glad I can make you forget and bring you such pleasure."

I lift my lips to his, claiming him as mine as I nibble on his lower lip. He groans in reply. I run my hands up his chest and wrap my arm around his neck. When I pull away, I yawn and push to crawl on top of him but he's like an immovable rock. I stare down at him with pinched eyebrows, confused as to why he won't let me move him.

"You're exhausted and we should talk about what our next moves are." I'm instantly disappointed but I lie back on the bed, realizing he's right. It's already hard for me to keep my eyes open and we should try to figure things out.

We stay up half the night talking about what we should do. But after talking through them, none of our plans seemed to end well, so we decide it's better to get a good night's sleep.

It's nice lying in a cushy bed wrapped in Allister's warm, comforting arms. His presence always makes me feel completely safe, even in my sleep. I haven't had a night terror since the first night here, when I woke him up and asked him to cuddle with me. I hate to admit it but he's right, cuddling does keep the night terrors away.

But like all great things it had to end. Morning eventually came which meant we had to get out of bed and pack. I take a couple blankets with us too. It's getting later in the year meaning the nights should be getting colder. Around this tree is perpetual summer, but it should change as we move further away from it, further north. I really don't want to be out in the elements with nothing but my bedroll.

"I'll let you down with the platform, bring it back up and climb down the tree myself," Allister says as he walks up behind me, wrapping his arms around my middle. The black fighting leathers he again has on, squeak at the movement.

I turn in his arms and stare up into his mesmerizing purple eyes, his long ebony hair is pushed forward over his shoulders. The sword strapped to his back gleams in the sunlight. "You don't have to do that! I know how much work bringing the platform up and down is."

He squeezes me once and shakes his head. "I want you to have some time in your mother's room alone. Maybe being in there will bring you a little closer to her somehow." He smiles down at me as I open my mouth. He lifts a finger to my lips, effectively cutting my words short. "I've had plenty of time in her room reading those papers. I feel like I got a chance to catch back up with her, now I'd like you to do the same."

My face heats and I dip my head. "Okay, thank you." I seriously don't want to get any more acquainted with my mother than I need to. I thought we talked about this. If I get more acquainted with who she was before she was turned into the monster I met, then I killed my own mother. I don't know if I could deal with that.

I walk over to the platform where my weapons and saddle bags, full of our things and Allister's satchel, already wait. But before I step out onto the platform Allister grabs my arm and spins me back around. My vision gets blurry, and I get a little lightheaded from the force of it as I feel his lips meet mine. I suck in a quick breath, completely thrown for a loop. My eyes shoot open, and as the world normalizes, he shoots me a wink.

"Um thank you," I say as I let him guide me onto the platform.

He chuckles and starts lowering me down. "I'll see you down there in a bit."

It's not until I'm halfway down the tree that it hits me what I just said. Did I seriously thank him for kissing me? How embarrassing! I smack myself in the forehead as my cheeks turn to liquid fire. What is wrong with me! Who does something like that? Ugh, how can I ever look him in the eye again? I shake myself before the platform hits ground level.

I drop my saddle bags and weapons as I climb off of the platform, making my way to my mother's room. I won't stay long. I need to grab some more of her tunics anyway and I might grab a book on the slim chance I'll get some time to read again. I used to read every night back in Daruk and I miss it. I can't pass up the chance to dig my teeth into a new story.

I grab my necklace and put it in the keyhole in the twisting colored tree bark. The door opens and I step in. I stride over to my mother's dresser, pull the tunic I'm wearing over my head, and leave it on the ground in a heap as I pull a new one on. I pull out a few clean tunics, enough so I can rotate them as needed. I pull a green one over my head and lay the rest of them over my arm. I make my way to the rounded wall covered in books. I don't take the time to read any of the titles. I simply run my hand over the spines and pick a beautiful red one up, tucking it into the crook of my arm along with the tunics.

I turn around and start to make my way to the door, but something catches my eye. The purple bed sheet flies up and I see something sparkling underneath. There had to be a gust of wind just now right? I cautiously walk over and lift up the bed sheet. I immediately throw myself backward, the tunics and book skittering out of my hand as I catch myself.

Under the bed is armor.

My mother's armor.

No way, why would she leave it here?

How is it possible the bed sheet lifted at the exact moment I would be able to see the sparkle of the armor? I scan around the room searching for some entity who could have made the sheet move, but of course, find nothing.

I tentatively crawl back to the edge of the bed and reach my hand under it. The feeling of cold, hard metal bites into my hand. The armor scrapes loudly against the ground as I tug. I fall backward as I yank it out from under the bed, dragging the armor into my lap. I expected it to be heavier than it is. It's surprisingly almost feather light.

I lift it up and see it's plated armor with chainmail between each plate, which must give the wearer complete range of motion in battle. It's one continuous piece reaching from the shoulders all the way down to the thighs. At the points of the shoulders are dark silver roses in full bloom. I lay the armor in my lap and grab my rose necklace. It's the same rose. I scan the front of the plates and realize the rose stems arc and twist all the way down from the shoulders to the thigh pieces.

I gaze around the room. Oak said he thought the tree was alive. Is the tree looking out for me? Does it know I'm Titania's daughter? "Thank you," I say meekly to the tree above me. I feel like a fool but some part of me knows this tree is alive and consciously trying to protect me. Honestly, right now I can use all the help I can get. "I'll come back. I won't let you sit alone for decades again." I hear a slight creaking of the wood and take it as approval.

I stand, easily pulling the armor over my head and like the tunics, it fits me perfectly. I do a few stretches to try out how well I can move in it, and I'm surprised to see it doesn't inhibit my movements at all. It's like I'm wearing nothing at all. The weight is just like I shrugged on a jacket. I wonder how this would hold up in a battle, it must be too lightweight to be of much use against a sword. But it's better than nothing. I pick up the tunics and book and stride out of the room.

When I'm outside, the door closes behind me and I'm met with Allister's smiling face. "How did..." he trails off as his eyes drift down my body and his mouth falls open. "Where did you find that?" He asks as he grabs me and spins me around.

I let him turn me around once but then shrug off his grasp. "It was under the bed. I happened to see it and figured I might as well use it."

"I see you found your mother's armor. Good, you'll need it," Hazel says from high atop a branch.

I tilt my head up and ask, "What?"

Allister whispers, his eyes locked on my shoulders, "I haven't seen this armor in decades." He reaches out a hand and touches one of the roses on my shoulders. "I always assumed she took it with her when she left." I now realize he's talking more to himself than me.

I roll my shoulder, forcing his hand off of it. "What are you mumbling?"

His eyes lock on mine. "Your mother wore this armor when she left Shadow Mountain on the Day of Destruction."

"What? How did it get here then?"

He shrugs his shoulders. "I don't know."

Almost as if on cue Raven trots up next to Allister. "What's all the commotion?"

I step up to her. "Raven, do you remember coming here after you guys left Shadow Mountain?"

She shakes her head. "I've haven't been here before."

I turn around and stare up at the wondrous tree. "So, either mother and father made a special trip to bring this armor here or this tree is more magical than I thought." I stride over to the tree and place my hand on its chromatic bark. "Thank you for this truly amazing gift you have bestowed upon me. I can't describe how blessed I feel. I will right the wrong in this world and I will return when it's done." I wrap my arms around the tree's trunk, well, I attempt to. Surprisingly I breathe in the smell of lavender, the aroma instantly calming me.

Allister clears his voice and nervously laughs out, "Umm — Attina, what are you doing?"

I hear Hazel from above us. "Shut up boy," and then a hmph noise tumbles out of Allister. How does she know what I'm doing? Maybe she's old enough to understand what this tree is? I'll have to remember this.

I spin around and happily say, "Is everyone ready?"

Allister throws his hands in the air. "We're not even going to talk about how you were just hugging a tree?"

Hazel and I simultaneously shout "Nope!" I make my way over to Raven and hug her baby doll head. "Ready to head out on another adventure girl?"

She eagerly bobs her head before saying, "Nice armor, where'd you get it?" I simply point behind me. She doesn't say anything, she only gazes at the tree with wide eyes, but when her eyes make their way back to me, I know she understands.

"Great so everyone gets what's happening besides me? Wonderful," Allister whines.

I admonish him. "Oh shh you big baby." I should explain it all to him but it's too much fun picking on him.

Allister stops pouting long enough for him to help me saddle up Raven. I throw my saddlebags on her, sling my weapons on me, and we're off.

I take one last glance behind me at the massive tree we called our home for a few weeks as we leave the clearing. The tree almost sparkles in the sun before disappearing all together, like it was saying goodbye.

I gaze down at Allister. "Hey. Turn around, the tree is gone."

He turns and when he faces me again he shrugs his shoulders. "I guess it only shows itself to people it wants to. Makes sense people walk right by it and never see it. I wonder how alive that tree really is."

I wonder the same thing. At first it was just like any other tree but now I'm not so sure.

I lift my face to the sky where I can barely make out Hazel's silhouette slicing through the air. "Hey, are you all right up there?"

She shouts down, "All clear as far as I can see!"

Then Allister yells up, "Hey can you keep an eye out for Talon?"

She hoots in reply, which I assume means yes.

"Who's Talon?" I haven't heard the name before.

"Talon is Henrik's Fae hawk. His top spy even above his slayers. He's sneaky. He told Henrik I was traveling with you."

"What? How did you get out of that one?" I ask, shocked.

A sly smile crosses his features and I swear one of his eyes sparkles right before he winks. "I'm an adept shit talker."

I tilt my head, and grimace. "Yeah apparently to everyone but me." I put my hand on my hip in emphasis.

He turns and locks his eyes on me, his gaze intense. "I've *never* shit talked you. You're my mate. I will always be honest with you."

I know he's sincere simply by his demeanor, but I also feel it in my bones. He's someone I can count on through thick and thin. I smile in reply.

20

ATTINA

When the sun starts its descent we all decide it's time to stop for the night. The nights are starting to get colder, as I thought they would. I'm glad I grabbed the blankets from our tree house. While I unsaddle Raven. Allister leaves to hunt down some firewood. I call after him, "Hey could you see if you can find some sticks I can use to make more arrows?"

He stops, turning around to pointedly nod at me.

"You know what to search for right?" I ask, suddenly uncertain. I haven't ever seen him actually shoot an arrow. Would he even know to search for an ideal arrow shaft?

He places his hand on his side and juts out his hip in a ridiculous display. "Of course I know which sticks to search for. You continue forgetting I'm the king's top slayer. I could make a weapon out of a piece of parchment if I had to."

I giggle and seductively stride over to him and say, "Well aren't you the manly man," before I quickly peck him on the cheek.

His eyes widen and he draws in air. When our eyes meet

again there's something dark and mysterious behind his. "You beautiful, frightening thing."

He turns and runs off and I make my way back to Raven. "You two are disgusting, you know."

"Get used to it. That's how mates are," Hazel says from her spot perched on a branch above us.

When Allister returns, his arms are chalk full of wood. In his hands are a few straight, long, sturdy, but thin branches which will be perfect to make arrows out of. I snatch them out of his arms greedily and excitedly squeak, "Thank you!"

He sets up the logs and grabs a bit of kindling from around our camp as I search down in my saddle bag for a leather pouch I have stuffed in there. Inside of it is the things I need to make arrows, except the shafts. There's a sharp knife which I only use to whittle down arrow shafts, a few feathers I've found over the years, some string to tie them on the stick, and some extra arrowheads.

Behind me I hear, a voice say, "Hey you gonna start this fire or do I have to do it the hard way?"

I spin my head around and glare at him, then glare at the fire. I tug on the pull in my gut and a second later a small ember is growing in the kindling. Allister crouches down and adeptly blows on it until the ember grows into a fire.

I turn and sit down with my back against Raven's shoulder and begin whittling the sticks the way I want them. After the fire is roaring Allister walks over and sits down next to me, hands wrapped around his knees since he doesn't have anything to lean against. He asks, "How long have you been making your own arrows?"

"A long time," I answer.

But the question makes my mind wander and I decide

instead of telling him the answer to try to let him *see* my answer. I clear my mind and think *I'll show you. I first learned how to make my own arrows after the last time I fell from a tree. After James was done berating me for being ridiculously careless he brought me home where I was laid up for a few days.* I show him the green forest around us and James's brown, glittering eyes bearing down into me.

Allister pulls his head back and by the one small gesture I know he's seeing what I'm seeing. I jump to me lying in my room back in Daruk. I have my bandaged leg up on an extra pillow. My father sits on the edge of my bed, with a handful of sticks in one hand and a leather pouch, the same one I just pulled out, in the other.

"He's your father? You two have the same eyes." I hear the awe in Allister's voice.

I cut into the memory and answer, "Yes," before I continue with the memory.

Father says, "Since you won't be able to get out of bed for a few days while your leg heals I thought I would teach you something your mother taught me." His eyes sparkle with happiness and love as he stares at me before he reaches down into the leather pouch, and I cut off the memory.

I blink back into the here and now. Allister's positioned himself so his body is completely facing me, and he reaches his hand out, placing it over mine. "Your father loved you so much, Attina. I can tell by the way he looked at you. He would be extremely proud of you."

I wipe the beginnings of tears from my eyes, but I don't glance up at him. I simply continue my work and say, "I hope you're right." Father is still a hard topic for me. I miss him so much. I have this huge gaping hole inside of me now since he and Oak are gone. I didn't know the people who leave you could take a piece of you with them, but they sure do.

All of a sudden Allister's fingers are on my chin, pulling my face, forcing me to stare into his eyes. "I mean it Attina. I didn't meet him, but I know from what you showed me he would be incredibly proud of how far you've come. You've become so self reliant, strong, and capable." Tears fill my eyes, and my chest tightens in on itself hard enough I have to drop my shoulders toward my chest to relieve some of the pain. He continues. "I've told you I knew your mother and I did meet Oak when they were in that mountain of hell with me. Both of them would be honored to call you family."

I pull my chin out of his hand and turn away.

"What's wrong?" I hear the worry plain in his voice, but I can't bring myself to turn and face him.

I shake my head and angrily wipe the tears from my cheeks. "I—" My voice catches. "I just can't okay!" I don't mean to, but the words come out in a yell. I barely notice as Allister pulls back away from me in shock. But I can't deal with him right now, I lift my head up to where I know Hazel is perched in the tree above us instead. "Hey Hazel, can I steal some feathers?"

She answers, "How many do you want?"

"Hmm how about like ten? Does that work?"

"Holy crap! Why do you need so many?"

I gaze down to the sticks in my hand. "Well I don't *need* any, but my mother made arrows with Fae hawk feather fletching and they shot farther and straighter. I figured your feathers would do the same thing."

She glides out of the tree and gracefully lands in front of me. She settles in and puffs out her feathers. "They will. It's only a little painful pulling them."

I sit up straighter, shocked. "Painful? I don't want to hurt you!"

"It's not bad pain. Think of it as someone pulling out a few of your hairs. Hurts for a second and you get a little tender afterwards." She flings her wings out wide. "How about you take two feathers each night?"

I lean forward and run my fingers along her wing. They're surprisingly soft but also somehow rigid. I haven't ever touched an owl feather. Owls hunt at night which meant they weren't out when I was doing my hunting for Daruk. "Sounds good to me. Thank you, Hazel." I quickly pluck two feathers before she has a chance to stiffen up. She jerks so slightly I almost miss it. I scrunch up my face. "Sorry, Hazel."

She brings her wings back to her side and shakes her head. "No, it's all right, thank you for making it quick. And hey maybe we'll see Talon and we can kill him and take his feathers. Then you wouldn't have a need for mine." She winks at me before taking back off into a tree. I hear as she lands and settles in for the night.

I run my fingers along the rigid spine of the feather. I turn my head toward Allister and see he's staring at the ground. I can see blowing him off like I did hurt him by the way his body crumples in on itself and how his brows are furrowed. I reach my hand out to him and his eyes meet mine. "Hey, I'm sorry. I shouldn't have snapped at you like I did."

"It's okay, I just don't understand. I was so excited when I figured out you were Titania's daughter. I thought I'd finally have someone to talk to about her, but you don't want to. I know we discussed why, but I was hoping after you got what you needed to get off your chest we could talk about her more. Now we can't talk about your father either?"

I take in a deep breath and bite the inside of my cheek. I don't want to cry so hopefully the pain will help stop me from doing it. "She's hard for me to talk about. We talked about it once. The wound father and Oak left is still too fresh. It hurts too much. I don't know what else you want from me." He grunts and his eyes revert back to staring at the ground in front of him. I see his hands grab tighter around his legs. I reach my hand out and place it on his arm "Hey." He turns back to me, hurt clear in his eyes and the sight of it breaks something in me. "We can talk about them if you'd like. Can you give me a few days to gather my thoughts?"

"Of course," he answers, and I see some of the hurt leave him with the big breath he releases. His shoulders relax and his face softens, his eyes even begin sparkling.

He wiggles over next to me until our hips are touching. He doesn't lean against Raven who is now deeply sleeping. "Want to show me how you do that?" He points his chin toward the freshly made arrow in my hands.

My mouth drops and I put my hand dramatically to my chest while I lean back away from him. "You mean there is actually something I know that the big powerful Fae doesn't? How could such a thing be possible?"

He narrows his eyes and sucks on his cheek. "Haha, very funny. I might be trained in all kinds of weapons, bows included, but I haven't made my own arrows."

I chuckle. "Yeah, of course I'll show you."

We make arrows until there are nothing but embers left in the fire pit, and I can barely keep my eyes open.

I decide I better check on my blackbird before I fall asleep, so I close my eyes and open my mind to her. I'm instantly back in that black void with her at my feet. Her feathers are ruffled, blood still coats them, but it's her stillness which worries me. I can see her breathing, but barely. I've seen this before; she's going into shock. Birds aren't the toughest creatures, even a bad scare can send them into shock and either they snap out of it, or they die. I need to pull her out of this.

I bend down and reach my hand out to her head. She had soft downy feathers before but now they're rough and tacky. My hands come back red. She lifts her head a fraction of an inch, not even enough to see who's touching her. I lift her stiff body into my arms, and it seems to pull her out of whatever kind of shock she's in. She fully lifts her head and peers directly into my eyes, a smell of tangy iron hits my nose and I know it's the smell of her blood.

"Hey you," I whisper.

I can tell she knows who I am. Her ruffled feathers smooth out at the sound of my voice, and she almost melts into my hands.

I hold her out away from my body and up to my face, her claws biting onto my hands, "You'll be all right. You're a tough bird." She lifts her head and sharply nods her head, obviously believing my words. I'm glad I came to check on her. My presence alone seems to have pulled her out of shock. "You're not about to let that stinky serpent beat you, are you?"

She shakes her head and throws her wings out. She flaps them, and in a flash she's up in the air. She gives me a wink and is off flying into the night.

I open my eyes and I'm back in the here and now, cuddled up next to Allister. I wiggle back into him and in his sleep he pulls me in tighter. My mind races. What if I hadn't checked on her? Would she have been able to pull herself out of it or would she have simply died? Would Allister have woken up with me dead by his side? My gut twists and I know I won't be able to fall asleep now.

WE CONTINUE on our way north toward the Eastern Fae over the next few days. The nights keep getting chillier. Each night, I'm happier and happier I brought those blankets from mother's room in the tree. The blankets are surprisingly warm for how lightweight they are.

By now I have my quiver full again with regular arrows and six Fae owl feathered arrows. I'm walking between Allister and Raven when Hazel screeches. I throw my head up, and I can barely see a dot in the distance above her. "What's she going on about?" I turn my head toward Allister.

His eyes narrow and a scowl crawls across his face, his voice is grave when he answers "Talon."

My eyes spring open. "Henrik's hawk?"

"Yes." He glances down at me. "We need to catch him. If we let him get away he'll run back to Henrik and tell him where we are and where we're heading. By now it's obvious we're traveling to the Eastern Fae."

"What do you suggest?"

He doesn't answer me but peers up at Hazel and nonchalantly says, "Hey, Hazel, you must be tired. Why don't you fly down here and hang out on the saddle for a bit."

I watch as she silently glides down to us and lands on the back of the saddle. I'm again surprised by her massive size, she's probably about as big as I am when I sit in my saddle. "So, what are we thinking? He just now found us, but he definitely saw us."

I turn my gaze back to Allister as he answers, "He'll want to see who you are Hazel. He won't leave until he knows for certain you're the late queen's owl. With you down here he'll have to get closer." He peeks down at me. "Attina, do you think you could pretend to be fixing an arrow?"

My brows furrow. I'm confused. "Yeah? why?"

"Maybe you could sling your bow in the crook of your arm?"

All of a sudden what he's saying clicks and I almost miss a step as it hits me. "Oh! I get it. You want me to shoot him."

Allister vigorously nods. "Yes, but don't kill him. Only clip his wing so he can't fly away. Can you do that?"

I smile a sinister smile. "If you have to ask that question you underestimate me sir."

As the hours tick by, Talon drops lower and lower, he must be feeling more secure we can't see him since, as we know, he's rarely noticed by others. He's getting too comfortable, which makes him sloppy.

I casually pull my bow over my head, like it's in my way, as I chat with Raven about what she wants to do when this is all over. She tells me she wants to settle down and have a family. I laugh at her answer before realizing she's not joking and try to hide my chuckle with a cough. I pull out a Fae owl feather arrow, one I was working on last night, as I pat her on the neck.

"I'm sure there will be plenty of other Fae horses where we're going. Maybe you can make some friends there."

She stares into the distance, something akin to longing covering her features as she stares off into the distance and sighs heavily.

I busy my hands with the strings attaching one of Hazel's feathers to the stick, double checking they are safe and secure. Along the way Allister was able to discreetly get into his satchel and pull out some rope he had stashed there. He acts like he wants to hold hands as he slides me the rope. It's the same rope he used at the tree for the platform we used to get up and down from the tree house. I didn't see him put any of it in his bag, but man am I glad he did. This will make things much easier.

I turn my attention to Allister as I tie the rope to the arrow. "You know? I could really use a good luck kiss."

His eyes widen and I can almost hear his heart beat faster as he sharply inhales but he doesn't miss a beat as he stops and leans down to kiss me. I stop and bring my hand around the back of his head, pulling him into my kiss. I slide my body up along his, allowing me to I feel every inch of him along my body. A spark jolts my entire being as our lips touch, but I don't let it cloud my head.

I hear Raven from behind us making a fuss. "Oh eww! Seriously you two! I'm right here, do you have to make out in front of me?"

I smile into his lips. Her reaction is exactly what I wanted.

I drop the bow into my hands, slide the Fae feathered arrow down, and nock it as I take one quick step back. In a flash I have the arrow with the rope tied to it flying through the air.

21

JAMES

We're farther north than I've ever been in my life. None of the maps I've ever seen went this far north. How is it possible I didn't know the world extended this far? Have I truly been left in the dark for this long?

The commander and Ned seem to see this as normal. I know they've gone on plenty of missions when they were younger but why wouldn't they at least add this territory to the maps in Sanctuary?

What else have they been hiding?

I decide to ask them straight out. "Why isn't this on any of the maps at Sanctuary? I know we've passed the last town mentioned on any map I've ever seen."

I sit on my horse waiting for a reply which doesn't come. The commander and Ned ride silently side by side ahead of me. Ned towers over us on his warhorse he calls Mylo. They keep peeking back and forth like they're searching for something. I guess they didn't let me in on whatever it is they're searching for. I'm surprised they're still this chummy, I really thought I'd driven a wedge between them back at Sanctuary.

I clear my throat and ask again, louder this time. *"Why isn't this..."*

"Shut up, boy," Ned snaps in a low tone.

That's it, I'm done playing nice. I ride up between the two men, pulling out my dagger. I bring it up to Ned's throat as I shout, *"You are not my superior. I do not have to—"* but before I can finish I'm slapped on the back of the head. My head slams forward, and I drop the hand holding the dagger forward to wrap my wrist around the horn in front of me to keep myself upright.

"Shut the hell up boy!" The commander hisses next to me. "He *is* your superior. He decided to come out of retirement which means you better listen to his orders or face the consequences."

My face falls and my mouth goes dry. He's back in the military? This means if I kill him I'll be killing an officer. I would be tried as a traitor, which would mean certain death.

From my side the commander whispers to Ned, "You all right over there?" Why is everyone whispering, what the hell is happening? I gaze up to Ned's face. He's grinning at me, and I finally notice his neck. When I fell forward I sliced his throat. Blood coats the front of his tunic, but only a little cut mars his neck. I scrunch my face in confusion. With that much blood there should be a deep wound there. Ned winks at me as I watch his neck stitch back together on its own.

My mouth drops open and I inhale in a deep breath. I pull back on my reins, getting as far away from Ned as possible. "Comm—Comm—" I stutter. Ned's gaze follows me, his venomous sneer gets wider and wider the more I can't get the words out. I swallow and brace myself as I shout, *"Commander he's a Fae!"*

The commander ignores me, turns to Ned, and exasperatedly says, "You seriously had to show him? What happened to keeping it a secret?"

Ned shrugs his shoulders. "He sliced my throat. I couldn't help him seeing it knit back up."

I yank my horse to a stop completely. *"You knew?"* I yell.

The commander turns backwards in his seat to face me. I can tell by the pained expression on his face that doing it, with how massive he is, is uncomfortable for him. "Yes, now shut the hell up; we're in enemy territory!"

"The enemy is right here!" I say as I point to Ned.

The commander rolls his eyes and opens his mouth but doesn't get a chance to say anything. Ned interrupts him, his voice is grave, "It's too late. They're here. I can hear them; they heard the brat."

"Who's here!" I shout. I'm so frustrated. I haven't been told anything. The commander knew Ned was a Fae and he allowed him to stay in Sanctuary and fight alongside our people? The commander is a traitor to our kind, and we let him lead us? Before I get an answer I'm yanked off the back of my horse. As I fly through the air I see the commander and Ned take off running opposite ways, leaving me to my fate.

I hit the ground harder than should have been possible. All I see are elongated ears before everything goes dark.

22

ATTINA

Talon sees it a second too late and my arrow hits its mark, in the middle of his right wing. I hear his pained screech and for a second I almost feel bad for him. But then I remember all the lives he helped end and the feeling quickly vanishes.

I could have simply clipped his wing but then he might have been able to glide away and who knows if we ever would've found him. This way, with the arrow in his wing, attached to a rope, I can pull him down to us.

The arrow hits with such force the entire thing goes through his wing. His whole body lilts sideways and he heads into a tailspin, careening down towards us. I thought he'd pull himself out of the fall by now, but he hasn't and he's getting dangerously close to the treetops. With his size, I'm not sure I could catch him with my powers.

"Hazel!" I yell.

She shouts, "On it," before launching off of Raven's saddle. Her huge wings spread and there's barely enough room for them between the trees. She makes it to him in a flash and we're lucky she's as big as he is because he slams into her full force, knocking her off kilter but at the last minute she rights herself and glides down to us safely with him on her back.

It's not until they make it down to us I actually see how big Talon truly is. While he's sleeker than Hazel, he's just as tall as she is. It really was a stroke of good luck she was able to catch him and carry him, she's much stronger than I ever gave her credit for.

Hazel lands in front of me and tilts her body allowing Talon to roll off her back. It's only then I see he couldn't catch himself because the impact of my arrow knocked him out cold. I take a step forward and lift his wing to inspect his wound. His main body is white and red speckled, while his wings are black and white speckled. His sharp, deadly beak is black but there's a red, bloody sheen to it like he killed something not too long ago. I lift his wing and see the gaping hole left by the Fae arrow. Lucky for him, being a Fae animal, he's already healing. I watch as the flesh stitches itself slowly back together.

He wiggles in my hand and his red tail flops up and down. He's starting to wake up. I have to act fast. I cut the rope from the arrow and quickly pull the arrow through his wing. I chop off the bloody section of rope and throw it to the side. I don't know if there are any Solis in the area but if there are I don't want them being drawn to us by the tangy, iron-like smell of the blood. I wrap the rest of the rope around his leg and tie it off.

Just as I finish tying the last knot his ochre eyes shoot open. His pupils dilate before focusing on me. He jumps back and away from me. He obviously knows who I am. He spreads his black and white wings out wide, and I notice his wing is fully healed, no remnant of a wound to be seen. The only difference is now he has a bald patch of skin where there once were luscious feathers. He flaps his wings and takes off into the air but is quickly met with a hard tug on his foot. It's enough to bring him down to the ground hard. He lands in a pile of body parts and feathers.

Talon gets back up and shakes his head. He lifts his foot and inspects the rope attached to it. He pecks at it with his beak, obviously trying to get free of it. I tug on the rope again, throwing him off balance so badly he flips over and lands on his back. When he gets up this time his gaze follows the rope to my hand. I hold the rope up for him to see, smile, and wink at him. "Nice to meet you, Talon."

He doesn't answer, instead he scans the enemy in front of him. He scans past me and seems disinterested when he peers at Raven with Hazel on her back again. But when his gaze finally falls on Allister I can see the anger coating his features as he opens his beak and huffs, his breathing hitching up. I'm starting to wonder if he can talk like all the other Fae animals I've encountered. I would have thought he'd be yelling and screaming by now.

I turn to Allister and watch him tilt his head and wave his hand, "Hey buddy! How you doin?"

Before I can turn back to see Talon's reaction he's on Allister, trying to scratch his eyes out with his sharp, deadly claws. If it wasn't for my Fae speed he would have met his mark too, in the last second I'm able to yank him away and down to the ground. I peek back at Allister and notice a small scratch is stitching itself back up on his cheek.

Allister's hand travels to his check, wiping away the small trickle of blood and he chuckles. "Well ole' Tal, was attacking me really necessary?"

"Traitor!" Talon croaks out. I know he's trying to scream, but it's as if he hasn't used his voice in so long the words are a strain. "I knew you were a traitor. Your honeyed words might have fooled Henrik, but they didn't fool me for a second."

Allister takes a step forward and puts his hands on his hips, bending over toward Talon. "Oh? And your master wouldn't believe you? No wonder you always hated me so much."

Talon's eyes narrow but he stays quiet.

I take a step forward now in line with Allister. "Do you know who I am?" Talon inclines his head. "And who they are?" I ask as I bring my arm out and behind me, pointing to where Raven and Hazel stand.

"The horse I don't know, and I thought Hazel was dead a long time ago. I could have gone a lifetime without seeing your ugly mug again." His gaze snaps up to Hazel.

"Same goes for you," Hazel answers.

"The horse is Raven. She's Oak's daughter. I'm sure you knew my mother's mount, Oak."

He gazes around like what I'm saying is inconsequential. "I didn't realize the old nag had any offspring."

An anger wells in my gut. I want to burn this bird alive and bask in the ashes of his body. Old nag? Oak was no old nag, he was magnificent. I feel fire rising in me but as I take a deep breath, I'm reminded that's an action Henrik would take and I will never be like him. I quell the fire in me and instead I call to the earth under Talon and fling him into the nearest tree. He hits hard with a thud.

I hear as everyone around me sharply inhales but I don't care, he deserved it. I stalk over to where Talon is picking himself up off of the ground and shaking his head, probably trying to get his senses back. "You *will not* speak ill of the dead. He was her *father*," I say as I point behind me to Raven.

I hear Raven behind me. "Girl, leave it, he's not worth it." But I ignore her, it's worth it to me.

"And he was *my* mount! If you ever speak of him in that manner again I will not hesitate to burn you to ash!" I shout.

Talon finally peeks up and meets my gaze, his eyes are wide but then a smirk stretches across his beak. "You can wield fire? And that temper of yours is exactly like your grandfather's. Are you sure you wouldn't be happier on our side where you can do as you wish? Kill as you wish? Rule over all?"

I glare down at him. "I may be able to wield fire, but I am nothing like my grandfather."

"Sure, I believe—" Talon starts, but I cut him off.

"*If* I was like my grandfather you would be a pile of ash on the ground right now instead of running your trap like you think I don't have the upper hand. I shot you out of the sky. I control your movements now." To emphasize my words I pull on the rope and he hops over to me to stay upright.

He shrugs his shoulder by lifting his wing. "You're just young, it will come with time."

I lift my hand and step toward him but as I do I feel Allister's reassuring hand warming my back. "Attina, he's not worth it. We have more important things to do."

I lean into his touch, the skin under his hand jolts with electricity. I turn my gaze up to him. "You're right but I need to do one last thing."

His brows furrow and he tilts his head. "What?"

I smirk but don't answer him. I turn back to Talon and will a band of air to wrap around his body, clamping down tight on it. He wriggles, fights, and squawks against the restraint I've now put on him. Watching him fight brings a little warmth to my heart. I'm sure he's watched many a creature wriggle and struggle because of his actions, it's a sort of poetic justice.

Stepping forward, I bend down, plucking five feathers

from him, and sweetly say, "Thank you for these." I take a step back and motion toward Hazel. "Hazel has offered up some of her feathers for my special arrows but now because of you she won't have to have any more of them taken from her." I release the hold I have on him, and he collapses to the ground gasping for breath.

Maybe I restrained him a little too tightly—darn.

When he gets himself together he glares up at me and snarls out. "You'll pay for this, half-breed."

I shrug my shoulders and happily say, "Maybe. Maybe not. We'll see, I guess." In a more serious tone I say, "Now we're leaving and you're coming with us."

He lowers his head and stares up at me from under his brow. "Make me."

I lift the hand with the rope still in it, I loom over him, and smile. "We can do this the easy way or the hard way." He lifts his head but stays silent. "The easy way is you fly above us and follow us, I hold on to the rope as a precaution, and everyone is happy."

Allister lovingly wraps his arms around my shoulders and pulls me into his chest. I don't break eye contact with Talon though. I watch as his eyes zero in on where Allister and I make contact, studying us. "The hard way is you refuse to do fly with us, and I drag you behind us."

He cocks his head and thinks for a second before answering. "You did just shoot an arrow through my wing." He lifts the healed wing, showing us the bald spot. "Can't I ride on the horse—"

I cut him off. "She has a name."

He corrects himself. "Can't I ride on Raven like I watched Hazel doing before you shot me out of the sky?"

Crossing my arms I pretend I'm thinking about his

words. I narrow my eyes, turning my gaze into a harsh unflinching one and simply answer, "No."

He throws his wings out and screeches, "Why not!?"

I chuckle and point to his clawed feet. "So you can tear up my saddle?" I lift an eyebrow. "Not even all the gods could compel me to let you do that." It might seem petty. I know I've already beat this bird thoroughly, but I've had my saddle my whole life. It fits perfectly to my body after years of wear and tear. I know if I let this bird in my saddle he will ruin it beyond repair merely out of spite.

He doesn't even say a word to my reply, he simply shoots into the air. He catches me off guard as he flies away so fast the rope yanks on my hand, making me almost lose the rope completely. I grab on with all my might and yank down on him. I watch as he falls from the air a bit before catching himself. I quickly tie the rope around my wrist in case he tries it again.

We must look like one of the strangest band of misfits as we continue our journey. Everyone is quiet for a minute before Raven pipes up. "You shouldn't have been so hard on him."

I slice my gaze to the right where she walks at my side. "He's been by Henrik's side for who knows how long. Do you realize how many people he's been a party to murdering? He had a hand in our father's murders remember?"

She slowly bobs her head. "Yes but we don't know his side. Maybe Henrik made him do it."

"And maybe he's just as evil as Henrik."

Now Hazel decides to throw in her two cents from where she glides above us. "But you heard Henrik wasn't always evil. Maybe Talon has a similar story. Besides we should still aim to be better than either of them."

I throw my hands up, which is a feat in itself with how

Talon is pulling the rope taut, flying as far away from us as the rope will allow. "Seriously, you two?"

"They're simply looking out for you, Attina." Allister coos to my left, his hand grabbing onto mine as his fingers twist through mine. "You were a little vicious back there." He leans in and whispers, "I completely approve. The bird had it coming, but they worry about that cold-hearted side you sometimes show. Let us in your head a little bit more. I know it's hard, but we will never hurt or betray you. You're our queen and we love you."

I pull in a deep, calming breath of air and lose myself in his words. I knew he loved me; he's hinted as much before. I mean I'm his mate, but this is the first time he's said it out loud. His eyes shoot open as the realization of what he said hits him. I feel his hand slink out of mine and he brings it up to rub the back of his neck. "Oh um...um." But he trails off.

Raven takes the opportunity to push into me. "Yeah girl, we all love you and only want to see you flourish. Back there was a little more torture than we expected, and we're worried about you losing control."

I gaze back at Raven, and Hazel above her, my eyes soften. "I will admit my first instinct was to light Talon on fire and watch him burn to ash." The group as a collective stops mid stride and I turn to them and hold up my hands. "*But* I didn't."

Hazel glares down on me from where she's landed atop Raven's back. "If you have thoughts like those again tell us. We all need to be open and honest." Everyone nods in agreement.

"I promise I will."

We walk for the rest of the day, until dusk, when we decide it's time to start making camp. As a group we decide it's safest if I wrap my band of air around Talon for the night. Preventing him from getting away and alerting Henrik to our whereabouts. Hazel sleeps on a high tree branch while I get more arrows made. When I'm finished I put away the arrows I've made before I crawl under the blankets between Raven and Allister.

23

NED

I made it out of the Fae's clutches. I'm not sure how I did it, but I did. Maybe they heard James yell about me being Fae so they didn't chase me? I shake my head. No, that's not right. I would have to be from Shadow Mountain then. If I were them, getting a Fae from Shadow Mountain would be my top priority. Especially over some humans, if even just for a little payback. John and I knew we were heading into Eastern Fae lands, but the damn boy refused to listen. When he started throwing a fit I didn't knock him down because I figured there wouldn't be any Fae this far away from the stronghold but I obviously miscalculated.

Now here I am racing through the night. I have no idea where I'm going or what to do next. Thank the gods we were on our horses at the time, and I had the fastest horse of the bunch. I reach down and pat Mylo, I wouldn't have made it out of there without him. It only now hits me he shouldn't have been able to out run those Fae horses I spotted behind us after we took off. Maybe they simply gave up on me, choosing to chase after weaker and slower prey but I'm not certain.

I lean forward and tilt my head until I can barely see his face as the moon streaks down on it through the trees. "Are you sure you're not a Fae horse buddy?"

He keeps moving like I didn't say anything, but I'm sure I saw his eyes turn back toward me in recognition. Or maybe I'm just delirious from lack of sleep. I haven't really slept since we left Sanctuary. I knew James would try to kill me in my sleep and I was right.

The bastard.

I pat Mylo one last time. "Let's find somewhere safe to stop for the night and get some rest. We'll figure out what to do in the morning."

24

JAMES

My eyes flutter open. I'm lying on cold, hard rock with my back up against something solid. How did this happen? I was just on top of a horse. Then a splitting pain in my head hits me like a stampede. "What the?" I say as I lift my hand to the back of my head, it's soaking wet.

Blood.

I don't have to be able to see my hand to know it's bloody. Not like I could see it if I wanted to. It's pitch black where I am. Then it hits me. We were riding, searching for Attina and the Fae. I was arguing with Ned and the commander, then I fell from my horse, something hit the back of my head and the world went blank.

I sit up and lean against the wall my back is against. Reaching out, I only feel more rock. I don't dare try and stand with the amount of blood I've lost, but I have to figure out where I am. I start crawling my way around the room I'm in.

I inch forward on my hands and knees keeping the wall of the room to my right. I reach a wall which is perpendicular to the one on my right and follow it. This one ends at an open space. I reach my hand in front of me and swing it in a big arch. It hits something cold and circular. I run my hand up and down it.

A bar.

I move to my left and find another. There is bar after bar lining one wall of the room. No, not a room.

A cell.

I press my head against the bars to see if there is any light around. Anything that could help me see where I am, who has captured me, but there's nothing.

I call out, "Hello! Is anyone out there?"

Someone calls back, "Shut your mouth! They'll come back if you keep hollering like that!" I instantly recognize the voice.

"Commander?"

"Yes. Now shut up. You wouldn't listen to me out there and you see where it got us. Now shut up and get some rest. I will do the talking from here on out. If I hear you again, consider yourself banned from Sanctuary."

If we ever make it back I think to myself. I make my way to the back of my cell and sit down, leaning my back against the wall with a loud huff. I rub the back of my head. The blood seems to have stopped flowing, but barely.

25

ATTINA

I'm awoken by Raven getting up and a flap of Hazel's massive wings. Before I know it I'm standing searching for my sword. I was in such a deep sleep it's a little disorienting to all of a sudden be awake and moving. It takes me a second to realize I was lying on top of my sword— a second which could have cost me my life.

I reach down and pick up my sword, noticing Allister is already at the ready with his hand held before him. I scan around our campsite. Everyone is staring into the trees, but I don't hear anything.

"What's going on?"

No one answers.

I close my eyes, comforted in the fact that I know Allister will protect me if anything happens. I feel the ground beneath me and instantly realize there is someone or something walking toward us. I can feel four feet but by the weight of those feet its either a horse weighed down by a saddle and body or something much more sinister.

I open my eyes and whisper, "They're about forty feet in and coming straight for us." I take in a deep breath and wait.

I think about grabbing my bow and arrows but in the trees it wouldn't be much help. I can do this. I can take on whatever is coming at us. I need to believe in myself. Before I truly feel ready, a horse breaks through the tree line. But the horse is far enough away, it's only the silhouette of one, but I can tell it's a horse with a rider.

I hear a noise from my right. "Mylo."

I turn my head to Raven. "What?"

"I can smell him. It's Mylo. But I can't tell who's on top of him."

Without a second thought I swing onto Raven's back. It's not until I'm up there though that I realize I easily did it one handed with a sword in my other hand, and I didn't kill myself doing it. That's even better than how I got on her bareback at the tree. I could get used to this Fae strength.

I smirk. "Well why don't we go give them a proper welcome?"

Raven shakes her head as I grab her mane, kick her, and we're off racing through the trees. I sense Hazel in the air at our backs as Allister yells behind me, "Attina wait."

I hear, *Get back here,* shouted in my mind but I ignore him. We race ahead, dodging trees as we race through the night.

We get about halfway to Mylo when I lift my sword in the air and shout, "Who are you!"

I hear, "Attina?" Then Raven slams on the brakes, almost sending me flying over her front end. Since I'm not in a saddle it takes latching my legs down on her with all of my Fae strength to keep myself astride her. I end up with the front half of my body wrapped around her neck, good thing I had the presence of mind to hold my sword out away from Raven. When I collect myself I sit up and see Ned and Mylo trotting over to us. I throw my leg over Raven's back and the ground catches me gently as I land.

"Ned!" I shout as I race over to them. In my mind I tell Allister *It's Ned! Get over here!*

Ned stops Mylo, hops down, and runs over to me. He shocks me by wrapping me in his arms, picking me up, and spinning me around. I lift my sword high into the air to keep from accidentally cutting either of us.

As he puts me down, I feel Allister walking up behind us. I take a step away, allowing the two men to greet each other. To my surprise Ned walks up and wraps his arms around Allister like he's welcoming a brother.

As they pull away I ask, "What are you doing out here? How did you find us?"

Ned lets out a gust of air and rubs the back of his neck before answering, "It's a long story."

From above I hear Hazel groan, "Now, can we head back to camp? I was in the middle of an extremely nice dream."

Ned lifts his head. "Um who's that?" He says as he points to the tree Hazel is hidden in.

I chuckle and shake my head. I lift my hand in a follow me motion. "Let's head back. We have a lot to tell you too."

I revive the embers of the fire with only a thought, and we sit down in a circle, just like the old days as we traveled across Arealea. I gaze over the fire and study Ned; his appearance is the same. As the fire bounces off of him, it accentuates his ferocious scarred burns down the right side of his body. The scars he got when Henrik murdered his parents and burned his family's home to ashes. He rubs his hand across his bald head and widens his bright green eyes at me. "You did that?" He points at the fire in front of him. I scan him up and down. His gray sweats from Sanctuary are stained with dirt and disheveled. But it's his swollen, dark circled eyes which tell me he hasn't slept in at least a week, which worries me.

Allister passes him some of our deer jerky and I ask, "Are you sure you want to do this right now? You look beyond exhausted. It can wait until morning."

He shakes his head. "No, let's get this over with now. I'm so beat because James has been trying to kill me every night for the past week."

I furrow my brows and tilt my head. "You came out here with James? Why in all the gods would you do such a thing?"

He leans back, holding his weight on his hands behind him and gazes up into the sky. The trees are thick here but there are still patches where you can see the dark starry sky peeking through. He begins his story, telling us what happened when he beat James back to Sanctuary. He tells us how Commander Demarco was suspicious, and he had to join the army again to get John back on his side. How calm and collected James was, telling his story so confidently and swaying John to his side.

"We came out here searching for you so James could prove you were with a Fae." His eyes move to Allister. "But each night James would try to kill me, which meant I never got to sleep. We finally made it into Eastern Fae territory." Allister crosses his arms next to me, drawing my attention. I glance back to Ned as he continues, "But that stupid kid wouldn't shut up. The Fae found us. They attacked us quick as lightning, hitting James over the head, knocking him out. John and I ran in separate directions."

He glances over to Mylo, and I do too. I see him rubbing his head against Raven's neck. She on the other hand is leaning away from him like he's crazy. I chuckle as I say, "So he outran Fae horses? How's that possible?"

He shakes his head as he turns back and gazes into the

fire, "No idea. I'm not sure he's only a regular horse. I think there's something more to him the longer I'm around him." And if on cue Mylo lifts his head and locks his eyes on Ned.

I shrug. "Hey, maybe you found your Fae companion. Closing my eyes, I rub my face trying to take in all he's told us.

Allister is the first one to say anything. "So, now James and the commander are prisoners of the Eastern Fae?"

Ned grunts, his eyes slowly closing. I get up, walk over to him, bend down, and wrap my arms around him. After a moment I pull back and lock eyes with him. "Get some sleep, we can finish this in the morning or whenever you wake up. We need you in top shape for what's to come. You're of no use to us like this."

Ned yawns. "You're right, I better get some rest," he immediately lies down in the dirt and falls fast asleep. I chuckle and shake my head as I stand, walking over to Mylo. I unsaddle him and pull Ned's saddle bags off of the saddle. They're surprisingly light, which is strange. Ned knew he was coming out into the cold. Why would he pack this light? I dig through them and realize they're this light because all he has is a bed roll and a change of clothes. He must not have been carrying the food and water or maybe they ran out of food and water?

I bring over his bedroll and put it under his head. He has a thick heavy cloak on, but I still grab one of the blankets I brought from the tree and throw it on top of him. That should be enough to keep him warm. I quickly check the tree Talon is lying under and I can barely see he's still sleeping on the pile of leaves I left him on earlier. My air band is still tightly wrapped around him. I walk over to the tree, and my movement wakes him, and he glares up at me. I reach out and yank on the rope securing Talon to the tree.

I'm satisfied he won't be able to break free in the middle of the night, so I leave him to his sleep.

I make my way back to where Allister has already gotten back into our makeshift bed. He lifts the blanket, inviting me in, "Well, I guess we'll have to share tonight," he says as he smirks at me.

I drop to my knees and crawl in. "Sorry, I couldn't let him freeze."

He smirks, wrapping his arm around my middle, and pulls me tight into him. "Do you hear me complaining?"

I suck in a breath as I feel his long length against my backside. "Allister!" I screech.

He tugs on me once. "Can you blame me? I'm cuddled up to my mate, I can't help it."

I quickly sit up. "Ned is right there sleeping." I point over to him as I stare down at my beautiful mate. My eyes drift down to his scrumptious taut arms wrapped around me, making my cheeks heat. Everything in me goes slack. He grins up at me like he knows what merely gazing at him does to me. I shake my head, clearing the fog thinking of him has caused. "What are we doing about James and the commander?"

Allister lies back on the ground and puts his arms behind his head as he gazes up at the night sky. "What do you mean? They were captured. We can't do anything. Besides, does it really matter?"

I glare down at him and curtly answer, "Yes, it matters."

He turns to me. "Why? Let's say they *are* still alive which I *highly* doubt. They're locked up in some dark cell far from our reach. Besides, one of them is James, he could use some cell time. And the other is this commander, and I haven't heard anything to make me think he's a terribly delightful man himself."

I'm flabbergasted for a minute. I mean he's not wrong. Neither of them are wonderful people. As I'm about to drop the subject it hits me. "The commander is the leader of the humans. We will need him on our side, we can't do that with him locked up in some cell."

"Shit," slips out of his mouth.

I smile cockily knowing I'm right. "See. We need to save them."

"Them?" He cocks his head as he gazes up at me with his hands behind his head. "All I heard was we need to save the commander."

I don't answer, I narrow my eyes down at him instead.

Allister huffs out a loud sigh and rolls on his side. "Fine, you're right, are you happy?"

I bounce in my seat and smile. "Quite happy actually."

He wraps his arm around me and yanks me down into his arms. Laughter bursts through me as he says, "Let's head to bed mate, we can figure it out in the morning. Ned isn't the only one who's exhausted."

He wiggles his arm under my head, and I say, "Goodnight" as Raven and Mylo begin bedding down for the night. I hear Hazel make one last rustle in the tree above us and I think to myself, *I love having my whole family back together.*

Allister answers, *I love having a family.*

26

ATTINA

We all wake with the rising sun, Ned included. I open my eyes, but I don't move for a second. I don't want to leave the warmth and safe feeling having Allister's strong arm draped over me brings. It takes a second for my thoughts to straighten out as the shock of having Ned's back with us hits me all over again. I sit up and rub the sleep out of my eyes as Allister props himself up on his elbows next to me. I peer over at him. It's extremely unfair he gets to look this gorgeous right when he wakes up. I know my hair must be all over the place at weird angles, but here he sits, not one hair out of place. How does he do that?

"Good morning beautiful," he says as his purple eyes sparkle against the morning light.

I shake my head and chuckle. "You're definitely the beautiful one out of the two of us."

His hand reaches up to my cheek and cups my face, his hand is so toasty I just want to melt into it. I close my eyes and lean into the warmth, letting it fill me from my cheek all the way down to my toes. "You're the most beautiful thing I've ever seen."

My eyes shoot open as his words process. I give him a pitiful smile. "You have to say those things, we're mates, you're stuck with me."

His eyes harden, he sets his jaw, and shakes his head. His long black hair swings around his face from the motion. "No. Even before I knew you were my mate, your beauty about knocked me off my feet. You're more beautiful inside and out than anyone I've met in my whole life. I could watch a million sunsets over three lifetimes and their combined beauty wouldn't hold a candle to yours."

I smile, placing my hand over his. I turn my head and kiss his palm whispering into it, "Thank you."

I turn back to him as he drops his hand to my leg, "You still don't believe me. Do you?" I scrunch my face up and shake my head instead of answering.

I turn behind me and check on Talon, he's still sitting under a tree behind us in the pile of leaves I left him in. His ochre eyes meet mine. He glares at me for a split second before ripping his gaze from mine and staring off stoically into the distance. The rope tied to his leg is still tied to the tree at the other end. I wanted to make sure if my powers gave out in the middle of the night for any reason he wouldn't be able to cut the rope with his beak and get away.

I'd hoped we would hear him before that happened, but we were all so tired, who knows what would have happened. I still don't trust my powers completely. Maybe I should trust them by now, but I just can't yet for some reason. There's not a solid reason, but I can't yet. Not when my powers failing would mean Talon escaping and handing our location over to Henrik.

Allister squeezes my leg, drawing my attention back to him. "Then, I'll keep reminding you until you believe me, or I'll spend the rest of our lives reminding you how beautiful you are." A tender smile crosses his lips as I lean over and kiss his forehead.

I open my mouth to reply but a loud groan interrupts me. I pull my eyes away from Allister to peer over at Ned who's stretching his arms up and around his head. He quickly sits up and scans around him like he's trying to reorient himself.

"Good morning sleepyhead," I call over to him.

He spins and locks his gaze on me, "Oh! Hey." His hand lifts to his forehead. "I almost forgot where I was for a minute." He slowly stands up and groans again as he stretches his arms back above his head, arching his back, stretching the rest of his body. He twists his torso and as he moves he must see Talon because his eyes fixate on the tree behind me, and he freezes. "Um what is that? Is that the bird I heard last night? Why is it tied up?"

Hazel takes the opportunity to glide out of the tree above me and land next to Ned. He jumps up and his eyes shoot open wide as she says, "No, you heard me last night."

He doesn't have to bend down far to examine her since she stands up to him mid-thigh but watching him scan her over has me throwing myself back in laughter. Allister takes the opportunity to jump half of his body over top of mine, knocking me the rest of the way down, and wrapping me in a tight bear hug. My laughter turns up an octave and becomes more of a screechy cackle.

"What the hell you two?" Ned yells but he sounds so far away from mine and Allister's little bubble.

I barely make out Raven saying, "They've been getting more lovey and annoying by the day."

I hear some mumbling and then nothing. When I've got my laughing under control and Allister releases me, I sit back up. I notice Ned is gone. I turn to Raven, "Where did he go?" I say as I point to Ned's empty bedroll.

She rolls her eyes, "You two were being gross so he said he was heading out to search for some firewood to build a small fire. I think he wanted to get away from the two of you." I can see the fire in her glare from where I sit.

My cheeks heat and I stand up. I shouldn't be embarrassed, Allister is my mate, it's natural. So far I haven't been the girl who's done the love thing. I've never been touchy feely with *anyone* before. I don't know how to balance being around everyone and being around my mate. I walk over and put Ned's bedroll away. It's the least I can do since we pretty much chased him off. Allister is helping me put our things away when Ned comes back with a small bundle of wood tucked under his arm.

He walks over and places them in the fire pit and shoves some pine needles from the forest floor under them. Wordlessly, he strides over to his saddle bag. Is he seriously mad at me? He digs in it for a second and fishes out with a piece of flint he always used to start fires with when we were traveling together. I wait until Ned has bends down by the fire pit to feel for the pull in my stomach and tug on it as I stare at the logs. A roaring fire instantly sparks to life.

He turns to me and cracks a huge grin. I'm instantly over flowing with relief. "I guess this means you figured out your powers while I was gone?"

I shrug like it's no big deal and say, "Yeah, it was a walk in the woods," and wink at him.

He almost believes it until Hazel hops up next to the fire and fluffs her feathers. "She's only trying to impress you."

Ned peers down at her and tilts his head, "Not to be rude, but how did you join the group?"

She starts explaining to him who she is and why she

showed up. Peering over at me she tells him how she and Allister also helped me to figure out my powers. Then, Allister and I butt in and finish filling Ned in on what's happened since he was last with us. We tell him about Talon, the secret tree, how we found it's opening using his father's sword and my necklace, the prophecy, how the tree showed me where my mother's armor was, and all the things in between.

He points over to the tree Talon sits under. "So, let me get this straight. He's Henrik's hawk?"

I shrug my shoulders. "What were we supposed to do? He found us. If we left him alone he'd fly back and tell Henrik where we are. Then Henrik would for sure send one of his special projects out to kill us.

When I finish Raven doesn't give Ned time to respond as she walks over with Mylo close on her tail. "So what's the plan now? I'm assuming we're still heading to the Eastern Fae to get them on our side. What will happen when we get there? And what about James and the Commander, what are we going to do about them?"

Ned spits, "Let James rot."

I send him a withering glare. "That's not helpful."

From behind me I hear Talon shriek, "Hey half-breed! Unbind my wings. I'm rather uncomfortable."

I spin around and cross my arms. "You promise to be good?"

"I'll do anything to get this dirty magic band of air off me."

The words are barely out of Talon's mouth when I hear Allister. "Choke on your own spit and die?"

Talon doesn't say a word, he just glares at him.

I scoff and shake my head. "Again, that's not helpful." There's no answer from him as I release Talon from my magic. He slowly spreads his wings and stands up. He puffs out all his feathers and shakes his whole body. I hear a deep sigh release from him. I don't untie him because I still have to saddle up Raven and I can't saddle and hold him at the same time.

I turn back around to face my friends, but I hear Talon squeak out behind me, drawing my attention back. "You're traveling to the Eastern Fae?" He's waddling over to us like he's stiff from being tied up all night, but I don't let myself feel bad. It needed to be done.

Allister spins around. He's glaring and his face is pinched as he leans forward. The energy I feel coming off of him is like a band being pulled too tight and is seconds from exploding. I slowly take a few steps over to him, place my hand on his back, and lean around him so my face takes up Allister's vision instead of Talon. "Hey, it's fine. He can't hurt anyone else."

It takes a couple of seconds for Allister to register my presence, but I notice when he does because his eyes switch from glossy and vacant to focused on my face. He meekly asks, "How do you know?" He points toward the bird. "What if he gets away from us?"

I shake my head and step into him, wrapping my arms around him. "We're close to your home right?" He wraps his arms around me, puts his head down into my shoulder, and nods. "When we get there it won't matter if he gets away or not. Henrik won't be able to reach us."

Behind us Talon snarls out, "Henrik can reach you anywhere little girl. He will have you in his grasp. It might not happen today or tomorrow but mark my words, it will happen."

I pull away from Allister and shake my head. "We will be all right. It will all work out. I know it will because not too long ago my mate told me it would." I smirk at him. I don't know where all of this confidence is coming from. I'm completely shocked but also comforted in the fact that even if I don't fully believe what I'm saying, maybe I can fake my way through it.

"You're her mate?" I hear the shock and disgust in Talon's voice, and I drop my head in defeat. I tried to save him from Allister's wrath, I really did. I throw my hands up and step away. Shaking my head I throw my arm out behind me and say, "Go for it."

A menacing grin spreads across Allister's face and I hear a crack behind me. I turn to Talon and see ice incasing his beak. His nose holes are still open, allowing him to breathe, but the rest is glued shut by the ice. A satisfied smile replaces the menacing grin and Allister stands up a little straighter as he meets my gaze once more. "You should have let me shut him up a long time ago."

I peer over at Talon and chuckle. "In all fairness I honestly thought you would kill him. But yes, you're right, I should have let you do it a long time ago." I turn back to our family again and am surprised no one says anything. This group of big mouths has nothing to say about our last exchange.

When I'm just about to open my mouth and say something about it, Ned says, "While I'm happy you're more confident about our mission, I agree with Raven, we need to figure out what's happening and plan accordingly." Hearing Ned leading the conversation again brings a smile to my face. I know it's strange given the conversation we're now having, but I can't help it.

But, of course, Raven immediately notices my strange reaction. "Girl. I don't care if you're in the lovey dovey stage with Allister. This is not the time to turn into a mindless twit." My mouth drops open. "Hearing you say you have more confidence is great and all, but I know you, and I don't believe it for a second." She glares down at me which only serves to make me chuckle, causing her to seethe. "What the hell is so funny, girl!"

I shake my head and make my way over to her. When I get to her she lifts her head and takes a step back away from me. The action shows me she's unsure what my crazy ass is about to do. I fling myself forward and wrap my arms around her neck. As I pull back I pat her on the neck. "I was getting worried you had lost that snarky fire of yours, girl." I spin around and say more to the entire group than only Raven, "I'm just ridiculously happy to have my family back together I can't help smiling."

Ned and Allister's shoulders both drop and their features soften as they both stride over to me. Before I know it I'm wrapped in a group hug. I'm still surprised the boys are being this civil to each other, but they seem to have turned a corner in their relationship, and I'm happy for it.

Allister pulls away and lets Ned continue hugging me, knowing what I need even before I do. Tears fill my eyes as I breathe in his citrusy smell. "I missed you," I √ into his front.

"I missed you too, kid." He squeezes me tightly one last time before pulling back. When I can see his face I see there are tears streaking down his pinkened, scarred face too. Everything goes quiet for a minute while we all simply stand there together.

To break the awkward tension I peek around Ned to where Hazel is watching all this go down, still standing by the fire pit. "So you didn't want to join in on the love fest?"

She ruffles her feathers and shakes her head. "No. I'd rather die than be a party to whatever this is."

I lift my hands up and move around Ned. "Oh come on.

You know you want a hug! Just let me hug you." She brings her speckled wings out, flaps them, and she's up perched in a tree before I know it. I follow her with my gaze and pout when she lands. "Well that wasn't terribly nice, Hazel."

"Come on, they're right. Let's get serious. What should we do?"

I turn my gaze on Allister, surprised he's being this sensible. I notice Raven next to him has Mylo stuck to her side and she's not leaning away from him this time. He must be growing on her. "Well, you know the stronghold best. What do you think?"

Allister drops his gaze to the ground and kicks the dirt underneath him with the tip of his boot. "I was incredibly young the last time I was there I don't remember much. I only remember, unlike Shadow Mountain, it's a stone castle. There's an enormous wall surrounding the castle and the entrance is spelled to keep out everyone who has any ill will to any of the residents. They also have tons of patrols around the area we're about to travel into. I'd like to not run into them if it's possible because I do remember the soldiers were more the capture and ask questions later type. Now, that was back when I was a kid, but I don't want to chance it. I'd like to avoid the dungeons if at all possible."

I announce, "Agreed, I can handle the stealth portion of the trip."

27

ATTINA

Ned spins to me eyes wide, shocked. "How?"

I shrug. "I can encase us in an air bubble remember?" He peers up into the trees and his shoulders drop. I can almost see him finally remember all those mornings he woke up to me and Allister wrapped in our wall of air. "No one will be able to hear us or smell us. I can manipulate earth, which means I can hide our footsteps." His gaze returns to me, and I point up to the tree where Hazel is listening in, "And Hazel can tell us if we're anywhere near anyone who could spot us."

"When did you become this sure of your powers? I haven't been gone for a particularly long time." The question comes out rough like he's accusing me of not being able to pull this off, but his tone is soft and hopeful.

"I'm not. I wasn't even confident my air band would hold that one," I point my thumb over my shoulder at where Talon still sits, "all night. But when it comes down to it I trust my powers to take care of me and my loved ones." I answer as I stand up taller and stick my chest out. "My other powers, I haven't used long enough to know for certain they would help, but all I can do is keep practicing." I turn to Allister, "What'll happen after I get us to the gate? Is there a door we'll have to pass through? Will they kill us on the spot?"

He lifts his hand up to his chest and his face scrunches in thought as he quietly stands there thinking for a second. He inhales a deep breath and lifts his finger in the air like he has an idea. But before any words fall out of his mouth he releases a big huff of air, drops his hands, and his whole body visibly sinks lower. "I have no idea. I know there isn't a door, only a wide break in the stone wall, but honestly, they very well could simply kill us on sight."

I immediately hear a smacking noise to my left. I spin and watch as Talon beats his frozen beak against the tree he's still tied to. My brow furrows as I watch. That can't feel good.

There's a snapping noise and Talon is turning around to face us. "Show up with me in tow and they will definitely kill you on sight. All the Fae know I'm Henrik's bird. They will assume you are with Henrik."

I ignore his remark. He might be right, but I won't give him the satisfaction of letting him see me worry. I lift my hand and spin back around to my friends. "Also what happens if Henrik finds out we're with the Eastern Fae? What's to stop him from coming to the Eastern Fae and starting a war?"

"Henrik will—" comes from Talon before I hear a crack and he stops talking completely. I don't even have to turn around to know Allister froze his beak again and it brings a smile to my face.

"Henrik won't storm the Eastern Fae if that's what you're worried about. There's a reason he killed my father to become king of all the Fae. Henrik might have his slayers, but the Eastern Fae have the numbers Henrik does not. It's a vast region, I don't even know the number of Fae living in the East and I'm not sure Henrik does either. It was much easier for him to kill my father and marry my mother, than it would have been for him to fight my people in a fair battle."

"Okay, well I guess we have that going for us." I gaze around at everyone. "Well, I guess we need to get our things together and head out. We will simply have to figure out things on the fly." I peer over at Hazel who's still perched in the tree above us. "Can you scout ahead?" She curtly bows her head before soaring through the trees and out into the open air.

I pull my mother's armor away from a tree Allister and I were lying next to, and awkwardly yank it over my head. I fight with the armor. Finally realizing I was trying to shove my head through the arm hole. I sigh at my own stupidity and adjust the armor, and my head easily slips through. I take a big gasp of air when my head passes the head hole. I didn't realize it would be so suffocating in there. I'm sure at some point I will be able to do it gracefully, but today is not the day.

Ned's shocked voice calls to me, "Where did you get the armor?"

I search around camp for Ned. I find him standing over by Mylo, his hands holding open his saddlebags like he was just checking them. I lift my arms out and spin around for him to get the whole picture. "Remember, I told you, I got them from the tree my mother's room was in. Isn't it cool? They aren't heavy at all." I move my arm up and down to show him as I say, "And they don't impede my movement at all. It fits like a glove."

When my eyes meet his again I see his mouth is slackened in shock. He slowly makes his way over to me. Each second it takes for him to reach me makes me feel more like maybe I shouldn't have taken this armor. He must know the armor from the way he's staring at it.

When he makes his way over to me, he reaches his hand out and gingerly touches the dark metal rose on the shoulder of the armor. His eyes probe the armor as his fingers glide over it, like he's inspecting every inch of it. "How?"

I shift my weight from one foot to the other, all of a sudden feeling self conscious and nervous. "Um... well.. the tree showed me where it was."

He spits out, "What?" as his eyes slice up to meet mine.

I take a step back and my hand reaches up to fidget with my necklace before I realize what I'm doing. "I was in my mother's hidden room. I was taking clothes for our trip and all of a sudden there was a gust of wind inside the tree. Which, now that I think about it, is strange to begin with. How could wind get *inside* a tree?" My brows knit as I peer up at him.

He crosses his arms in front of his chest and tilts his head down at me like I'm being ridiculous, and says, "You're rambling."

I try standing up straighter, but it doesn't stick. I end up slumping my shoulders again and this time I start nervously picking at my fingers. I stare at the ground in front of me. "I know how strange this sounds but it's the truth. The tree sent a gust of wind into my mother's room, and it lifted the blankets on her bed enough for me to see a shimmer of metal. I bent down and saw this armor under the bed." I run my hand down the armor covering my side. "I figured whoever it belonged to wasn't using it again so I could take it and use it. When I walked out of the tree I felt something warm and inviting and I knew it came from the tree. Oak told me the tree was magical and it knew things. He was right." Ned places his hand on my shoulder, breaking my train of thought. I peek up at him. "Did I do something wrong?"

He chuckles and shakes his head as he wraps his arm all the way around me, pulling me in for a hug. "No you did nothing wrong. I was only shocked to see that armor again."

I pull back from him a bit, "What do you mean? You know this armor?" I peer down at my shoulder as best I can and realize what the rose on it must mean. "Oh, your father made it?"

He sighs, "Yes my father made it for your mother along with her sword and dagger. I haven't seen it since I was a very young boy. I was just shocked to see it." He pulls me in and wraps me in a bear hug. "I wasn't trying to scare or worry you. I'm sorry if I did. We should head out though."

He releases me and takes a step away from me before I call to him, "Wait! Do you want the armor back? It might fit you. Your father made it; it must mean a great deal to you."

He turns on his heel with a huge grin on his face "My father made it for *your* mother. I'm sure the armor means more to you than me. I have my memories of my father to cling to. Sadly, you only have a few trinkets she owned. You're the future queen, it could save your life. You keep it." He bows his head and turns back around heading toward Mylo. Then he waves his hand over his shoulder as he says, "Besides, who am I to doubt some magical tree? Maybe it knows best."

Allister walks over and bumps me in the hip, breaking my concentration on Ned. "So, that's why you hugged the tree before we left? You think it's seriously alive and cognizant?"

I shift toward him. "Does anything else make sense?"

He shakes his head and wraps me in a hug, holding me tight. I wrap my arms around him. I stand there in his embrace for a moment. I'm not sure why he needs this right now, but I can tell he does, so I stand there with him until he pulls away.

We get the rest of camp packed and I untie Talon from the tree. I say, "You know the drill," and he shoots into the air. This time he doesn't try to rip the rope out of my hand. He simply stays with me as I make my way over to Raven and climb on her back.

THE SUN IS SETTING, and I'm surprised we haven't had one hiccup yet. Hazel flies down and gives us reports of what she's seeing every hour. For the most part they're boring reports of nothing around us. She did see some Fae far off in the distance to our right, but they didn't give any indication they knew we were anywhere in the vicinity. My powers must be working then.

I've thankfully been able to keep the wall of air around us the entire day. I don't harden it like I did when I was having my night terrors. This allows the air to move and sway as we travel through the trees. Even Talon has been cooperating the entire day which is surprising based on all of our other interactions.

We've all been relatively quiet today. I'm not sure about everyone else, but I didn't want to press our luck by talking and possibly drawing attention to our little group. That's why I jump in my saddle when Ned whispers. "We should start thinking about where to stop for the night and make camp." I open my mouth to answer him but all of a sudden I feel Hazel's huge form slicing through the air above us.

The way she's descending is almost like she's falling. I lift my head and shout, "Hazel!" Everyone around me shh's me, but I don't care. Something is extremely wrong. I can tell she's about to fall through the trees right above us. Hopefully something bad didn't happen to her, but whatever's happening, it isn't good. She slams through the trees above us and as her amber eyes meet mine, I notice the feet behind us.

"Fuck!" I scream.

I reach my hand down to Allister who is walking next to me. His face is pinched, and his eyes are narrowed but he doesn't ask a question as he grabs my hand and swings onto Raven's back behind me. Before he's completely situated on her backside I kick Raven in the sides as hard as I can, forcing her to shoot off into a flat out run.

I don't have to turn around to know Ned is right behind me, Mylo easily matches Raven's speed. We dodge trees as I shout up to Hazel, "How did you miss this!"

She soars above us. "They came out of nowhere. Henrik must be controlling them somehow. How would he even know where we were? As soon as the question leaves my mind I have my answer. Talon, they must be connected somehow. Henrik must have known where we were because we have Talon.

"What's going on?" Allister shouts through the air whipping around us.

"Solis. A lot of Solis. Running faster than I've ever seen them run before!" I shout back loud enough for Ned to hear. I gaze over at him and see his mouth drop and the color drain from his face. "He must have some sort of connection with Talon. He must know where we are and that we have him."

"I'm gonna kill him!" Allister growls and I feel him moving behind me as he reaches forward for the rope in my hand.

I quickly smack his hand away. "No, he can still be of use to us."

A Solis jumps out from between the trees from our left. Before I have a chance to react, Allister unsheathes his sword, swings it, and chops the thing in half, blood squirting onto my leg. I notice Ned is doing the same thing as he runs next to us.

Behind me Allister says, "Just keep running straight. We can outrun them or chop them down until we get to the Eastern Fae."

I know he's wrong though. I'm not sure how far away the stone wall to the Eastern Fae is, but I know Raven and Mylo will eventually tire, whereas the Solis will not. They will keep pursuing us until their legs literally fall off.

A Solis falls out of the tree above us, but Allister cuts the woman in half. Blood pours on top of Allister and me. It's warm and sticks to my face and chest. I've seen a Solis bleed before, but I'm always surprised at how much it's like normal, living human blood. I wipe it from my eyes the best I can, but with how much is all over me, the movement doesn't do much.

Then, out of nowhere, I'm almost knocked off balance by the weight of what is now chasing us. Gigantic paws thunder on the ground behind us, shaking everything in the vicinity. I feel the weight of those paws slamming into the ground, leaving small craters in their wake. The earth groans under the weight of the beast. My stomach drops and I almost feel all the color drain from my face as the realization of what's chasing us hits me.

Instead of screaming over the sound of the earth shaking around us, I think, *Allister, I need you to go over and get behind Ned.*

What? Why? His voice is scared, almost frantic. I know he doesn't want to leave my side, but we don't have a choice right now.

There's a werewolf behind us. I can feel its weight impacting the earth behind us.

He takes a sharp breath before wrapping his arms around me. *There's no way in hell I'm leaving you! Raven can outrun it, right? You guys have killed one before.*

I shake my head. *We didn't outrun it. I can tell you the story at another time but right now I need you to get over on Mylo. We don't have the time needed to explain every single thing.* I take one of my hands off the reins and grab onto his arms wrapped around me. *Trust me. I need your help, but we can't do this if we're both on the same horse.*

Without a second's thought he answers, "I trust you." The quickness of his response. That he trusts me even in such dire situations, brings a smile to my face even as we face almost certain death.

"Hey, Ned," Allister shouts. "Don't ask questions and get over here. We need your help."

Ned turns his head toward us. I see his eyes narrow, and he glares at Allister, but he moves his hands down the reins, asking Mylo to move over.

I take the moment to go out on a limb and ask Allister, *Can you crush its mind like you did with your men back in Rawu?*

Allister leans his head against my back, and I feel his

shake his head back and forth. *No I can't crush animal minds only beings with a higher level of thinking like humans and Fae.*

I answer *I was worried that's what you'd say.*

Ned manages to get Mylo next to Raven even while dodging trees. That warhorse *must* be part Fae. There's no way he could be this agile, and able to keep up with Raven, if he was only a normal horse.

Allister yanks my hand behind me and kisses the back of it before he manages to stand on top of Raven and step over to Mylo's back. As soon as he is off of Raven I lean down and begin untying the rope attaching Talon to my wrist. Then I tie the rope to the swell of the saddle in front of me.

"Hey girl," I start, and I see her ears prick up in acknowledgement. "I hate to be the bearer of bad news, but we have a werewolf behind us."

"What!" she shouts and I hear the terror in her voice. As she turns her head I see her eyes are shot wide open. Her mouth hangs open so wide the bit bobs up and down in her mouth from her movements.

I pat her neck. "I need to spin around on you. You remember how we did this before, right? I need to stay turned around this time though which means I'll need you to stay as smooth as you can. If you need to dart one way or the other to avoid a tree or a Solis just try to yell at me so I'm ready for it okay?"

"Okay!" she shouts back to me. "But what are you going to do?"

I sit back up and throw my leg over her back, spinning in my seat. When I have myself turned around in the saddle, my legs held tightly against her sides, and my bow out with a Fae feathered arrow cocked, I answer.

"You'll see."

28

JAMES

I wake but my eyes don't adjust to the light streaming in because there is none. I might as well keep my eyes closed. I'd be able to see just as much with them closed as I can with them open.

I reach my hand back behind my head. Hissing as I feel the thick scab which has already formed. I must have slept for longer than I thought. I crawl over to the front of my cell. I feel less woozy now, but I still don't feel like standing would be the greatest idea in the world. When I reach the bars of the cell I wrap my hands around them and press my face into the cooling steel.

I quietly say, "Hello, is anyone there?"

I hear the gruff voice of the Commander in the cell next to me. "I thought I told you to shut up or you couldn't ever go back to Sanctuary."

I huff. "Yeah, *if* we make it back."

"Shut up, James. If it wasn't for you, we wouldn't be in this mess."

I ignore him and instead ask, "Is Ned here?"

"I've been calling out to him. He hasn't answered. Haven't you heard me yelling?" He sounds confused.

"They hit me pretty solidly on the head back there, hard enough to knock me out. I've been in and out of it ever since."

"Oh," he answers. "Well, no, I don't think Ned is here with us."

"So, he either took off or he was in cahoots with the Fae all along," I mutter, more to myself than him.

I hear him slam his hand on the floor. "Ned would never!" I would almost believe him by how much conviction he has in his voice—almost.

"Ned and Attina were with a Fae when I found them. We leave to search for Attina and are ambushed by Fae. But Ned somehow manages to miraculously get away? You don't find it a little odd?" Before, I probably would have yelled at him for his stupidity but not now. We're already prisoners, what would yelling at the Commander do besides make my throat sore?

"Hmm," he mumbles. "I've known him for years and years. I couldn't imagine him siding with the Fae. He hates the Fae. Henrik killed his parents. He would never side with them even if he is—" but he doesn't finish his thought.

"Even if he is what?" My brow pinches in confusion.

"Nothing," he quickly spits out. "I spoke without thinking. I don't know what I meant to say." He means to placate me, but it does the opposite. My curiosity is now piqued.

"He's gone. He ditched us and he won't find us here. Who knows if we'll even make it out of here." I take a deep breath. "Honestly, I highly doubt we will make it out. We're dead men anyway, you might as well tell me, even if it's merely to pass the time before some Fae comes down here and kills us or we starve to death." Everything is quiet for so long I give up and move away from the cell bars. I make my way back to the back of the cell and sit down, leaning my head against the wall.

I shut my eyes and then I hear the Commander meekly whisper, barely loud enough for me to hear, "Ned is half-Fae. His father was a Fae, and his mother was a human. It's why Henrik hunted his family down and killed them. I met him as he was wandering around after Henrik burned his family house to the ground."

My eyes shoot open as memories begin flooding back to me. Now I remember! I get a flash of holding my knife to his throat, cutting his throat, and watching as it stitched itself back together. I must have been hit harder on the head than I thought for me to forget something so crucial. "And you allowed him to live in a *top secret* compound with the last humans in all of Arealea? Do you realize what you could have done? He could have been a spy for all you know!" By the time I'm done talking I'm shouting at him.

He answers in a tone which tells me he doesn't think it was a big deal. "I was young and trusting. I guess in hindsight it was a bad idea, but by the time he told me what he was he'd lived in Sanctuary for a long time. We had been to battle together, and I trusted him completely. It's not like you can simply glance at Ned and know what he is. *You* didn't even know yourself."

I understand what he's saying. Ned has rounded ears like a human and whatever powers he must have, he keeps them under wraps. How could anyone know without him telling them? It should be a comforting realization but it's not. He was able to fool all the humans around him for decades. Attina is a half-Fae and now I find out Ned is too? How many of them are out in the world? What if a half-Fae who's working for Henrik infiltrates Sanctuary? We wouldn't know until it was too late.

"I hope you realize if we somehow get out of this he can't go back to Sanctuary, and we will have to figure out better security measures. We can't continue letting in half-Fae and assume they're not working for Henrik."

I hear him wiggle forward in his cell and wrap his meaty hands around the bars "What do you mean *continue* letting in half-Fae? Who else is half-Fae in Sanctuary?"

I sharply suck in air. Shit. I didn't mean to say that. "Um well..." I stumble out.

He growls. "Soldier, you better spit it out now or no matter what happens to me you won't make it back to Sanctuary alive."

I think for a second before answering. Attina won't ever be allowed back into Sanctuary if I tell him her secret. But if I'm honest with myself she'd never be allowed to go back anyway. We left Sanctuary to search for her because I told the commander she was in an alliance with a Fae. Did I really think she would be allowed back in after I proved myself right? There's no way she'd be allowed back in. Well I guess we'll just have to leave Sanctuary together and live on our own. That is, if I can get out of here and find her. No way to keep it a secret now.

"Attina is half-Fae too, Commander," I whisper barely loud enough for him to hear.

"What!" he shouts. "You knew this, and you let her live in Sanctuary! How could you?"

I calmly say, "How could you? You did the same thing with Ned." He doesn't answer and I know it's the end of our conversation, but I need to ask him one more thing. "How many days have we been down here?"

"Only a couple of days."

"And they haven't brought us food or water? Are they trying to starve us?" I'm not truly interested in his answer. I'm using this question so he doesn't find my next question too strange.

"There's water in the corner of my cell but no they haven't brought us any food. I haven't even seen another soul since we were brought here."

I start crawling around my cell. He's right. In the corner of the cell is a medium sized water bucket with a wooden cup floating on top of it. How did I miss this? I checked the perimeter of the cell the last time I was awake. I'm surprised I didn't slam into this as I was moving around before.

"Has anything weird happened since we've been here? Maybe, while I was sleeping?"

"No, the weirdest thing that's happened so far is you telling me I had not one but two *half-Fae* living in my *human* stronghold."

I don't answer and he doesn't say more. Nothing strange has happened. Good. But still, the change will happen soon, while we're stuck in here, together.

Fuck. I think as the realization finally hits me.

I wonder how he'll react to it.

This should be interesting.

29

ATTINA

Nocking an arrow, I pull the string on my bow taught. I gaze over at Ned and Allister. Allister now has himself turned backwards on Mylo, mirroring the way I sit on Raven. Ned nods to me and I hear Allister in my head. *I told him what was going on.* I lock eyes with Ned and bow my head to him.

I shift my gaze back to Allister. *Remember, I only have ten Fae feathered arrows. I need to be sparing with them. Don't let me use them too fast.*

Also, remember, kitten you can't be sparing if you're dead.

He has a point there. I lean back in the saddle, leaning against the saddle horn behind me. I feel the rope attached to Talon moving back and forth against my back. I glance up and see him erratically flying back and forth. He pulls on the rope and pecks at where it's attached to his leg, trying to escape.

I hear *chicken shit,* in my head and it makes me nervously cackle.

The werewolf is gaining on us. The earth around us is already shaking from the weight of the beast. I hear a far off noise which reminds me of the cracking noise you hear when you rip bark from a log. I sense how massive the creature is by how its body slices through the air behind us. The beast must be almost twice as big as the one Raven and I ran into around my father's campsite. How is such a thing possible? How could any beast be this unnaturally huge?

Have you seen a werewolf before? I ask Allister.

Not in person. I've only heard stories. Which is why I'm going to follow your lead on this one.

I take in a deep steadying breath as I bring my bow down. *This one is gargantuan. I thought I could handle it mostly on my own, but I can't. I need your help. Can you accurately shoot a bow?*

He sounds almost annoyed when he answers. *I'm the top Fae slayer. Of course I can.*

I pull my quiver over my back, putting the arrow in my hand back in it. *I need you to come over here and take this from me. I want to try to knock it back with my magic and I need you to shoot at it.*

He turns and I watch him say something to Ned. Ned peers over at us and starts steering Mylo toward us. In a flash the three of them are right at our side. It takes a couple of tries, the bouncing from the running horses throws us off a few times, but I do, eventually, successfully pass the bow and quiver to Allister.

As soon as Allister has the bow and quiver he flips the quiver over his back, somehow he gets it situated perfectly over his sword, and smoothly pulls out one of the arrows I made with Hazel's feathers. *Remember to be sparing with those.* He doesn't answer though, he turns his face toward me and exaggeratedly rolls his eyes instead. I ignore him. *Tell Ned he'll have to kill the Solis for you two.*

I watch as he does what I ask, but as soon as he's turned

back forward the ground shakes violently enough we both almost fall off of the horses we're astride. When I've caught myself, I gaze forward and can barely see something gray in the distance.

It's only a small gray blob at the moment, but I know it's because the thing is so far away from us. As it runs, a massive tree behind it smashes down into another. It ran into a tree and ripped it out of the ground so violently, it made the ground underneath Raven shake enough to almost knock me out of the saddle!

My mouth goes dry.

We're screwed.

We can't outrun this thing.

I call to my powers. A wall of earth forms directly in front of the werewolf, but it smashes right through it like it wasn't even there, boulders flying through the air. My eyes shoot open, and I forget to breathe for a second. I pull the earth out from under the werewolf, well I try to. I don't compensate for how fast the creature is moving. By the time my power reaches where the werewolf is, the crater I create is only under his back feet. He stumbles for a second but easily pulls himself back up, out of the hole with his front feet.

Allister says, *Try again.*

This time I account for the beast's speed and watch as the werewolf falls down into a gulley of my making. He disappears from sight for a second and I peek over at Allister with a huge grin plastered on my face.

That wasn't as hard as I thought it would be.

But almost immediately after I have the thought, the ground splits sideways from where my crater is, and I see two paws hold onto the edge. Then all of a sudden, like an arrow shot from a bow, the creature shoots up into the air. It almost gets level with the treetops before it deftly lands, not missing a step, and continues chasing after us.

This thing is tenacious. Allister whispers in my mind like he's in awe.

I'm unhappily surprised by its speed considering how massive the animal is. You would think it's massive weight would slow the thing down, but it doesn't slow it one bit. It's graceful too, maneuvering around thick trees, but mowing over the small ones as if they're not even there.

In a blink of an eye, a sheet of ice is formed in front of the werewolf. It notices it a second too late and loses any chance it had to jump over it. The beast's front legs cross and it stumbles forward, slamming its face on the rock hard water in front of it. It's body slides forward on its face and chest, the momentum of it throws the werewolf's back end over its head and it goes tumbling tail over head. It doesn't stop until its back slams hard into a giant tree. I watch as its body slides down the tree into a crumpled pile.

I don't have control over water very well yet, so I peer over at Allister who's sitting up ramrod straight with a giant, shit eating grin on his face. I smile back at him. That was awesome. He should be proud.

I gaze back to where the werewolf landed and watch as it gingerly untangles its limbs and sits up on its butt. The animal shakes its head like it's clearing his head and then his eyes immediately focus back on us. He howls once before he's off like a flash, chasing us again. Raven jumps left and a Solis barely misses her butt. I pull my sword out and quickly slice the thing's head off before re-sheathing it.

He's getting too close. *You think you can hit him from here?* I ask as I turn and pointedly stare at the bow in Allister's hands. *Those Fae feather arrows shoot faster and farther remember.*

Allister answers, *Yeah, I can do it.*

I'll try to slow him down. Try to hit him in the neck. His skull is probably too thick to penetrate, and you probably won't be able to hit his heart through his rib and collar bones.

Will do, he says, and I can hear the focused determination in his voice.

I take in a deep, steadying breath and try to focus all my attention on the air around us. I concentrate on hardening the air behind Raven. I push it and fold it in on itself like I did when I made the air bandage for Allister's arm when he got cut down by his soldier's sword. The only difference is this time I'm having to deal with about twenty times as much air. I feel all over the air wall I've built in front of me, searching for any weak spots. I don't find any, so I send the air wall forward, toward the werewolf.

I physically feel it in my chest as the wall slams into the werewolf's face. It throws its head back like it's been smacked. But his reaction, and him slowing down a bit is the only response I get from the beast. I guess slowing it down is better than nothing.

Try to shoot a regular arrow at it first. We need to experiment, and those Fae feathered arrows are too precious to waste.

He switches arrows and I hear, *Done. Now what?*

Shoot!

He looses an arrow aimed at the beast's neck. I see where the arrow will hit my wall and open up a spot big enough for the arrow to fit through. By some miracle I calculated correctly, and the arrow makes its way through my hardened air wall. It flies at the werewolf and the creature barely ducks its head, causing the arrow to bounce off of its chin, breaking the arrow in two.

Wonderful. Regular arrows will be a waste on this beast. We'll have to do what we can with the ten Fae arrows we have.

How much farther do we have until we make it to the wall of the Eastern Fae stronghold?

I don't know for certain, but we must be close by now.

All of a sudden I'm hit hard on my right side. I crumble to the ground in a jumble of appendages and metal. I'm surprised my armor doesn't crunch into my body anywhere, it melds like a glove over my body even when it's thrown in such extreme angles. A body lands on top of me and all I hear is snarls and growls as I roll over on top of the Solis who has my arm grasped in its mouth. Luckily, it grabbed on to me where the armor covers my arm, just the weight of its body flung me off of Raven.

"Attina!" I hear Allister scream as the pounding feet of the werewolf gets closer by the second.

I lift my arm and the Solis's head comes up with it. I take the Solis' head and slam it to the ground. The Solis's teeth break against my armor, blood pours down the corners of its mouth, but it still holds on. I pry my arm out of the thing's now toothless mouth and I'm shocked by its beauty. The Solis is a woman. Her red, matted hair must have flowed down to her hips when she was a human, but now it lies in knots. Her body is tiny and has curves in all the right places. But her eyes are what make me hesitate, they're the most captivating hazel I've ever seen. Bright green eyes with deep brown pockets in them lock on mine as she claws at me trying to get some kind of hold on me.

As I stare down at her, Allister flies past me on the ground and shouts, "Get in the fight, Attina! What are you doing!"

His yells bring me out of my reverie. I reach down into my boot and pull out the dagger Ned gave me when we left Sanctuary, sorry for what I'm about to do to this woman. I've never been totally okay with killing Solis, something about it has always felt wrong. I'm not sure why but something about this woman makes me feel more wrong for killing her. "Sorry," I whisper to the woman as I close my eyes and slam the dagger into the Solis's head.

"Attina!"

I spin around just as Allister and the werewolf are meeting. He slides past the werewolf on his knees and slices at the thing's legs. At the last second it jumps away. I pull my sword out and race over to where Allister is standing back up, sword at the ready.

Being as big as it is the wolf doesn't have to use much power to jump exhaustingly far away, but the Solis are still around us, crowding in on us. They simply stand there in a circle around us like the dinner bell rang and we're the main course. I take a chance and glance over to where Ned and Raven were running seconds ago. Glad to see they were finally able to turn around. Running as fast as they were, with their Fae speed, it isn't easy to safely slam on the breaks and completely turn around. Racing to Allister's side, I push my back up against his sturdy back.

Behind me, I hear the wolf slamming through the thick trees back toward us. Underneath, I feel trees being ripped from the earth, his weight making easy work of removing even some of the thickest ones.

In front of us, the Solis still just stand there, bent over, staring at us. Some are missing limbs but what's strange is they all have legs. In the past when we've run into Solis, even hoards of them, there were at least a couple with missing legs who only happened to run into us. Some drool like they're starving, but they all pant like they've been chasing us for awhile. Pushing their bodies to the absolute limit. I wonder how long it takes for an undead being to tire like that.

What are they doing? I ask Allister behind me, *Why aren't they attacking us? They appear worn out but how is such a thing possible?*

They're all undead; it shouldn't be possible, he answers. But before I really have a chance to think about it one of the bigger and obviously stronger Solis screams a guttural cry. Then, I feel the werewolf's big paw land right in front of Allister. I turn my head to where Ned and Raven are racing with all they have back to us, but there's no way they'll make it in time.

30

ATTINA

I scream back at the Solis as my eyes float over his gash riddled face and tattered clothes. My eyes sticking to his clothes though, because unlike most Solis I've seen. His clothes are tattered like he was poor without enough money to have them properly mended, not like he's been aimlessly roaming about for years, tearing them on branches as he goes. This one is different somehow.

As the screech leaves my voice I plant my feet wide, parallel with my shoulders, giving me the most solid stance possible. I lift my hands into the air, putting all I am into my powers, focus on the earth around us, and close my eyes.

Even though I'm focusing everything I have into this, I can still barely hear Allister behind me yell, "Attina!"

When I open my eyes I see the damage I've created. A gully surrounds me and Allister. It almost completely encircles us. There's barely enough of a bridge left to allow Raven and Mylo to get to us. The Solis are nowhere to be seen and I can barely see the werewolf off in the distance, where it must have jumped away from the earth falling around it. I can't even see its actual body. I spot trees falling down in a circle off in the distance and know it's already pursuing us again.

I fall to my knees, exhaustion taking over me. I see spots in my vision. And my head gets light right before Allister's warm hand is on my back, holding me upright. "Attina, are you all right?"

I struggle but I manage to get my sword back in its sheath as I answer him "I'll be fine, I just over did it."

Hazel screeches above us, "Hang on, Ned's almost to you Attina."

I nod but the movement makes me nauseous. I'm not sure how it happens but I'm being lifted up onto Mylo's back in front of Ned. I hear his calming voice. "Hey kid. You're gonna be okay."

I don't answer him before I hear Raven's angry voice next to me. "Girl you do not get to pass out on us, we're almost there."

We're moving again and I hear Ned beside me, he must be leaning forward. "We saw the castle spires, hang on a bit longer kid. I got you."

But as his last words leave his lips, I feel the thunderous pounding of the werewolf's feet behind us once again. Snarls of the Solis reach my ears from somewhere far off. It takes effort but I turn my head to gaze over at where Raven and Allister run next to us. Allister is turned around in the saddle. I peek under Ned's elbow and see ice spikes ripping up from the ground, slicing into the werewolf. But the werewolf isn't slowing down. He manages to catch the bigger spikes in his mouth and brush the other ones off like they're some sort of annoyance.

I turn forward and see what Raven and Ned were talking about. I can see the spires of the Eastern Fae castle ahead of us, peeking through the forest. It's hidden well. I can tell the roof is black but the rest of its covered in moss. It blends in with the forest surroundings perfectly. I bet someone could walk right by and not notice it. I smile, happy we made it, but before I can revel in my happiness I feel the snapping jaws of the werewolf on the air right behind Raven. I turn and see Allister's sword slam down on the werewolf's head, making it back off and shake its head. Blood streams down its face, but not enough to seriously slow down the beast. In a second he's running again and right on Raven's tail.

I peer forward and my heart drops as I realize we can't see the castle walls yet. Even if the Fae were to somehow come to our aid, by some miracle, they wouldn't make it in time. We're on our own and we've run out of time. The werewolf's jaws snap again and Raven cries out as the tips of his teeth make contact. Blood spurts from Raven and my heart drops as she almost falls to the ground. Her back leg has been torn into so badly she can't really run anymore. She's running as well as she can with three legs, but it's not much more than a quick hop. Only being able to use three legs is a death sentence for any horse.

My mount is about to die.

The werewolf is going to eat her along with my mate.

I scream out, *"No!"* Under me, Mylo squeals out along with me. He slows, but Ned kicks him in the side, willing him to keep running. Ned clamps his arms down on me

Hazel screeches above me as Ned says, "There's nothing we can do. You are the future queen. We must get you to safety."

I feel a burst of energy hit me and I chuckle, actually chuckle at his words. Like he could stand a chance at stopping me. I would rather die than watch my mount and my mate be eaten alive by a werewolf. I don't care about being the future queen in a world without them in it.

I pretend to be listening and slump in the seat. Hazel flaps her wings above us, and I throw a gust of wind up, knocking her off balance which does exactly what I want it to do. It brings Ned's attention off of me and onto Hazel.

I use the break in his concentration and reach down into my boot where I still carry the dagger Ned gave me. "I'm sorry," I say loud enough for Ned to hear. His attention comes back on me a second before I gently slide the sharp dagger across his arm. It easily slices through his clothing and the skin of his arm. I don't push enough to actually do damage, just enough to make him release me.

As he releases me I throw my weight to the left, allowing me to tumble off Mylo, on to the ground. I roll into a kneeling position and take off toward where the werewolf is again being bombarded by Allister's ice spikes. They're slowing the creature down enough to keep him and Raven from being eaten for the moment, but it won't last long. I'll give it to Allister, he's trying his damndest to keep the both of them alive. But ice spikes won't do it, and he can't crush this beast's mind like he did against his men all those weeks ago.

The werewolf notices me racing toward it. The creature stops its pursuit completely and allows Raven to limp off. I hear Allister shout to my right, but I can't make out the words he says, my entire focus staying on the werewolf.

Get Raven to the castle. Get her some help. Make sure Ned and Mylo follow you.

No! I will not leave you! Allister shouts into my mind. *You are my mate I will not leave you here to die!*

I imagine my hand caressing his hard sculpted cheek as I take a second to stare deep into his distant pooling purple eyes. *I do not intend to die. I need you to take care of our family while I cannot. I won't be able to take down this beast while I'm worried about our family. Please take them to safety.*

Then Ned's voice floods into my head. *I won't leave you!*

Ned, I don't have time for this. If you stay I will die. My eyes stick back on to the werewolf before I continue. *I need you to help Allister get our family to safety. I can't concentrate if I have to worry about anyone else.*

Silence fills my head before I hear, *fine.*

I'm surprised he agreed this easily but I'm glad I can count on him for this. While I think of all this, I watch as the werewolf turns its body toward me, widens its stance, and literally plasters a grin on its face. It's almost like the creature has been waiting for this moment. I thought this beast was after all of us, but it's now plainly obvious he was only here for me.

Henrik sent all these special projects of his solely for me. I could have saved my father, Oak, and now Raven simply by giving myself up. Well, I will not let any more death or suffering happen because of me. If this werewolf wants me, then he'll have to come get me.

I can't live without you. I won't leave you, Attina.

He needs to stop this and get them to the castle; Raven doesn't have much time. She needs to be seen by a healer if she's going to have *any* chance of survival. And Ned and Mylo have absolutely no business being out here with this monster. *I can't live without our family. If you want me, you have to save them.* I hear him as he debates within himself what to do. Always the warrior, he quickly weighs his options and realizes what he must do.

Fine, I'll do as you ask, but I will only take them to the gate, and then I'm coming back for you. Stay alive long enough for me to get to you.

I turn my head and nod to him as I shout, "Run!" All the

while realizing this monster will take this opportunity to pounce on me. I pull my sword from its sheath as I lean back and let the ground consume me. The monster pounces exactly like I thought it would and I lift my sword up to meet its fleshy underbelly.

The squelching noise and warm liquid which pours from its stomach tells me I hit home. I hear the beast screech in pain as I feel it jump far away from me, knocking down trees in its wake. I stand up and watch as it folds in on itself, trying to lick the wound I caused, like a dog.

I take the opportunity to turn and watch as Allister walks Raven as quickly as he can away from the fray. I notice Talon is being dragged along by Raven. My lip quirks up as I watch him reel backwards, flapping his wings with renewed vigor as he tries to flee the scene. Then I see Allister and Ned yelling at each other. I'm sure Ned wants to come help me. I don't know what Allister is saying to keep him from racing back to me, but I'm thankful for whatever it is because now they're all leaving for the safety of the castle.

Above me, through the air currents, I feel Hazel soaring through the air. I glance up to where she's watching me before I lock my gaze back on the beast which is now standing back up. The grin is gone from its face and replaced by a tightened, snarling mouth.

I hear Hazel above me. "Well Attina, if your plan was to piss it off you did well. Don't get yourself killed."

I lift my sword, pretending like I plan on taking this thing on without my powers. The thought makes me smile. Only a madman like my father and Allister would try to take on a werewolf with only a sword.

I chuckle and shake my head as I shout, "Get back to the castle. When Allister leaves, do whatever you can to make sure everyone is taken care of."

All I hear from above me is a flap of wings. But as I widen my stance and tighten my muscles, readying for what's about to happen, I hear her shout back, "I will." Just hearing those words warms my heart and solidifies my will. My family will be taken care of, no matter what happens to me.

I stand there staring at the werewolf. I'm surprised he hasn't made a move now, since he's up on all fours again. But he simply stands there, watching me. In short order I realize why he's only standing there, and it throws my plan out the window. My jaw slackens and my stomach drops as I see what's walking up. From behind him in the trees, the Solis start poking out, one by one.

The Solis I saw earlier in the tattered clothes is even there. My attack killed about half of them and maimed the others. But even a maimed Solis will chase after its prey until its dying breath, and right now *I* am the only prey around.

The werewolf lets out a loud howl and a bunch of the Solis surge after me at once. I wait until the first ones are right on me to throw up a wall of air, knocking down the ones who get closest to me. I move around them, piercing their skulls with my sword, giving them a true death.

At the same time, I call to the earth and make it move underneath the Solis who are running after me in the next wave. As they run the ground shakes, knocking them down. The Solis are fast but not too bright, which means moving the earth beneath them is enough to knock them to the ground. I move forward and start cutting down the Solis as they fall before me. I continue making the ground move under me which makes it impossible for the Solis to get back up, making the killing swift.

When I'm finished, I gaze back up to where the werewolf

still stands, snarling. Only a portion of the Solis still remain. I'm assuming these are the smartest ones, if such a thing exists. These Solis watched what I did to their brethren and decided to wait for a better opportunity at me. The man from earlier has moved forward and now stands to the right of the beast. The man peers up at the creature and growls at it. The werewolf in turn gazes down at the Solis.

Can they actually communicate? Such a thing isn't possible right?

The werewolf faces back to me and paws the ground in front of him, a snarling smile cracking his face. The man next to him screeches while he turns back and forth, all the other Solis spinning to him, like he is talking to them. I wish I had my bow right now so I could send an arrow straight through his brain. He faces me again and licks his smiling, rotting lips.

Oh shit, this can't be good.

The werewolf howls and all the Solis along with the werewolf take off at once. I take a step back but as I watch the werewolf covering ground, I know there is no point in trying to outrun him.

I only have seconds before the werewolf reaches me and I won't have to wait long until the Solis are on top of me as well. I force myself to drop my sword and close my eyes. I search for my powers inside of me. I call to the earth. I feel the air and hear the water around me. I pull on the knot in my stomach where my fire is.

As I open my eyes I see a swirling, eddying protective bubble around me. Water, earth, air, and fire swirl around me; encasing me. Almost at the same time as I open my eyes the werewolf slams into my protective barrier, slamming me back on my butt.

An oof noise releases from my lips, but my powers don't

fail me. I have all my powers encircling me which means the earth doesn't catch my fall this time. I'd almost forgotten how much it hurts to fall down.

Gradually, I crawl my way to my feet again. Using all my powers like this is exhausting and I'm finding it almost impossible to do anything but stand. The werewolf bats at my barrier with his massive gray paws. I see the claws of his paws, as they scratch down the surface of my barrier. They're almost as long as I am tall.

Then I notice a crack in my barrier.

Shit!

I take a deep breath, steadying myself. I push every single thing I am and every single thing I will be into the barrier. I push until I think I have nothing left and then I push some more, until I'm almost completely depleted. I need to hold on for a few seconds longer. I sway on my feet. I can do this. *You can do this Attina,* I say to myself, *hold on a little longer.*

The seconds tick by like minutes as I get weaker but finally it happens. The Solis finally reach my barrier. Having them all slam into it almost simultaneously is like being hit by the werewolf all over again. I stumble back but stay on my feet this time. I know if I fall now, I won't make it back up to my feet again.

Then I hear Allister in my head once more *Attina hold on. Our family is safe. I'm coming back to you.*

All I say in answer is, *I will always love you.*

I hear the panic in his voice as he screams, *Attina! No, just hold on!*

I don't have the energy to answer him. I vaguely hear him screaming in the back of my mind, but I have to focus. I'm glad he's far away, hopefully I won't hurt him with what I'm about to do. Taking in a final breath, I steady myself, feeling calmer than I thought I could be in this moment. I release a blood curdling scream as I shove all my powers out of me. Toward the beings attacking me. The same ones who tried to kill my family.

My barrier shoots out, slamming into the Solis and killing them instantly. I manage to stay on my feet and watch as the werewolf is thrown backward by my powers. Its body is thrown through the air like a ragdoll, slamming into trees as it goes. What's strange is I can no longer sense those trees being ripped out of the ground.

He lands in a pile of fur and teeth, and I see a tree has impaled itself in its chest. I watch him struggle to get up, he kicks and scratches at the air above him, slicing through the air not even registering with me, but he never makes it up. He puts up a good fight against fate for a bit but, in the end, no one outruns fate.

Just as I can't outrun my own fate.

I see all the Solis littering the ground around me as I fall to my knees. I try to call to the earth beneath me but instead I feel the crack of pain in my knees. In front of me I stare at the werewolf. His chest rises as his lungs take in one last breath before stilling completely.

A smile crosses my face. I saved them. I saved them all.

I fall backwards and feel a warm hand cup my back, keeping me from hitting the ground. I lean back into his hand as Allister's face is thrust in front of mine. I reach my hand up to his cheek and stroke it, just like I thought of doing earlier.

You made it. I think to him because I'm too tired to talk.

His gorgeous, swirling purple eyes fill with tears which slide down his face. His shoulder length black hair frames his face as he looms over me. His chiseled jaw tightens as he places his hand over mine and says, "I did. I'll be by your side forever, my love." But as the words leave his lips I see condensation leave his mouth. My hand slides out of his as my lungs fill with the sharpness cold air always brings. When my hand lands on the ground I feel a cold wetness there.

He carefully leans down over me, his cold, red nose is stark against his ashen face. I close my eyes as he places the softest, most gentle kiss I've ever felt on my lips. As he pulls away I realize his lips are salty from the tears coating his lips.

31

ATTINA

I wake to the dark place in my mind. I search around me but see nothing, pitch black surrounds me. Then a screech breaks the silence to my right. I spin, calling out to my powers in anticipation, but they're nowhere to be found.

Fuck.

Then there's a shriek from behind me, I spin around again with my hands up, ready for a fight.

But none comes.

I hear rustling off in the distance which makes me take a few tentative steps forward where I think the sound originates from. Out of nowhere my blackbird comes screeching to my feet, its aquamarine eyes, the same eyes I have, lock on mine. More glittering blood splotches cover most of her black body. Her orange beak shutters open and closed incessantly. I bend down, attempting to comfort her.

"Hey, it's okay, I'm here." I reach my hand out to pat her small head, but my hand drops right through her body, like a ghost. How's strange, I was able to touch her before, wasn't I?

The movement does the opposite of comfort her though.

It only serves to make her panic more. She flings her wings out, blood splashing onto my knees and the ground around her. One of her wings must be broken because it hangs at an odd angle.

Then my bird springs around and goes deathly still. I shift my gaze to where her eyes are fixated, where the white serpent slithers out of the shadows. Its lips pulled back, its fangs hanging outside of the thing's mouth. The serpent's red eyes seem to sparkle with bloodlust as it slithers closer. My little black bird turns and squawks at me like it's telling me to save myself. I simply shake my head at her, if she dies, I die, and running away won't change it.

There's no running for either of us now. But honestly my bird couldn't outrun the serpent for long with how beaten up she already was. Her beak almost droops as she gives me one last, sad look before she turns to face her impending doom.

In a flash the serpent is on my bird. Instinctively I scream. I reach down and try to pull the serpent off of her, but my hands move through their tangled bodies. I'm helpless to do anything but watch as the serpent winds its body around my bird, constricting it until all the life leaves those aquamarine eyes of hers.

"No!" I shout, lurching forward as something inside me breaks, pulling me to the ground in a ball of nothingness.

I watch from the ground as the serpent's lips turn up in what I can only explain as a grin right before he unhinges his massive maw and inhales my bird head first.

Everything I am falls away from me and I'm left with emptiness.

I wake with a start, breathing in as much air as I can. A warm pair of hands grab my wrists and I swing my arms wildly about. The hands don't release me, and I start to panic. My vision is black, but my eyes are open. Why can't I see anything?

I feel the pull in my gut. I sense the fire there is somehow stronger, almost twice the size it previously was. I push the fire into my arms, I imagine my arms turning red from the fire racing through my body.

I hear someone shout, "Attina!" The voice makes me freeze. I know that voice. I pull all my fire back into me.

"Allister? Where are you?" I peer around even though I can't see, force of habit I guess.

A hand makes its way to my face, cupping my cheek. His voice is soft, loving, as he answers, "I'm right here." And I realize he's the one who was holding my wrists.

I suck in a sharp breath, momentarily forgetting I can't see for worry I hurt him. Panic grips my voice as I ask, "Did I burn you? Please tell me I didn't burn you!"

He chuckles and I can imagine him shaking his head as he smirks at me. "We're mates. You couldn't burn me if you tried, remember."

Panic continues to grip me as questions spill out of me. "Why can't I see anything? Where are we? Will I be blind forever? What happened to everyone else? Is Raven alive..."

Both of his hands cup my cheeks as he lays his forehead down against mine. In his sweet, velvety, soothing voice he says, "Shh. Calm down. Your heart is beating a mile a minute. You're fine. We're safe. We made it into the Eastern Fae stronghold. The healers said there might be some after effects from what happened but they wouldn't be permanent. Your sight will come back. Kitten, you've been asleep for a week."

"*A week?*" I shout. "What happened?"

He pulls his head away from me and by the movement in the bed I know he's sitting straight up again, "Yes a week." Now I notice the anguish in his voice, the pain which still lingers there. He must have been worried sick about me.

"Is Raven all right? The werewolf ripped such a big hole in her." My voice catches at the end as tears fill my eyes. I really don't want to hear his answer. I think I already know the answer, but I need to hear it from him. I don't know what I would do without her.

"Raven is fine. She's absolutely beside herself with worry about you, but she's snarky as ever. She actually seems to be enjoying being around other Fae horses. And Mylo is sticking to her side like glue."

All of a sudden my body feels incredibly heavy, like I'm being dragged down through water. I can't keep my eyes open and I'm having a hard time keeping my head up, but I need to ask one more thing. I sit back up to keep myself awake. "Is Ned okay?" And I ask again, "What happened to me? The last thing I remember is thinking I was dying." I remember Allister's face and thinking this is it and then there was my horrible dream. It felt real but I'm alive and my powers still work, so it must have been a dream. Right? Then I wake up here? After a week? What's happening?

He gently guides me down back onto the bed as he answers, "Ned is fine. The Fae weren't too happy about a half human behind their walls, but we worked it out."

I yawn, making my voice comes out all squeaky when I say, "I bet they absolutely *love* having me here then." I half chuckle at the sound of my own voice.

Allister doesn't laugh in return; he simply runs his thumb from the top of my forehead down to my chin. "As to what happened to you, that's for a different time." Normally,

I would be mad at him for keeping something so important from me, but I'm so tired right now, I don't care. "I'll fill you in on it all when you wake up again. Now rest. You're safe. I'm right here in case you need anything."

I nod my head and push my cheek into his hand. "Thank you." I yawn one last time before I say, "I love you" and let exhaustion take me.

I OPEN my eyes into a black void. Or what I think is a black void? Maybe I'm still blind?

"Allister?" I call out, "Are you there?" There's no answer in return, but I hear a batting of something above me. Cloth? I peer up into the darkness, straining my eyes. Whatever it is flaps again. My brows knit. What in the world could it be? I scan around me again but still see nothing.

Panic grips me. My chest tightens the air out of me, and I grab at it, trying to ease the pain. The feeling I get when something can see me, but I can't see it instantly envelops me. Tingles run up my back and I break out in a sweat. I swing my head wildly around, searching for the danger but all I see is darkness. Then I hear the flapping noise above me again. I follow my gaze in the direction the noise came from, and I finally see something dropping down through the dark shroud above me.

A huge, red, taloned claw reaches down through the darkness above me. I try to move away, run from it, but I can't. I'm somehow stuck to the spot. I call to my powers, searching for any sign they're with me but feel nothing. No pull in my gut, nothing. What's going on now?

The talon turns into a leg, the thickest, scaliest leg I've ever seen. It reminds me of the lizards I would lie next to in the forests of Daruk, while I was lying in wait for a deer. It's not green like those were though. The red of the thing's talon moves up its leg to mix with other colors. Bright oranges and yellows mix and marble around the leg.

Then I'm again hit with a memory. I remember after my fight with the werewolf I passed out and went to where I saw my magical animal. I watched as the serpent ate my bird, killing it. Hazel said if your magical animal dies, you lose your powers and you die along with it. So, all of it was actually real? My powers aren't working because my magical animal died. But if my magical animal died wouldn't it mean I'm dead too?

No.

Allister wouldn't have been as calm as he was if it was the last time I'd ever see him. If I was dying he would be a mess. Our last talk didn't seem like he thought it would be the last time he saw me. He was caring and sweet like he was taking care of someone sick, not someone dying. Is that it then? Am I sick? Was seeing my magical animal eaten a dream?

Is *this* a dream?

The leg drops farther down, closer to the ground. Then the other leg drops into view. I notice there are only three toes on the ginormous foot. It must be some sort of lizard right? But what kind of lizard is this giant?

My breathing picks up along with my heart. I know what was watching me now. My instincts never fail me, but they do nothing to calm me. What if this thing, whatever it is, wants to eat me? If I'm in a dream, like I think I am, I shouldn't be afraid. This thing can't hurt me. But what if I'm not. There is a slight chance this is all real and if it is, then I'm definitely not getting out of this one alive.

I hear one more flap before those monstrous feet reach

the ground. A plume of dust flies up as those talons make contact with the ground. My hair is blown back as two wings peek out of the darkness and flap wildly above me. As they move back and forth I see a pair of auburn bat-like wings with thin skin stretched over a skeletal structure.

As the wings beat the darkness of the void around me is blown away. Behind the creature, I notice a dark black sky with sparkling stars blinking in the distance. I gaze at my legs as I try to move against whatever is holding me down, but like before, I can't budge an inch. In a last ditch effort I call to my powers again, but they are nowhere to be seen.

Then I peer up and finally see a mountain of a beast. The creature's full body. My eyes slide up the monster-like body as I take it in. Where I thought there were two feet there are actually four. What I thought was lizard-like skin is actually thick human shield sized scales. It has a broad beige chest which moves into a blood red and dark orange back. Its broad wings start the same color as its chest, but the bone-like edges are the same red and orange color as the rest of it. Atop a long curving neck sits an angular face. Thick menacing horns sit atop, its head leading down to its aquamarine eyes, then dip down to its nostrils. Those aquamarine eyes remind me of my own.

It simply stands there and breathes, smoke wafting out of its nostrils as it stares at me. I'm not sure why, but now, seeing the creature with my own eyes, all of the panic I experienced before is completely gone. Now I'm just curious. I want to know why I'm here, where here is, and what this creature is to me. I can feel this creature means something to me. I'm just not sure what it is.

I stand there staring up into its familiar eyes. We hold each other's gaze for what feels like an eternity before the beast opens its mouth. Before I even hear the words tumble out of its mouth I see the massive, sharp, and deadly teeth piercing out of its gums. Its canines must be as big as half my body. If it were to chomp down on me, I'd be down its gullet in a flash. If I didn't sense this connection between us I'd probably be scared out of my mind.

The creature says, "Attina. I'm glad you're here." By her voice I can tell whatever it is, is a girl.

"Where's here? And what are you?" I ask.

The creature bows its massive body down. Its neck stretches down to my height as it slightly crouches on its front legs. I notice sharp scales run in a row along the monster's back. Almost sparkling in the starlight. They must be razor sharp to sparkle like they do. The massive, mysterious figure moves until the right side of its face is mere inches from mine. I should pull away, but this only serves to pique my curiosity.

The beast tilts its head. "You don't recognize me?"

I shake my head in response but reach my hand out to its face. The creature allows me to feel the scales along its face. They're surprisingly soft, while also being somehow sturdy. They shine in the darkness like a liquid coats them, and with its coloring, almost appears like blood.

As I pull my hand away the beast locks its eye with mine. "I'm your Anima."

"My what? What's that mean?"

It blows smoke out of its mouth, in what I can only describe as exasperation, "I was a blackbird before. Remember? I was getting chased by the serpent?"

If I wasn't being held to the spot I would fall down in shock. How is this possible? How could this thing be my magical animal? It was such a cute, sweet, and little bird before. What happened?

"How did you become this?" I ask as I lift my hand with

a flourish indicating the new creature before me. "I had a dream you were eaten by that serpent. Was it not a dream?"

Pulling back, she closes her eyes and shakes her head. "No it wasn't. It actually happened. That horrible serpent really ate me. Its bite was so painful and toxic, I couldn't hold it off for long. When you used all your magical power to take on the werewolf, it was too much for me. It weakened me enough to allow the serpent to overpower me and swallow me whole."

I gaze down at the ground, it's still only a dark expanse, I can't make out anything except black, so I just stare at my feet in shame. "I'm sorry."

Surprisingly, I feel the gentlest nudge against my shoulder. Who would have thought a creature this immense could be this soft and tender? "Hey, don't be sorry. If you hadn't killed the werewolf we wouldn't be standing here talking. We'd both be dead."

I gaze back into the beast's eyes. "What are you? What happened? You used to be incredibly small and delicate." I move my hands up and down indicating her new body. "Now you're this," I say as sweetly as I can. Hoping to take some of the sting out of my words, I reach up and pet the bridge of her nose, because it's about all I can reach with how massive her head is.

"You saw me get eaten and then I don't remember anything after that. All I know is I woke up here in this body. I'm not sure how it happened. As to *what* I am. I'm a dragon."

"A dragon?" I think back to the books father read to me as a child, filled with white knights saving princesses from beasts called dragons. I scan my gaze over the creature before me. "Yeah, I guess that's exactly what you are. But how?" Then I realize something. "Wait, you couldn't talk to me as a bird could you?"

She shakes her head. "No, I couldn't. I'm not completely sure. I guess my form and the serpent form merged together?" She stands up a little straighter. "I mean look at me. I have bird and serpent features; they've just multiplied in size." She lifts her wings in display, "I still have wings, but now they're bigger and better. And look at these amazing talons at the ends of them." She brings the tip of her wing down next to me for me to inspect. The talon on the end must be almost as long as I am tall and it's deadly sharp. It wouldn't take much for her to eviscerate me.

I reach my hand out and gently touch the dark bone-spiked talon. "This is wonderfully scary." I peek back up to her eyes as she continues showing off, like an excited child. I smile. I'm glad she's this happy after being in so much pain and terrified for as long as she was.

Her eyes almost cross as she tries to gaze at her own mouth, "And I have this wondrous beak, but now it's full of these sharp teeth." She smiles like she's showing off a new toy. "And my feet are still like my old body but they're bigger, deadlier, and there's four of them now."

I chuckle. "Yes it is all very miraculous. You also have a long body and tail like a serpent." I squint my eyes up toward her mouth, "It also seems like you have a forked tongue like a serpent?"

She sticks her tongue out to inspect it. "I do!"

"So, where are we?" I ask, trying to get us back on topic.

"Your subconscious of course. This is where we've always talked. I was just too little before, I couldn't clear away all of the fog blocking it, that's why it appeared like a black void all the other times."

It makes sense. I know she resides somewhere within

me, but I didn't know where. "I wonder if you and the serpent merging allowed you to speak."

She cocks her head, the gesture somehow funny and frightening at the same time. "What do you mean?"

I cross my arms in front of my chest. "Well, you both were magical creatures right?" She purses her lips and inclines her head as she follows my logic. "Maybe merging all of so much magic not only changed your body but changed your abilities too. You must be stronger now."

She flaps her wings and the gust of wind released would knock me down if I could move. "I would say so."

"So it's not too far of a stretch to believe your ability to talk came from your transformation."

She lifts one wing and places the taloned tip under her chin, precisely like a human would if they were thinking about something intensely. I don't want to interrupt her as she sits for a moment making some kind of noise I can't make out, like she's talking to herself. "Hmm I guess it's possible."

"So what do I call you?" I ask. It really would be much easier if I had a name for her.

"You can call me Kaida." She puffs out her chest.

"All right Kaida, how do I get out of here?" I ask.

"Oh that's easy, you simply wake up."

32

JAMES

I pace in my cell. Guards have brought us food a few times now but it's really sporadic, like they keep forgetting we need food to live. I wonder if they even care if we survive or not.

In my mind I can see them now in some guard house talking to each other. "Did you feed the humans?"

The other guard shakes his head as he answers, "No, I thought you did."

As I pace I think about what I can do. I have no clue where we are so even if I wanted to break out, I'd be breaking out into only gods know what. I would have no clue where an exit is or how to get there. I'd be caught in a matter of minutes and would have angered my captors in the process, which could only spell trouble for me and in turn the commander. If the commander gets killed, who will lead Sanctuary?

I walk over to the front of my cell and call out, "Hey Commander?" He doesn't answer; he only grunts at me. I take it as a sign to continue "Hey, what happens if you don't get back to Sanctuary?"

He sounds annoyed when he answers. "What are you prattling on about?"

"Well, you're Sanctuary's leader. What happens if you don't make it back? Will they send out a search party? Will they even know where to search for you?"

He huffs and even though I can't see his face I know he's exasperated simply by the noise. "You were there boy you know we didn't give anyone our destination or where we would end up. We didn't know how long this god's forsaken mission would take or where we would end up." He blows out a loud puff of air before he continues. "I guess, if they haven't heard from me in a few weeks, they'll send out a search party. But I'm not sure what they'll do when they can't find me. They'll either assume we were turned into a Solis, or the Fae took us."

"What happens if they assume the Fae took us?"

I hear a thud noise and then a sound like clothing being rubbed against the cell bars in the cell next to me, making me assume he leaned and then sat against the bars. "If they assume the Fae took us, there will be war." He says it so nonchalantly, like it isn't a big deal, but it is definitely a big deal.

"What!" I shout. "Will they have a chance?"

I hear a slight scratching noise from his cell. "Without me? I doubt it. We don't have the numbers. I don't know how vast the Fae empire is, but with their magic, they don't have to have big numbers to squash our army. We would lose."

Which reminds me. "How did you even know we were walking into Fae territory before we were captured?" I ask, thinking back to when I was arguing with him and Ned before we got caught. I didn't believe them at the time, I thought they merely wanted me to shut up. I never knew there were more Fae than the ones in Shadow Mountain.

"Boy, you keep forgetting I was a warrior while you were still in your momma's belly. I have traveled all over Arealea. I know more about the world we live in than you could ever dream of."

I hear him stand and walk away. I know our conversation is over. I also stand and make my way to the back of the cell. I sit back down and wrap my arms around my legs. I can't let Sanctuary head to war with an enemy they can't possibly defeat. I need to find a way to get the Commander and myself out of here and back to our people.

I'M AWAKENED from a deep sleep, covered in sweat, my heart pounds in my chest. It pounds so hard against my ribcage the bones ache.

Panic rips through me. *No, not now.*

I despise this part of me. This weakness. I knew this was coming but I thought I had a couple more days, I thought I had more time. A yell releases from my lungs as each one of my bones begin breaking and realigning, starting with my ribcage. It's like my heart beats so fast and hard, my ribs have to move out of the way to keep my heart from breaking through.

I hear the commander in the cell next to mine shout, "James! Are you all right? What's happening?"

I don't want the commander to see this part of me. I hid this part of me extremely well from everyone around me, Attina included, but now it seems my secret will be out for the world to see.

I will be exposed.

This wicked creature is coming out whether I want it to or not.

33

ALLISTER

As I stare down at Attina's sleeping form, empty sadness spreads through me. I've been incredibly worried about her this whole time. But now, knowing she's fine, I worry about the other things I've learned since being here.

How am I ever going to tell her what I've found out?

How will she take this news?

34

ATTINA

I open my eyes and hiss, instantly regretting my decision. The sun engulfing the huge room I'm sleeping in streams right across my face, into my eyes, burning them.

"Are you all right?" I hear Allister's worried voice next to me.

I rub my eyes and sit up in bed. When I open them again I take in his beautiful face before me. He leans over the side of the bed, his hands on either side of me. My eyes lock onto those gorgeous, purple, pooling eyes of his. I smile. "Yes, I'm fine. Just felt like my eyes were burning out of my head when I opened them." I tilt my head. "I guess being able to see isn't all it's cracked up to be after all."

His eyes widen as he cradles my face. "You can truly see again?"

My breath hitches at his closeness, the smell of him permeating my senses. All of a sudden I'm hit with it. I can sense each of his movements around me. I remember when he told me he could feel me even when we weren't together. I know I could find this man anywhere now. It feels almost like he's become another appendage. There's this constant awareness of where he is but it's not overwhelming, like how you always know where your legs are. I open my mouth to say something but find it dry as the sand I trekked through on the way to Sanctuary in. So I nod instead.

I notice the vast room around me has vines running up the walls. The interesting thing is, there don't appear to be any vines on the floor. I wonder why that is. His shoulders slacken, he lets out a big huff of air, and he hangs his head. "Good." He lies down on my chest, takes a deep breath, and slowly releases it before he repeats himself. "Good."

I lift my hand up and almost hesitate before I lay my hand down on his head. I'm not sure if he wants this comfort or not but there's only one way to find out. I stroke his luscious hair, the black strands weaving through my fingers. Then I smell roses and lavender, I lean my head down and smell my shoulder. The smell is definitely coming from me, but how is that possible? We were on the road for awhile, and I was passed out for a week, so I haven't been able to take a bath.

I move my head so I can peek at his face a little. "Did you give me a sponge bath while I was passed out?" My cheeks heat as the words leave my lips, did he see me naked already?

He solemnly nods his head but there's no other reaction. No snarky comment, nothing. I'd almost felt violated that he bathed me without my permission, but his reaction cut down the feeling before it could bloom. It feels like a hand wraps around my heart. What's going on with him? We both sit there in silence for a minute as I stroke his hair before I realize his shoulders are shaking. Is he crying?

I gently grab his shoulder and sit forward, and the blue, silk sheets almost sigh as I push him back into a straightened position. As he sits up straight I see the glimmer of tears on his cheeks. When we lock eyes I see his are full of tears and blood red. He must have been crying for a long time for them to be this red, more than just the little bit he's done now. I was so enthralled by the color of his eyes earlier I didn't even notice. I would be embarrassed at my pig headedness if I wasn't so worried about him.

"Hey, what's wrong? Are you all right? What happened?"

He dips his head back down and violently shakes his head before launching himself on top of me again. I'm thrown back onto the plush bed, my head grazing the headboard. His arms are wrapped around me solidly like a serpent, but also softly enough to not hurt. He buries his face into my shoulder and inhales deeply. I move my arm and he releases barely enough for me to pull my arm out from his grasp, before he locks his arms back down on my body. His body wracks with tears.

I bring my hand up and begin stroking his hair once more. I shush him, trying to comfort him. "Shh. It's okay. I'm right here."

He lifts his head a fraction of an inch and I barely make out what he says through his trembling voice, "You were dead!"

I pull back as much as I can, trying to gaze into his face. "What? What are you talking about? I'm fine, I'm right here, Allister."

He dives his face back into my shoulder and shakes his head.

I begin rubbing his head again feeling his silky hair under my hand and I give him I squeeze him before saying, "I'm right here. Nothing happened to me, I only slept a little too long, that's it."

He huffs out a big sigh before rolling on his side. He rolls me over with him, making our chests meet and I'm gazing up into his face. Even with the snot spilling out of his nose it's a glorious sight. I swear this man has no flaws.

He wraps his leg around my lower half, his arms still around my top half. I should feel embarrassed, but after all we've been through and all we've shared this seems like the most natural thing possible.

He shakes his head, his hair rubbing on the soft down sheets beneath us. "No Attina. You died out there with the werewolf."

I furrow my brows. What is he talking about? Obviously I didn't die. I'm right here in his arms talking to him. No, I couldn't have died. Right? I do remember thinking I was dying but then I woke up here in this soft bed. I'm alive right? I run my hand through his hair again, the motion grounding me somehow, reminding me this is real. "What are you talking about? I'm so confused. Spit it out Allister. You're freaking me out."

He pushes me away and stares intently into my eyes. "When I made it to you, you had already hit the ground."

I roll my eyes. "Yes, I remember and then you picked me up and I passed out. The next thing I know, I'm waking up here."

His eyes tighten and narrow as they grow hard. He moves to lie in the bed next to me, facing me. "No, Attina, you died in my arms."

I shake my head, shock washing over me. I know he believes what he's saying. There's no other explanation for how he's behaving. He's acting like I did when I thought he died, like he really thought his mate left him forever.

"You did. You told me you loved me and stopped breathing. I couldn't hear your heartbeat. There was nothing I could do. I don't have your magic. I couldn't bring you back the way you did with me. I tried breathing air into your lungs and pushing on your chest to get your heart beating but nothing worked."

My breath catches. I have to push through a knot in my throat to get the words out as I say, "How am I alive then?"

He pulls me back into him and I shove my head against his chest suddenly insecure. I'm not sure what I'm insecure about but it's the best way to describe what I'm feeling right now.

"I picked you up and raced you to the Eastern Fae stronghold. I ran through the gate screaming for a healer. One came to my aid, but he could do nothing for you. He pronounced you dead as I sat on the ground with you in my arms." At this point in the story he completely breaks down again. His body wracks with the sobs coming out of him, but by now they're more like pained screams than actual sobs.

I get a flash in my mind of the scene. Allister on the ground. His face covered in dirt and grime, with my limp body in his arms. The ground around us is covered in frost and ice. My clothing is torn away in spots, which I assume happened when I released all of my power. My face is pale as a ghost, my chest unmoving. A blonde man in a long black robe bends over me and places his hands out flat, against my chest for a moment. The man then peers up at Allister with a drawn, sad face and shakes his head. Allister throws his head back and lets out the most guttural, pained scream I've ever heard a man scream. Ice covers everything in sight and snow begins falling heavily. His water powers unleashed from the pain inside his heart.

I huff out a breath, throwing my arms around him. I wrench my arms down on Allister until my arms feel like they will pop from my shoulders. I rub my face into his chest as tears fill my eyes. In his memory I sense the pain and anguish he felt when he realized I was dead.

"I'm so sorry I put you through all that, Allister. No one should have to suffer through the pain of thinking they lost their mate."

Allister pulls away from me once more. I gaze up at my mate. We sure are a pair in this moment. Both of us weeping like babies with snot running down our noses. He leans down and places a soft kiss on my lips, tears and snot mingling together.

We stay intertwined for what feels like hours, but I eventually pull back and gaze into his reddened eyes. I need answers. "So, how did I come back to life?"

His face pinches and he shakes his head. "I'm not sure. I brought you down into the infirmary. The Fae here keep their dead there, in a separate room from the patients, until they can build a pyre. I was there with you. I refused to leave you." He chuckles as he says, "I actually punched Ned in the face."

I push on his chest and pull back further, my body sliding against the bed sheet. "You did what? Wait, what were Ned and Raven doing during all this?"

"Raven was being seen by another healer so she had no idea what was happening. Ned was right there with me. I came through the gate, and he was right behind me the whole time."

Makes sense why I didn't see him in the memory.

"When you died and I broke, he tried to comfort me." He now has the good sense to appear a little ashamed. His cheeks slightly heat, and he wraps his arms around himself. "When I finally moved to get up, he tried to take you from me to help me stand up." His eyes break contact with mine like he's uncomfortable. "He didn't even touch you before I punched him square in the mouth."

"Allister!" I shriek as I push on his chest. "He was only trying to help!"

His eyes turn soft as he looks directly at me, the intensity of his stare making my cheeks flush. "I know. It was just an instinctual thing. I wasn't angry with him but you're my mate and I'd lost you. I thought he was trying to take you from me. Or at least that's what my body was telling me." He then quickly adds on, "He doesn't even have a bruise anymore!"

I quirk my eyebrow and tilt my head. "You still have to apologize."

He shakes his head and I open my mouth to argue but he cuts me off. "I already did. He understands. He even said he shouldn't have done what he did. We're fine, there's no ill will between us. You don't have to worry; our family is still intact." Then he leans down and kisses me on the forehead.

"Where are Hazel and Talon? You said Mylo is stuck to Raven's side but what happened to them?"

"Talon is in a cage in the dungeon. Ned made sure they put him somewhere he couldn't escape and explained who the bird was. Hazel, on the other hand, I'm not sure about. She took off before I brought you back and I haven't seen her since. I'm not sure if she even knows what happened."

"She knows; she has to know. That bird knows everything," I answer as I place my forehead on his chest. I breathe in the forest-like scent which is distinctly Allister.

He pulls my head into him and asks, "So how do you feel?"

I think for a second. "Tired. But otherwise, I feel fine, maybe even stronger."

"Stronger?" he asks as he holds me away from him, his head cocked.

"Yes. I can't be sure but something inside of me feels

more... grounded I guess? I'm not really sure how to explain it." I reach up and grab at my necklace, insecurity washing over me. "There's... also something else I need to tell you."

Allister places his finger under my chin and lifts my head until our eyes meet "What is it, love?"

My eyes bulge as I croak out, "Love?"

He chuckles. "Yes, love. I've accidentally blurted it out once and you said it before you died. I think I'm allowed to call you love now." I gulp in a sharp breath. I completely forgot I did that. How did I forget such a major thing? Oh yeah cuz I was *dying*. My whole body heats, starting at my head and drifting all the way down to my toes. I must be beet red by now.

Allister moves up onto the arm underneath him so he's hovering over me. His face is pinched in confusion. "You don't remember telling me you loved me do you?"

I quietly and quickly shake my head. "No, not at all."

"Oh." His shoulders fall in on themselves as he visibly deflates.

I quickly wiggle out from under him as I scan around the room, gazing at the gray brick walls, the vaulted ceiling, and the sconces on the wall. Staring anywhere other than his face. I don't know how to do this. I don't know how to be vulnerable like this. "I mean it's not untrue... I just..."

He crawls back over me, and his hand moves my face back to his. His eyes show an intensity I haven't seen in awhile. He slowly reaches over me, encasing me, leaving me no room to escape. Not like I would if I could, though. The realization surprises me, I thought I'd be nervous being this vulnerable, but I find I'm not.

He leans down and gently places his lips on mine. The warm electricity when our lips meet is intoxicating. How can kissing someone feel this wonderful? Our mouths move, every movement brings a new sensation. His tongue grazes my lips and I invite him in. I throw my arm around his back, grabbing onto the back of his black tunic, pulling him into me. He groans into my lips, his tongue thrusting inside my mouth before he gently pulls away and placing his forehead on mine, both of us now breathing heavily.

I decide I'm done being timid with him. I grab on to him, pushing him sideways, rolling him off of me. I seize the chance and climb on top of him, his strong body rubbing against my thighs.

He will be mine.

35

ATTINA

I WANT THIS.

I will not die again without making this man mine. I lean down and press my lips against his. Electricity shoots through them like it always does. I hope this doesn't ever change about us. I hope our kisses stay literally electrifying forever.

He runs his hands up my legs and digs his fingers into my thighs. Goosebumps start where his fingers touch and spiral out, dotting the rest of my body. I deepen our kiss. He opens his mouth, allowing my tongue can mingle with his as his hands roam up my waist to palm my breast. I moan into his mouth.

He must not want to ruin the moment so instead of pulling away to ask me something, he asks into my mind. *Are you okay with this? You're sure? You're not worried about your fire?*

I answer back in his mind as I pull away slightly, placing kisses on his cheek, his neck, down his chest. *I've never been more sure of anything in my life. I barely came back from the dead. I'm done being timid with my mate. You are mine and I intend to show you so. If I burn this bed down, so be it.*

He groans into my mouth as his motions become fevered. His hands move to cup my butt, grabbing on like he's worried I'll run away. The movement feels surprisingly pleasurable, making me grind against him. I feel the length of him underneath me and I realize I completely mean what I say. Even when it comes to this epic adventure. I started this to please other people, not for my own reasons. But right now I want this man for me, selfishly.

Then all of a sudden Allister grabs me around the waist and back, throwing me onto my back. I gasp in surprise but before I know it, his lips are back on mine. He mirrors where I was just kissing him. His lips trail down to my chin, my neck, my chest. His strong hands roam down to my thighs, pulling up the gray tunic covering me, over my head. I lift my hands in the air, allowing him to gently slide the fabric off of me, leaving me bare beneath him. I'm incredibly exposed, but it feels right. It's like I'm exactly where I should be. Like I'm meant to be in this castle, with this man, in this moment.

He sits up and a growl escapes him as his eyes rake down my body, taking in every bit of me. He pulls his black tunic over his head, leaving only his pants on as he flops his body down over me, on his hands again, like a bear covering its quarry. I watch as his bulging muscular arms and chest flex to hold his weight.

"You're the most beautiful thing I've ever laid eyes on, have I told you that before?"

My cheeks heat and my mouth goes dry as I stutter out, "Umm...I..." But then I remember, this is my mate, I *just* said I was done being timid. I steel my back, unintentionally causing my breasts to push out. His eyes lock on my chest. I reach up, hooking my finger under his chin and pull his gaze to mine. "You've told me once before, but I'd love to hear it again."

He groans out, "You're the most beautiful thing I've ever laid eyes on." He leans down, putting one of my nipples in his mouth, sucking on it.

I feel fire course through me as I arch my back and let out a loud moan. His hand drifts to the button on his pants and unbuttons them, he deftly shimmies them off. Then he opens my legs with his knees. When I look down and see his impressive length, my body goes weak and taut at the same time my mouth dries. Fire instantly flits through me, melting everything in its wake. Any doubt or embarrassment, gone in an instant.

He crawls back over me and gently kisses me, making me moan. He pushes himself up against me, only stopping his feverish kisses long enough to stare into my eyes. "Are you sure about this?"

I silently nod and he puts his mouth back on mine. I lift my arms and wrap them around his neck. Opening my eyes for a split second I see my skin is again red. I gasp and Allister pulls away. "Are you all right?"

I don't answer him but by his reaction I know my face is just as red as my arms. I let go of his neck and turn my face away from him. Ready for him to pull away, to tell me it's too dangerous. But instead he grabs my chin in his fingers and pulls my face to his. "Do you realize how much of a turn on this is?"

I shake my head, hope springing forth in my chest. "You don't think I'm strange?"

"Strange?" His brows knit. "Are you kidding me? I'm turning my mate into liquid fire. This is the most amazing thing I've experienced in my life." His mouth is back on mine in a flash, drawing me to him, allowing our bodies to touch every inch of each other. My moan turns to a scream as he thrusts himself into me, making us one. Being so close with him, sharing this, feels right. I feel something click into place as he moves over me. His moans of pleasure make me want to scream loud enough for everyone in the castle to hear our love. He moves in me, over and over again, until I'm screaming his name in bliss.

When we finish he rolls off of me and wraps his strong, now sweaty arms around me. I hear a crunching noise as he moves and a burned smell floats to my nose. I must have burned the sheets.

Then, I feel his hot breath on the shell of my ear as he whispers, "Attina, I love you with everything I am and everything I will be. I will love you for the rest of my life, until my dying breath. I am yours until the stars fall from the sky and the ground beneath us turns to dust."

My mouth goes dry as I lift my hands to his cheeks. I pull his head down to mine. I kiss him again as I feel tears slip down my face. "Allister," I say as I choke back a sob. He hears me and pulls back his eyes widened in shock. "I love you." I might never be as eloquent as he is, but I know my words hit home when he throws himself on top of me and wraps me in such a tight hug, I have to tap his shoulder like we used to do while sparring to tell the other one we gave up, they had won.

He pulls back. "Did I grab you too tight?"

I chuckle out, "Just a bit," as I sit up in bed. He follows me so we're sitting side by side in bed. "I need to tell you something."

"Can't it wait?" he asks as he leans over and gently kisses my neck.

I answer, "You're already ready *again?*" But as I move my

body closer against him I can tell he's definitely already ready. How is such a thing possible? I move and expose my neck to him more. Give him more places for him to land those soft, luxurious kisses on. I almost give in, but this is too important. I straighten back up and raise my shoulder to my cheek, cutting off his ability to reach my neck. I grunt as I try to get my wits back about me, and clear my throat, "No Allister. I want you again, but this is important, it's about my magical animal."

I notice those words get his attention as he stills. "What? What happened to it? Last you told me it had been bitten by that damn serpent."

I dip my head. "Yes, and it got eaten by the serpent."

"*What!*" he shouts and he's instantly in front of me staring into my eyes, his hand grasping mine. His words fall out as an almost beg as he says, "Tell me everything."

So I do. I tell him about what I saw after I fought off the werewolf and what I saw in my subconscious mere moments ago. I tell him about Kaida.

He doesn't say a word until I finish saying what I need to say. He appears to look past me as he says, "No wonder you died. It makes complete sense now."

I jack up my face, completely lost as to what he's saying. "What do you mean?"

In a flash, he jumps out of bed and quickly throws his black tunic back on. I almost hate how hastily he gets it on because it gives me less time to devour his body with my eyes. Then he begins pacing the stone floor before the bed I'm occupying. His head down, his hair moving in front of his face, hiding it from me. He places his hands behind his back as he begins. "Your magical animal got eaten, so it essentially died. What did Hazel say? If your magical animal dies, you die.

"Yours died, so you died." He lifts a finger but continues his pacing. I realize now he's not actually talking to me, he's merely talking things out to himself. "But your animal came back to life as a dragon, so you came back to life."

"One more thing. I can feel you now." I feel my cheeks start to heat but I'm not sure why I'm embarrassed by this after what we just did. Allister faces me, his brows knit in question, and he opens his mouth to say something, but I push on instead. "How you can feel me wherever I am. I can feel you now too."

A wide, proud grin crosses his face. "You can? Finally, I wonder why it took this long. Maybe having two magical animals prevented you from feeling me?"

I nod as I find my clothes and wiggle back into them before I throw my legs over the side of the bed, determined to take control of what's going on around me. I find I hate feeling helpless and being stuck in this bed is definitely starting to make me feel helpless. I take a second to spin around and confirm I did singe the sheets during our romp. I'm surprised to find I'm not embarrassed about it at all. If my mate likes this side of me, then I should learn to like it too.

In a flash Allister races over to me, kneeling in front of me, worry written on his features by his creased brow and slackened jaw. "Are you sure you want to get up? We could stay in bed one more day, make sure you're healed. You did just die. I could use a little more time, only the two of us."

I lift my hand to his cheek as warmth spreads in my chest. I know he's worried about me, but I can't simply sit here doing nothing. "I'm so sorry I put you through so much, love." A broad smile flashes across his features at the nickname. "But I have to see what I'm capable of now. I have to see my family and make a plan to take down that tyrant Henrik."

He sits there and stares at me, for a second I think he'll refuse me and try to keep me locked in this room for another day for my own good, like James would. But then he stands and holds out his hand to me, wiggling his brows. "Don't you want to take a bath with me first?"

I peer over at the bathtub in the corner of the room longingly, wishing I could melt into warm water and allow it to take all my aches and pains away. "It'll have to wait until I make sure everyone is safe."

Allister doesn't even miss a beat. "Fine, but I want you to see the healer first. Deal?"

I gaze down at his hand before placing mine in it. As I stand I answer. "Deal." Then I walk over to the corner of the room, where I spotted my armor, sword, bow, and dagger leaning against the wall beside the nightstand.

I bend down to pick it all up before Allister coos behind me, "You won't need those here."

I spin my head around while I'm still bent over and say, "You actually feel that comfortable here?"

He wiggles his eyebrows. "I wouldn't have done to you what I did if I didn't." My face falls in annoyance when he pointedly stares at my bent over form. "But you can stand there as long as you want. I'm enjoying the show."

I glare at him and shoot him an obscene gesture before standing upright. "Fine, but I don't trust this place as much as you do. I'm still bringing my dagger."

He raises his hands, saying, "Fine by me," as he turns to open the door to our room.

I finish dressing and throw my dagger in my boot before hurrying after him.

36

ATTINA

As we stride through the castle I'm surprised by the muted tones surrounding me. It all seems distinctly—natural here. Vines grow along the walls and what I must assume to be Fae animals scurry around inside the castle. Buds of flowers even dot along the vines. I notice, instead of windows, there are only open frames along the walls. Which is curious, because even though I can tell winter is near, by the chilly breeze flowing in, the castle is warm. There must be some sort of magic keeping the warmth in.

"How do you know where we're going?"

He chuckles as he glances over his shoulder at me, walking down some stairs. "You forget, you've been asleep for over a week. While I did stay by your side most of the time, I did have to scrounge up some food and search for exits in case we needed to escape quickly." He moves to the side and stops, waiting for me. When I take the few strides to reach him, he cups my cheek in his hand, his eyes softening as he stares down at me. "You couldn't protect yourself. I had to make sure if anything happened I could get you out of here safely. I don't remember much from when I was a boy here, but the little parts I do remember haven't changed"

I scoff and shake my head. I sense a pair of Fae walking further down the same flight of stairs we are. One of them says beneath us, "Do you smell smoke?" The other answers in turn but by then they've moved too far off for me to hear

My cheeks heat, that was me. I always forget the Fae have amazing senses. I need to be more careful around here. I'm not sure who could be listening. So I say into his mind, *Always the warrior.*

He grabs onto my shoulders, turning me to face him and shakes his head, "Firstly, there are others in this castle who can read minds like me. Which means there's no point speaking mind to mind until I have the time to teach you to block them out. Secondly no, I might be an amazing warrior but I'm more about always being the *protector*—"

I cut him off. "And extremely modest."

He ignores me. "But I only ever wanted to protect my people from Henrik's wrath. If that meant killing others then so be it."

My mouth drops open and I take a step back from him, my back pushing against the stone wall behind me. "How could you say such a thing? The people you killed were innocent. They didn't deserve to die."

He closes the distance between us until his body is pushed up against mine and I'm pinned between him and the wall. I have to tilt my head up to peer into his eye, my face barely reaching his chin. "Attina, you grew up in a much gentler world than I did. The world I grew up in was kill or be killed. There was no love, no happiness."

"Oh Allister." I reach my hand out and wrap my arms around his torso. I know how awful my grandfather was and is, but it never hit me how terrible Allister's life must have been while he lived under Henrik's rule. I'd assumed he was the greatest warrior, so he had it easier than the rest. But I guess I was wrong

"If you weren't useful you either starved or were killed. If you went against orders there were... other consequences."

Instantly my heart begins racing. "What kind of consequences?"

He huffs out a breath of air and turns from me, sitting down on the stone steps beneath us. He pats the ground next to him, inviting me to sit. He hangs his head and his shoulders sag, like he's defeated. "I have to explain something to you about the last time I was at Shadow Mountain."

My eyes narrow and my heart starts beating faster. What could make him this upset? I sit down before I ask him, "What is it?"

He places his elbows on his thighs and starts picking at the nail of his ring finger. "The last time I saw Henrik, I told you he slapped my mother, what I didn't tell you was he threatened to kill her if I betrayed him."

"He what?" I shriek.

He sighs, places his hands behind him, and leans back. "Yeah he did. But there's nothing I can do about it. I can't leave you—"

I cut him off. "Yes you can! I can handle this. I can't be the cause of your mother being murdered. I couldn't live with myself, and you wouldn't be able to look at me the same way, knowing I was the reason your mother died."

He straightens up, turns to me, and grabs my face in both his hands. "*You* would not be the reason she died. *Henrik* would be the reason she died. I know the issues you have with your mother, but my mother and I have our own issues."

I cock my head. "What issues?"

He places his forehead on mine for a split second before he moves back to his leaning position. He lets out a big breath of air before throwing his head back to stare at the ceiling. "My mother is basically already dead. She died the night her mate died."

"Your father..." I encourage him to continue.

"Yes, ever since the night my father died, all those years ago, she's been a ghost. When I was a child we were almost inseparable, but after my father died, she's just plain gone."

"What do you mean gone? She lives in Shadow Mountain with you," I ask, confused as to what he means.

"I don't mean physically gone. I mean vacant, like there's no one behind her eyes. The only time I ever see her is when I have to see Henrik. And when I do see her she simply sits on her throne with an emptiness in her eyes like her body is here but she's somewhere else completely. Henrik can abuse me or threaten my life and she doesn't say a word. She just blankly stares off in the distance like she's not seeing what's happening right before her very eyes. Losing her mate broke something in her. It's like I lost my father and mother on the same night."

I wrap my arm around his and he stops staring at the ceiling to peer at me. "I'm so sorry Allister." I lean forward and place a kiss on his stubbly cheek.

"But we have Talon now, so at least Henrik must be kind of in the dark. Hopefully he still thinks I'm his spy."

I stand and reach my hand out toward him, inviting him to stand with me. "We should go find Talon and see if we can get some information out of him."

He ignores my hand, narrows his eyes at me, and puts his hand out to the ground by his side, leaning against it. His voice is accusatory as he says, "You're not trying to get out of seeing the healer are you?"

I shake my head, my hair swings around me touching and tickling my cheeks. "Even with how much I don't want to see the healer, I agree I should probably be seen by one. But after we're done there I want to see Raven and Ned. We can interrogate Talon afterwards."

"Agreed," he says as a broad, stunning smile cracks along his face. He places his hand in my still outstretched one. "I'm glad you're *finally* listening to reason."

I rip my hand back and turn around, making my way down the stairs. I call back over my shoulder, "You make it seem like I'm unreasonable." I lift my nose in the air as I bob down the stairs. Instantly, I realize how much more sure-footed I am. How even the stone calls to me, telling me where to next put my feet. If I'd tried this before I had my powers I surely would have fallen down the stairs in a bloody mess.

I hear him burst out in laughter behind me, but I don't turn around I simply keep moving forward. "And this is how you choose to prove you're not unreasonable? By leaving me, the person who knows where they're heading, on the stairs, and taking off on your own?" Sarcasm leaches from his words as he finishes. "Yes, it sounds like you're a *completely* reasonable person."

I spin around, my hand on my hip, trying to appear annoyed when I'm really not. I wanted to cheer him up by taking his mind off of all he's divulged. Scanning him up and down it's obvious my plan worked. Now there's a satisfied grin plastered on his face, and he even stands straighter. His muscled shoulders pull at the fabric of his tunic as they slightly shake, quietly laughing.

I wave him down. "Well, get down here all-knowing one. We have places to be and people to see." I bend over, laughter spewing out of me, as he bounds down the steps two at a time to reach me.

We have to walk down flights of stairs for what seems like eternity before we get to the infirmary. Like Allister said before, it's under the castle, which means we must have been in one of the top rooms of the castle's spires. Why would we get a room this high up? Do these Fae know who Allister is?

I glance over to Allister as we make our way down a dark hall which he says opens up the infirmary. "Hey, I just realized, how come we're not in the dungeons or something? They don't know who we are, and we get our own room? Why would they do that?"

He continues staring forward but I notice how his jaw clenches before he answers. "I told them who I was," he says, like it explains everything.

As we walk I roll my hand in front of me in a flourish as I awkwardly half bow and sarcastically ask, "And they simply believed you, your highness?"

He turns toward me and glares down at me. He must not think I'm as funny as I do. His face becomes tightly pinched, "Well, no. They didn't, but I was able to convince them enough that they want to test me to see if I'm truly the heir to the throne."

We make it to the bottom level of the castle, turning down a darkened side hall. The smell of chemicals tickles my nose.

37

ATTINA

I stop walking and turn to him. "Test you? What does that mean?"

He keeps walking to the wooden door to our right and opens it before saying, "I'll explain it all after you're seen by a healer. We're here." He walks through the door and holds it open so I can follow.

We enter the room and I'm instantly hit with the smell of rubbing alcohol mingled with something I can't place. The scent is so strong it brings tears to my eyes. As I blink the tears out of my eyes, I see shelves covering all four walls and an old wooden table sits in the middle. On the shelves are all manner of concoctions. Some have liquids in them with every color imaginable. Others have what appears to be animal parts pickled in them. As I move further into the room I see oddly shaped glass containers containing a heart, an eye, and even a horse hoof. All are immersed in some sort of semi-transparent brownish liquid. Finally, my nose adjusts to the smell and my eyes stop watering

While I'm taking in the room around me a door is opened from the wall to my right. A man with an off-white robe and pointed ears poking through his long gray hair, backs into the room. When he turns I see his arms are full of more liquids, the glasses make a scratching noise in his arms. When he lifts his head and notices me and Allister he jumps a bit, and the containers fall out of his hands.

I lift my hand and call to my powers. I watch as the air around the glasses slows down their descent and the ground under them cradles the fragile containers. I lift my gaze to the old man and see him staring at me. His mouth is agape, his long beard hanging down almost to his belly button where a rope is holding his robe shut. His eyes reveal his shock, making me tilt my head in confusion. Everyone here must have magical powers. He can't be shocked I can use mine to stop his glass containers from breaking.

He must notice my confusion because he shakes his head and stutters out "Th—thank you. I shouldn't have tried to take so many at one time."

"You're welcome. Are you the healer who's been keeping an eye on me right?" Allister and I move to help him pick up his containers.

He crouches down and starts collecting them as he answers, "Indeed, I am. But I'm not sure how much help I was. I simply made sure you were still breathing and checking to see if I could do anything." He lifts his head and tilts it toward Allister. "Your mate is actually the one who was keeping an eye on you."

Allister's head shoots up. "How did you know we were mates?"

We pick up the rest of his containers and the old man chuckles as he stands up. "A Fae would only react the way you did when she died, if it was their mate who died." He places the glass containers on an empty space on one of the shelves before turning toward us. "Let's call it an educated guess."

I notice Allister's cheeks heat all the way up to the tips of his pointed ears as he puts his armful on the shelf too. I follow suit and when my hands are empty, I rub my hand up and down Allister's arm, trying to comfort him.

"So, are you here to get a check-up?" the old man asks me. His gray eyes surprise me. They're gray but almost white, like he's losing his sight, but he doesn't walk around like he's losing his sight; he's so sure in his movements.

"Yes, sir, I am."

He chuckles and gestures to the wooden table in the middle of the room. "Go ahead and leap up onto the table, I need to take a gander at you. And please call me Kalven. I've never liked people calling me sir. It makes me sound so old." He turns around and makes his way to the other side of the room.

I feel Allister's arm move up and down against my back as he chuckles. I spin my head and shoot him a withering glare before making my way to the table. I jump as the coolness of it penetrates my tunic, surprising me.

Kalven asks, "I know you two are mates, but would you like him to step out while I examine you?" He indicates he means Allister with a dip of his head.

I shake my head and grab on to the table under me. "No, it's fine. He can stay."

Kalven turns around and begins inspecting the concoctions on the shelf behind him. His head moves as he scans the shelf. "Okay, I didn't want to assume anything. A patient and their healer should have absolute trust." His head stops moving and he makes an ah ha noise as he grabs a glass full of green liquid off of the shelf before him.

Turning around he downs the liquid and explains, "This

potion lets me see what's wrong with you beneath the surface, I can see your bones, muscles, innards and even your Anima's aura." He narrows his eyes and scans my body up and down. "Hmm nothing seems to be wrong with you physically. He narrows his eyes and brings his hand up to his chin. "Although your Anima is something different entirely. Can you tell me what happened? I've never seen anything like this before."

I turn to Allister. "Anima?" He merely shrugs his shoulders as he shakes his head and lifts his hands in the air. I turn back to Kalven.

His head swivels between Allister and me, "You don't know what your Anima is?" He faces me, from what I've gleaned from your mate you didn't know you were part Fae until recently. He turns to Allister and points. "But *you've* known you were Fae your whole life. How do you not know what your Anima is?"

Allister crosses his arms over his chest and narrows his eyes at Kalven. "How about you stop talking to me like I'm a child and spit it out. Tell me what the hell you're talking about."

Kalven takes a step back like Allister's slapped him and his mouth gapes open but only for a second before he calmly composes himself. "Your Anima is your spirit animal, it's a part of your soul, where your magic stems from."

Allister's eyes budge as realization washes over him, "Oooohhh, you mean your magical animal. Yes, I know what that is, I haven't heard it called Anima before. It makes sense though; animal and Anima are pretty close names."

"So in the west you call it your magical animal? Why would they change the name? It's such a dumbing down of what the word truly means. Your Anima isn't merely your magical or spirit, it's your soul, it's your life force, without it we cease to be. Why would Henrik allow such a thing?" He spreads his arm out to encompass the room. "Do you even have a healer with such potions in the west? Are there any of the old ways left in that cursed place?"

Allister scans the room around him. "I've never seen this many potions in one place. We don't have a healer like you. We completely rely on our own healing ability. If one of us becomes critically injured they simply die, there's no one there to help." He tilts his head and shrugs his shoulders. "Our people also starve while Henrik gets fat on his stored supplies so I'm not completely shocked."

"Hmm, it's upsetting hearing he's lost his way entirely, but I'm not surprised though. Something needs to be done about him. He's leading our brethren down such dark a path. Fae are meant to be one with the world around them, not master of the world. I will have to talk to our leader about this."

I cock my head and furrow my brow. "Why would your leader lend you his ear?" Then I lower my head and wiggle in my seat. "I don't mean to be rude, but I just don't understand how you could have influence on what your leader does."

He smiles down at me, the movement pulling at the wrinkles of his eyes. "The Eastern Fae are a very spiritual people. The healers of our people are considered high ranking officials. And out of the few healers, I'm the one with the most seniority. I'm seen as a source of wisdom, which makes me almost like our leader's right-hand man. So yes, I have a great deal of pull with our leader."

My eyebrows lift but all I can think to say is, "Oh."

Kalven lifts his hand and makes a motion like he's trying to clear the air. "So tell me about yourself, what you've gone through, and what happened to your Anima. I can tell there was recently some change. Its aura has a mixture of colors, which isn't normal, but the colors marble together which means two Anima must have become one. I haven't heard of such a thing happening before." He grabs a chair I hadn't noticed before from the short side of the table and places it before me, sitting down in it. "I heard you are Henrik's granddaughter and the rightful heir to the Western Fae throne. Is that correct?"

"How did you know?" Allister asks.

Kalven doesn't even peek at him as he answers. "I know more than you think boy."

Allister opens his mouth to say something, but I interrupt him and take off on telling him my story. Kalven is quiet through it all, the only indication he's following along is how he nods his head occasionally. When I get to the part of my Awakening he drops his head and interrupts me. "I'm so sorry for your loss. Losing your father and your companion in the same night must have broken your heart. I see you brought in another horse, though. Is she your new companion?"

I smile and stare at the floor below me. "Thank you. Yes, it was extremely hard. I haven't had time to mourn their loss yet, either. There's no time to feel everything I've lost since that night. But, yes, Raven is my new mount. She was Oak's daughter and my late father's mount. She hated me when I was growing up, but she's become my best friend."

I gaze up and he's smiling, but there's a gleam of sadness behind his eyes, like he really feels for me even though I'm a stranger to him. "I'm glad she's become your best friend; a companion should be your best friend. You two will live side by side and share your lives. I'm glad you have each other. But you need to grieve. You can't move forward if you don't lay to rest those feelings. You'll never be able to remain a force of good and take on Henrik without grieving. Losing someone dear to you creates unbridled darkness in your heart."

I lean back on the table and lift my head to the ceiling. I sit there quietly as I try to keep the tears from flowing and keep myself together. *Allister, could you continue for me? I need a moment to get myself together.*

Of course, kitten. Allister clears his throat and draws Kalven's attention. "Attina needs a moment. I'll fill you in on what I can."

Kalven's eyes move back and forth between us, "You two can read minds? Both of you?"

Allister shakes his head. "I can but she can't. She can hear my mind because we're mates, but she hasn't shown any signs of having the same powers as me. Her powers are element manipulation."

Kalven turns his seat toward Allister, "Good to know. So what can you tell me about her story?"

Allister tells him everything he knows, even about what James has done to me. He gets to the point where we faced off with the werewolf before he chokes up. He clears his throat and simply says, "Well, you know the rest of the story already, so now you're all caught up."

By the time he finishes his retelling of our journey together I have myself put together enough to continue with what I have to say. I don't give Kalven a chance to comment on what Allister explained before I say, "I had two Anima to begin with."

Kalven slices his gaze toward me. "What?"

I take in a deep breath. "Yes, I started off with two Anima, a little blackbird and a serpent like my grandfather. The serpent was hunting down my blackbird. I was frightened for a long time, because I was told if your spirit animal dies, you die, and I didn't think my blackbird would win the fight."

Kalven's face twists and his eyes harden in thought. "How is this possible? I haven't ever heard of such a thing."

I shrug as I peek over at Allister. "When I died I saw the serpent devour my blackbird. I thought it was merely a dream, but it turns out it wasn't, it really did happen." Allister moves over and places his hand on my back. I'm not sure if he's trying to steady me or remind himself I'm still here. "While I was sleeping I saw my Anima. The two beings have merged into one. Now instead of a blackbird and a serpent my Anima is a towering crimson dragon."

His mouth drops again. "Two Anima merging into one? I'm astounded something like this could happen. I've heard of dragons before, they're part of an ancient, extinct world. Nearly all Fae Animas are creatures from this world. I only know of one other Fae whose Anima is an ancient beast."

"Who?" Allister and I demand simultaneously.

Kalven lifts his hand to his chin. "Henrik's Anima is a three headed Hydra."

38

ATTINA

I open my mouth to say something, but Allister beats me to the punch, "No, his magical—I mean Anima is a serpent, everybody knows that."

"If his Anima isn't a serpent why would my other Anima be one?" I glance back and forth between Allister and Kalven. Pointing my thumb at Allister, "We thought I had a serpent because I was bitten by a Solis and some of Henrik's power leached into me from the kernel of power left within it."

I follow Kalven with my gaze as he stands up and starts moving around the room searching shelves. He stops at the shelf behind me, and starts moving containers around, like he's organizing. Over his shoulder he says, "No, that's only what he tells everyone." I notice him slightly shrug, "I mean it makes sense for him to tell people his Anima is a serpent. No one knows what a Hydra is anymore. They wouldn't question his authority and allowing them to think his Anima is merely a serpent, makes him seem weaker than he truly is."

He cuts his gaze to me. "Do you know what a Hydra is?"

I shake my head and say, "No, I don't."

"A Hydra is a gigantic three headed serpent."

I jump in. "So the serpent attacking my animal *was* a kernel of his power!"

I thought Kalven was done with his line of thought, but I realize he wasn't when he says, "With one immortal head."

Allister shouts, "Immortal? Does this mean Henrik is immortal?"

Kalven leans forward onto the table next to me and lets out a big huff. "I honestly don't know, it's definitely not a good sign though."

I cut in, shaken by this turn of events. "Are you telling me he might be immortal *and* he's more powerful than anyone knows?" We already know Henrik is the most powerful Fae in all of Arealea with the power we know about. If Kalven is right, then how do I have any chance at stopping him?

He turns to face me and moves back to gently lean against the shelf behind him, careful not to shake it. "I know how powerful he is from experience."

Allister shouts, "How is this possible!" I notice him move toward me protectively out of the corner of my eye. "There's no way you could have met him and lived."

Kalven's eyes turn dark as he lowers his head and his shoulders stiffen. "Boy, do not presume to tell me who or what I know. I've lived a whole lifetime more than you have."

Allister's eyes go wide as saucers as he shuffles back a little, "Um—I'm sorry." Almost as an afterthought he drops his head and says, "Sir—I mean, Kalven." I'm surprised by his reaction, but it comes out like he's only now remembering Kalven is his elder, has helped our family, and hasn't tried to hurt us.

Kalven lifts his head and a smile tugs at the corner of his mouth as he shakes his head, turning around to continue his organizing. "You're just as presumptuous and spunky as you were as a kid, Allister."

Allister's hand rubs the back of his neck as he kicks at some invisible speck of dirt. "Well, I'm not so sure of that." Almost as soon as the word leaves his lips though he stands up ramrod straight and races in front of me. He grabs onto Kalven's shoulder and spins him around, slamming him into the shelf behind him. About half of the containers skid off the shelf and fall to the floor. With only a thought I catch the containers as they fall through the air, then gently let them tumble to the ground I've already softened.

Kalven pushes against Allister's hold and peeks around him, locking eyes with me. "Thank you, Attina. Some of those were extremely rare potions." I only stare at him though. This is between him and Allister, I'm not getting involved in whatever's going on. I just thought it would be a shame for so many unused potions to go to waste when they could possibly help someone in need.

Allister growls as he brings Kalven forward and slams him back into the shelf, almost knocking off some more potions in the process. "Don't even look at her until you tell me what the hell is happening. Who are you really?" He lifts Kalven slightly in the air by his throat.

Kalven squints his eyes and his face gets tight. Obviously Allister is pushing against him hard enough to hurt him. I slam my hands on the table drawing both men's attention. "Allister, maybe you should let up on him a little. I don't think he can talk with all the pressure you're putting on his neck."

Allister turns to me for a second before turning back and I hear Kalven choke out, "Thank you, Attina," while he still stares at Allister. Not once peering in my direction just as Allister told him not to. "I had hoped you would have remembered me, my king." At Kalven's words, Allister drops him. Kalven bends over coughing and gasping for air.

Allister gawks down at Kalven and says, "What did you just say?"

Kalven peeks up and meekly says, "My king." He's still bent over so he throws his hand out in a flourish like he's actually bowing and not simply bent over in pain.

"How—" Allister stumbles back against the table next to me. I lean forward and wrap my hand around his, trying to lend him some of my strength to deal with whatever is happening between them.

Kalven stands up straight and rubs his neck, "I'm not surprised you forgot about me; you were such a young lad the last time I saw you." He steps forward and places his hand atop Allister's shoulder. "But it's wonderful to see you again, little cub."

I'm watching Allister's face as the words tumble out of Kalven's mouth, meaning I can see his reaction to the nickname Kalven calls him. His eyes water and he lets his mouth drops open in surprise. I even feel his hand begin to shake a little. His voice is meek as it comes out. "The only person who ever called me little cub was my father's best friend."

Kalven steps forward and wraps his arms around Allister's shoulders. "Again, it's wonderful to see you again little cub. I didn't think I'd live to see the day you'd return. I thought you were lost to us forever, corrupted by that evil tyrant." He pulls away with his arms still on Allister's shoulders. "But here you are barging into your people's castle with your own strange family and Henrik's own granddaughter, who also happens to be your mate, in tow. The one person who could take down Henrik and unite this nation." His eyes move over to mine for a second before pinning them back on Allister. "I'm so proud of you. Your father would be incredibly proud of you too. Your mother must be beaming." Allister almost crumples into the table behind him as he rests his head on Kalven's shoulder.

Kalven wraps his arms back around Allister as Allister's shoulders shake. I give his hand one tight squeeze before letting go. As soon as I release his hand Allister wraps his arms around Kalven.

He peeks at me from around Allister's shoulder and winks at me. I smile at the both of them reunited. As I sit and watch their interaction, tears start welling in the corner of my eyes. Allister thought he lost everyone, from the sound of it even his mother was lost to him, but now things have changed. Now, he has someone here from his past, someone who remembers him, who loved him.

Allister releases Kalven and moves over to me, wrapping me in a warm embrace. As he pulls away I see how reddened and wet his face is from crying. The redness in his face surprisingly brings out the ruby hue in his eyes, making them appear more red than purple. As he faces Kalven again he moves closer to my side and drapes his arm around my shoulders.

"I thought our entourage was killed along with my father. How did you escape?"

"You won't like this." Now, it's Kalven's turn to appear uncomfortable as he rubs the back of his neck and shifts his weight back and forth. "Your father knew he would be killed. He found a secret passage into Shadow Mountain and sent me back through it."

"*He what?*" Allister screeches in the highest pitched voice

I've ever heard fall out of his mouth. "He sent you but didn't leave himself? He knew he was going to die, but he chose to stay?"

Kalven puts his hands up in a placating gesture, "You have to think about how it would seem. If your father left, Henrik could say your father murdered his father and your father taking off in the middle of the night was proof of his guilt. Henrik could have then easily have called a blood feud against your father which would have resulted in all out war. Your father was trying to save our people by sacrificing his life."

I cut in, "What's a blood feud?"

Kalven's eyes swing to me. "A blood feud happens when a Fae kills a member of your family. Which, as you can tell, happens often. When a member of a Fae family is murdered, a Fae from the victim's family would kill the murderer of said family member. Which in turn leads the other family to kill the Fae who murdered their family member."

"So it's a vicious cycle? How does it ever stop?"

Allister says, "It does when both families annihilate each other. My eyes grow wide. "But my father ended the barbaric practice long before I was born."

Kalven adds in, "He simply made murder illegal."

"It wasn't before?" I ask, shocked such a thing could be allowed to go on without punishment for hundreds, maybe thousands of years.

Kalven shakes his head. "You forget what vicious creatures Fae can be. But when Allister's father took the throne the first thing he did was make murder illegal. Then he outlawed blood feuds. If a person murdered another Fae they would have to answer to the king. If someone acted on the blood feud they would also be punished by the king."

I'm still confused, so I ask, "If it was illegal why would Henrik have been able to call a blood feud?"

Allister shakes his head and leans on the table. "Just because it was illegal in the Eastern Fae territory does not mean it was illegal in the Western Fae territory. Blood feuds still happen there. Henrik doesn't care about his people's well-being like my father did."

I ask, "So your father let him finish out the blood feud knowing no one here would retaliate and it would be finished with? But he had to have known he would then have control over his territory, right?"

Kalven breathes out, "Yes, but he assumed I would be able to sneak his mate and child out of that hell hole. He must have thought we would take the Eastern Fae territory back from Henrik."

Allister takes in a deep breath and drops his head, he almost whispers, "Well, my father could have simply sent me with you, and I could have this kingdom back already."

Kalven lowers his hands and his shoulders sag. "The same could have been said about you or your mother leaving. It's not rare for young Fae children to kill people, we're a vicious bunch. But one member of the royal entourage missing? I doubt Henrik ever gave it a second thought." Allister silently nods in agreement. His words flabbergast me. This is actually well known in their world. It's semi normal for Fae kids to *murder* people. How could such a thing possibly be real? How often has this happened to become an accepted norm? I quietly remind myself to take note of any children I pass in the castle.

Kalven steps forward and places a hand on Allister's shoulder. Allister peers up at him. "Your father entrusted me to save you and your mother by any means necessary. He was trying to protect you both while keeping his people from having to face a war against Henrik." Kalven drops his head to his chest in shame. "He entrusted me with the most precious things to him and I failed him. I couldn't find a way to get either of you out without it turning into a full scale battle."

Allister swings his arm around Kalven's neck and drags him into another hug. "Father wouldn't be disappointed in you. You kept his people alive and safe until I could fight my way back and reclaim the throne."

Now it's Kalven's turn to cry, but instead of the silent shaking of the shoulders like Allister did, he full on sobs into Allister's shoulder. Allister just stands there and holds the man while he falls apart. It takes Kalven a minute to recollect himself but eventually he does. He pulls away from Allister as he wipes his face and nose on the sleeve of his off white cloak.

I internally cringe at the sight, but a thought hits me. "If you're the right hand of the leader of the Fae then why does he," I point at Allister, "have to do some trial to prove who he really is? Can't you simply tell the leader who he is, and he can be crowned king again?"

"Well, for one, since Henrik married," he glances at Allister, "your mother, we haven't had an official king. Since your mother was your father's mate, technically Henrik is our king through marriage."

Allister's eyes enlarge but he stays silent.

"Still... you didn't answer my question," I reply.

Allister turns to me. "Fae love power. Their leader won't just give up the crown simply because Kalven tells him I'm king." He turns and puts his hand on my knee, staring into my eyes. "There won't be an easy way to go about this either. If I pass, he will probably claim I cheated somehow and challenge me to a fight to claim the crown. If I fail, I will have to challenge him to a fight."

I knit my brows and place my hand over his. "But you're the rightful heir. You shouldn't be capable of failing whatever test he sets right?"

Kalven moves forward next to me and answers. "You're assuming he'll play fair. Gerald didn't become our leader by playing fair. There were *many* Fae who fought for the position after Allister's father died, but Gerald beat them all in combat to win the title."

Allister shakes his head. "I still can't believe Gerald is the leader. When we talked after I showed up here, he acted like he didn't even remember me, but I sure remember him."

"He remembers you. Everyone who was old enough to know you, remembers you, but no one wants to say it and risk incurring Gerald's wrath. It's all a calculated move on his part."

"You remember him from when you were a boy?" I ask Allister.

He smiles sadly. "Yes. As a boy I enjoyed playing soldier. I would, try, and fail miserably, to run drills with my father's men. Gerald was the one person in the whole group who'd go out of his way to knock me into the mud or kick my legs out from under me. I was told the other men asked him why he did it once and he said it was his way of trying to toughen me up, but I know that was a lie. He acted on malice and hatred. Not to mention his face would give me nightmares as a child."

I sit back. "You don't mean that do you?"

Allister chuckles and shares a look with Kalven who smiles before Allister answers, "Just you wait until you see him."

I finally jump off of the table I've been sitting on and

cross my arms. I want to ask the questions which have been gnawing at the back of my mind since Kalven revealed who he truly was. "So you really think I could defeat Henrik, and do you seriously want me to unite the nation? You don't want to turn the humans into slaves like Henrik wants?"

39

ATTINA

Kalven turns his gaze down on me. "I want what Allister's father, Rufus, always wanted, a untied nation where Fae and humans could live peacefully together." He takes a deep breath before continuing. "And as you are right now? No, there's no way you could take on Henrik."

I roll my eyes and huff in annoyance. That's all anyone has ever told me. I need more training. I can't take him on unless I have more training. I'm sick of it. Will I ever be good enough?

You're more than good enough for me. I glance up to Allister as he smiles down at me.

Kalven lifts his finger and clears his throat, breaking my concentration on our thoughts. "Whatever you two are saying, stop. I'm not done." His eyes move back and forth between us expectantly, when he's decided we're done talking to each other through our thoughts he continues. "You're Anima *just* merged together. Give yourself some time to figure out what such an event will do to your powers. You're the first person I've ever heard of who's had something like this happen to them. Let's be practical and take some time to figure things out."

I cross my arms and stick out my hip. "I've waited and trained long enough."

He shakes his head. "I know you have, but I'm begging you, please give yourself time to settle into your full magical powers."

I cut him off. "We don't have time. Every day Henrik lives is another day my future denizens suffer, and I can't allow it anymore."

"Only the winter. Give it until spring. It will give Allister time to reclaim the throne, we can make a solid plan to overthrow him, and you can get used to your new Anima, and whatever changes in your powers come along with it. Will you do that?"

Allister moves to face me, and I turn to him. "I think we should listen to Kalven. Remember the prophecy? We can't simply ignore it and run off half cocked. We need to do this the right way if we're to have any chance of winning against Henrik."

"Wait!" Kalven interrupts. "What prophecy?"

Allister explains what we found out at my mother's hideout, and I begin pacing the room. I know Allister is right, but how can I just sit here while Fae and humans suffer? I'm supposed to stay in this warm cozy castle, the most beautiful place I've ever seen in my life, while others suffer? I've never been able to sit around idly. I have this horrible mothering complex. I want to take care of everyone, it's part of why I hunted for the people of Daruk daily. I wanted to make sure everyone had the food they needed to fill their bellies. But by the time I make it to the other side of the table I know what I must do.

As soon as Allister finishes talking I say, "Fine. I'll stay until spring, but not a moment longer."

A wide grin cracks along Kalven's face. "Great. Now I want you both to get some rest. You've had a long journey, and you could use it."

I shake my head and put my hand on the table in front of me, leaning on it. "No. I've slept enough." My gaze shifts to Allister. "Where's Raven, I need to see her."

But it's Kalven who answers. "Actually, I'll come with you two to see her. I wanted to check up on her and give her another potion."

I stand up straight. "You're the one treating her? But I thought you were—"

"A human healer?" Kalven finishes for me.

"Well, yes," I answer.

"While I can't treat regular animals, I can, however, treat Fae animals. The fact they are able to tell me what's wrong helps a lot. They're not much different than treating Fae in all honesty, and the biggest difference is dosage."

"Hmm, well how is she doing then?" I'm only now realizing how much I miss her. She must be worried sick about me. I've been asleep for so long and there's no way she could have visited me up in the tower I was sleeping in.

"Honestly, it was a little touch and go there for a little while but she's doing much better. She'll have a nasty scar for the rest of her life, but she doesn't seem to care."

"Touch and go? She was really as bad as I thought then?" My eyes dart to Allister's whose sad eyes and pouty lip tell me I was more right than I know.

"She had a huge chunk of her rump ripped out by the werewolf. It's a miracle she made it here on her own and as you well know a horse being unable to walk is almost always a death sentence."

I start pacing the room. I need to see Raven. See how bad she is. I'll stay by her side in the stables for months if need be. I can't lose her.

Allister reaches his hand out to me, halting my movement. "I know you want to see her right now, but we have to do something first."

I meet his purple eyes and plainly state, "No."

He clenches his jaw which makes his lips press into a tight line. "Attina, I must take you to Gerald—"

I cut him off and cross my arms over my chest, "No. I want to see Raven. I will see Raven now."

He mirrors my stance and glares down at me. "She's all right. I told you she was fine. Don't you believe me?"

From my side I hear Kalven burst out in laughter. I spin, glaring at him and notice Allister does the same. He's bent over laughing and hitting his knee. He takes gasps of air before he stands up straight and says, "I see you found someone even more stubborn than you, cub. I didn't think such a thing was possible." He lifts his hands and wipes a tear away.

I gaze over to Allister whose face softens but I don't allow mine to as his eyes draw to mine. "Yeah, I guess I did. She's lucky I love her."

My cheeks heat, the words making my resolve falter. I'm still not used to him saying he loves me, and this is the first time he's said it in front of someone else, it almost feels too intimate. I shake myself out of my reprieve, "Still, I'm not going anywhere other than to see Raven." I cross my arms over my chest again, but I know it doesn't make as much of an impression as it did the first time I did it. Damn him for throwing me off my game.

Kalven says from my side, "He's right. She's fine." I don't pull my gaze from Allister until Kalven walks over and places his hand on my shoulder. I peer up into Kalven's gray eyes, "I have to make a potion for her anyway. It will take me a bit to make, instead of waiting here for me to finish, why don't you guys head off to see Gerald. By the time you make it back I should be done with her potion, and we can go see her together. How's that sound?"

I drop my arms and tentatively nod. "I suppose we can do that." I cut my gaze over to Allister. "We'll see him." I lift my pointer finger, "but not for one more second than is absolutely necessary."

Allister shakes his head and chuckles. "Yes, kitten. Anything you say."

I turn to Kalven and give him a wide, toothy grin. I almost giggle as I see him momentarily frozen in place. He shakes himself loose and says to Allister, "I never thought I'd see the day you would yield to anyone."

Allister moves next to me and lazily throws his arm over my shoulders. "Neither did I."

Allister and I leave Kalven to make his potion and we make it back into the main part of the castle. If you were to walk through the castle doors you would see the stairs we came down to the left, which lead to our room, and a long hallway directly in front of you. We make our way down the hallway and almost instantly a shiver runs up my spine.

"When we meet him I want you to refer to him as my liege," Allister says solemnly.

I spin my face towards his. "What? Why? He's not my king."

Allister doesn't look at me, he simply faces forward toward the doors we're walking up to. "He's a bastard, Attina. He'll twist your words and use them against you if you're not extremely careful. You forget how evil Fae can be." He brings his hand up and rubs the back of his neck, a gesture I've come to realize he does when he's nervous. His eyes grow dark as he instructs, "I want you to be tremendously curt with him. Answer his questions, but don't elaborate. Remember we can't talk mind to mind here, and most importantly, keep your attitude in check."

I turn my gaze back toward to the doors we're approaching. Now we're closer and I can truly take in their beauty. Like the rest of the castle, vines barely crawl up the doors. The stone doors themselves run up high above us, almost three times the length of Allister. More vines and leaves are carved into the door, and I notice a cougar on each door hiding in the foliage. I quirk my head at Allister. "Isn't your Anima a cougar?"

He stops at the doors in front of us and places a hand on the massive stone door. "All my blood relatives have cougar Anima. It's our symbol."

"That's why Kalven calls you cub," I say but then a thought tickles the back of my mind. "Is that why you call me kitten?"

A devilish smile crosses his features, and he turns into me. His presence pushes me against the wall next to us. The vines soft against my back. "I was wondering how long it would take you to pick up on that." He leans forward into my space and my knees get weak, my breath coming in short gasps. His eyes travel down the length of me and he growls right before his lips are on mine. To my surprise he grabs my lips with his teeth, the shock and pain is almost sweet, making me release a moan. When he pulls back he straightens his tunic, all business again, and pulls me back toward the door. "You ready, kitten?"

I shrug like what happened didn't affect me. "As ready as I'll ever be."

It's obviously a heavy door because Allister has to lean

into the stone to heft it open. As the doors widen I train my face to appear disinterested and stride behind Allister into the room.

The room is massive. I try not to let my gaze wander around it. I try to school my features back into a disinterested look but it's hard. It's big enough to be a ballroom but with how drab it all is, I doubt they do. Everything is stone gray, even the sconces sprinkled on the walls. Vines make their way up the walls here too, ever a staple in this castle. I almost smirk at the thought of all this life forcing its way into such a boring room.

A long black rug is laid out from the doors, leading up to a dais which encompasses a quarter of the room. A Fae man sits on a throne up five vast steps. I only use the word man because creature would be rude, but creature would be a better term to describe the man.

As we walk the distance to the bottom of the stairs Gerald crosses his leg. The action somehow comes off as superiority. The green of his tunic sparkles and I realize it's because there are golden leaves sewn throughout. The crown on his head sparkles as red and blue gems on it hit the light given off the beautiful chandelier above. I only get a glimpse of it but I can tell it's in the shape of vines with candles lit here and there.

When we make it to the base of the dais Allister bends to one knee, a fisted hand travels to his chest. I stand there in shock for a moment before I follow suit. I can't believe he would kneel to anyone, especially this false king. This must all be some play of his.

Allister's voice is loud and strong, making its way all around the room as he says, "My liege, I brought Henrik's granddaughter, Attina, to you as you commanded."

Gerald's voice on the other hand is meek, making strain

my ears to hear, another power play, I'm sure. "Thank you, Allister. I'm glad to see you've finally found your place." A fire heats in my chest. This man definitely knows who Allister is and yet he's still claiming the throne? Gerald lifts a hand. "Attina, rise and make your way up here."

I do as he commands and crawl up the stairs to him. And when I say crawl I mean literally crawl. The stairs are comically too big, I'm not sure if this is some power play to show everyone around him he's higher than everyone or what, but it's dumb. First thing we're doing when Allister gets his throne back is demolishing this podium of pomposity. I can sense Allister at the base of the stairs and simply knowing he's here backing me up helps me feel more confident.

As I make it to the top stair I can take in his ghastly face. It's bloated and puffy, making it appear bumpy, even his pointed ears are lumpy. His dry, cracked lips open as he says, "Get over here girl. Let me see you."

I take a step forward but no more.

He chuckles, the movement making his too big body wiggle and his brown eyes crinkle. The hook on his nose almost reminds me of a fishing hook as it moves with his words, "So you're Henrik's granddaughter?"

I try to keep the disgust out of my features and voice as I coldly answer, "That's what I'm told." As an afterthought I add, "My Liege."

"How do I know you're not here to overtake my lands?"

I cross my arms over my chest. I know Allister said to keep my attitude in check, but come on, did he seriously think I'd be able to with this Faehole in front of me?

I cock my head down at him. "Now let's think about this logically. If you were Henrik's granddaughter, the granddaughter of the most powerful Fae in all of Arealea, do you think you would come knocking on the door of a place you wanted to overtake? Or would you simply take it?"

He leans forward, uncrosses his legs, and steeples his hands in front of him as his brows knit and those brown eyes of his glare at me. Before I might have cowed at the look he gives me, but now? Now, his glare only annoys me, like a gnat buzzing in my ear. What could this man do to me?

"And if you were a king and that granddaughter came onto your lands would you murder her right away? Or see what she has to say?"

I cock my head and tentatively answer, "See what she had to say."

"And if she did intend to take your throne, wouldn't you take her injured horse companion, treat its life threatening wounds, and offer her friends asylum, in the guise of being helpful instead of holding them hostage?"

I stand up straighter, staring down my nose at him. "I suppose I would if I was afraid of her."

He leans back in his throne and smiles a sickeningly sweet smile. "I wouldn't have to fear her. She would be too worried I would kill her friends." His eyes leave mine and land on Allister for a second, "Or her mate." His eyes return to mine with his horrible, evil smile still plastered on his face even through the blatant threat. "Good thing you're not here to steal my throne."

I uncross my arms feigning defeat. "Good thing."

He lifts his hand in a sign of dismissal. I awkwardly bow before spinning on my heel. I jump down the stairs, making the descent less awkward. I notice Allister brings his hand back up to his chest as I pass him. He stands and follows close behind.

As soon as we're out of the throne room Allister whispers in my ear, "What happened?"

I don't bother whispering though. I'm already over this charade. "He threatened to kill our family if I try to take his throne."

Allister grabs my shoulder and spins me toward him, "He what?"

"You heard me. He threatened to have you all killed if I try to take his throne." His eyes narrow. "We will talk about this with Kalven."

40

ATTINA

We make it back to the infirmary and tell Kalven about the exchange I had with Gerald.

"He's scared of you. He wouldn't have gone out of his way to have you brought to him only to intimidate you if he wasn't."

I wave him off. "I made it seem like I was defeated by his threats, hopefully we won't have a problem."

"Hopefully? I told you to check your attitude!" Allister yells at me like this is all somehow my fault.

I slice my gaze to his and give him a withering glare. "You thought I could do that with such a pig of a Fae?"

He throws his hands up in the air and huffs in exasperation. His thumb and forefinger pinch the bridge of his nose. Kalven walks over to him and places his hand on Allister's shoulder. "It's not her fault. We will figure something out."

Allister peeks up at his friend and smiles. He lifts his arms up, an invitation for me to wrap myself around him. So I do. I could use the comfort right now, even if he is acting like an idiot. When my arms are wrapped around his torso he leans down and places a soft kiss on the top of my head. "It's not your fault. I'm sorry."

I peek up at him. "Like you always say, we will figure this out together."

He sighs and his shoulders slump, then Kalven cheerily says, "Well, why don't we head out to check on Raven together?"

I squeeze Allister once before moving away. The three of us make our way out of the examination room, Kalven in the lead with Allister trailing behind me. Tables line one side of the next room. Gleaming saws, pliers, needle-like knives, and a multitude of other instruments line the walls. I take a big nervous gulp. "Is this where you treat sick patients?" I ask the back of Kalven's gray head.

As he moves out of the room into the open, chilly air, he lifts his hand and twirls it in the air as he says over his shoulder. "No, I treat sick patients in the room we were in. If someone needs more in-depth care they stay in the room to the right of that room. It's a room off of my own quarters, allowing them access to me day or night. This room is where I examine the dead."

I stop in my tracks. "You what?"

He keeps moving forward so Allister pushes me from behind, urging me to keep following him. "I haven't used this room in decades. I only use it if someone dies of unnatural causes. It's only so I can determine why they died and if whatever killed them was contagious." He turns around as he keeps moving throughout the courtyard we're now walking through. The ground and walls around us are covered in low greenery. I love how natural my surroundings seem. I keep forgetting I'm surrounded by walls. I thought this place would make me feel like I did in Sanctuary, like the walls were closing in on me. But it's all so open and full of life here, it's refreshing. "Actually, the last time I used it was when a Solis happened to stumble close to the perimeter of the castle."

"Find anything interesting?" Allister asks and Kalven turns back around, lacing his hands behind his back and tilts his head.

"Surprisingly we did. They're not truly dead. I know that's what humans say about them but it's not completely true."

I ask, "How could that be? You're either dead or you're not. There's no in between."

By now we've rounded the corner of the castle and a huge, aged barn comes into view. The double doors are swung wide open allowing goats, sheep, chicken, horses, and everything in between to meander around the building. The pointed roof and all the sides of the barn are again covered in grass, weeds, and dark green vines. The whole thing is covered *except* where the animals could reach up or over and munch on the greenery. I stop listening to whatever Kalven is saying and race over to the barn.

I race through the opening and yell, "Raven! Where are you?"

The barn is much bigger on the inside than I thought it would be. Stalls of all shapes and sizes line the sides, big pillars dot the structure throughout. The middle of the building is a vast open area, but past it I can see more stalls. In the middle of the open area I see Raven lying on the ground, a huge bandage on her hip. Her dark fur almost glistens in the light peaking through the windows scattered around the building. Behind her stands Mylo and all around her horses and other animals stand as they listen to her talk, like she's holding court.

"Raven!" I shout. She turns her head toward me, her eyes

soften as recognition hits her. I hold my breath as I race through and leap around the other animals. Coming *way* too close to some of the animals' back ends, I'm honestly surprised I don't get kicked. It's not until I have my arms wrapped around Raven's blood red neck and my body laid across her that I can take a calming breath. Tears stream down my face as I take in her earthy, homey smell, and weep into her blackened mane. "I'm so glad you're alive. I was ridiculously worried about you when I saw that werewolf slice you open."

She manages to nudge her head into mine, making me pick up my head to look at her. "It'll take more than some dirty dog to keep me from you kid. I don't give up that easily."

I know she said it to make me laugh and to comfort me, but it only makes me cry harder. I flop back down on her as I lose control of my tears. I'm just so happy she's really okay. While the sobs are wracking my body I feel two warm hands grab onto my shoulders, picking me up off of Raven. I throw my hands back, trying to get the hands off of me but before I know it I'm being embraced. I breathe in the smell of rain and forest, and I know its Allister. I lift my head and peek up at him with my swollen eyes.

He smiles down at me. "Kalven needs to treat her and he can't do it with you splayed across her, I told you she was all right. I can't believe you didn't believe me. Why would I lie to you?"

I shake my head. "I didn't think she would be this okay. I thought you were only saying she was all right to keep me from having a meltdown."

He lowers his head on top of mine as he holds me into his broad sturdy chest. "I would never lie to you about

Raven. I know how important she is to you. Even if it meant I would meet my death I will tell you the truth."

I squeeze him tight once before rubbing the snot and tears from my face and turning around. Kalven is now kneeling down inspecting her wound. I move to where I can get a better peek, I need to see what we're dealing with. As I walk away Allister mumbles, "I'll have to deal with one shortly anyway," but I ignore him. If it doesn't have to do with Raven I don't want to hear about it right now.

I move over to Kalven's side as he gently lifts the edge of a huge piece of cloth he has wrapped around her rump. Under it I can see where a giant divot was taken out of her flesh. I draw in a steadying breath and at the same time I feel Raven nudge my foot with her muzzle. I turn to face her, more tears pouring down my face. "Knock it off right now you big baby. It looks worse than it actually is. I'm feeling much better, I promise. You're the one who died, not me!"

"Well I did tell you I would die before we left, you were warned," I chuckle out through my tears. Kalven stands and I sit down, wrapping my arm around Raven's wither and leaning against her.

He walks over to her head. "It's getting much better. I'm happily surprised at how quickly you're healing." He reaches out to pet her head, but I notice Mylo shoves his head between Raven and Kalven. Mylo pins his ears and lifts his lips in a snarl at the healer.

Kalven moves away from the threat. Raven throws her head up, it doesn't hit Mylo, but it doesn't need to for her to get her point across as he rears his head back away from Kalven. "Knock it off! I've told you he's taking care of me, so stop being such an insanely possessive male!"

I glance over to Allister and see his shoulders shake as he covers his face, chuckling. What in the world is going on?

Kalven moves back to Raven, but this time Mylo simply stares daggers at him. He pulls out a large vile, yanking a cork out of the top. "It's time to take your medicine. Sorry I know it tastes terrible." She doesn't fight him as he tilts the vile back for her, allowing her to drink it all down.

He takes a step back and glances around him. "Okay, well I have other patients to check on." His eyes land on Allister and me for a split second, "I'll talk to you two later." I nod and he makes his way over to Allister wrapping him in a bear hug saying, "I'm glad you finally came back." He then pulls away, turns to me, bows his head, and walks out of the barn.

I turn back to Raven and pointedly gaze between her and Mylo. "So what's happening here?"

She wiggles where she lays and scans around the barn, searching for anywhere to stare except my face. "Um... it's hard to explain. Ahh—"

Then from behind Allister I hear someone say, "They're mates. Who knew Fae animals could have mates?"

Allister turns out of my way, and I see Ned striding up behind him with a cocky grin plastered on his face. I notice he's holding a grain bucket before him. In a flash, I'm up and running at him, so happy to see him again. He drops the bucket right before I reach him. Grabbing me up in a big hug. He lifts me and spins me around. "You're awake! I'm so glad. We've all been so worried."

When he puts me back down I see tears sparkling in his eyes. I didn't realize seeing everyone again would be this emotional. I take a page from Raven's book and answer, "It'll take a lot more than a dirty dog to keep me from you." I hear everyone chuckling behind me, but Ned doesn't get the joke and he cocks his head in confusion, his brown tunic moving with the motion. I'm almost taken aback, I've only ever seen him in drab gray sweats, this is a nice change for him. I wave my hand in front of my face. "Raven said the same thing to me earlier."

"Ooohh," he says as he picks up the grain bucket and makes his way over to Raven. I follow him as he places the bucket down in front of her. She greedily shoves her head into it and chomps down on the contents.

I don't want to interrupt Raven's eating so instead I ask Ned, "They're mates?"

He stares down at Raven. "Raven said as much. I guess I was right about him being half-Fae too."

Raven has yet to pick her head up to breathe. I squat down and pat her head, "Hey you wanna take a breath there, girl?" She doesn't even answer me, she merely snorts at me.

Ned answers for her. "The meds doc gives her make her ravenously hungry. He said food helps her heal, and for her to heal as fast as she is, she needs to eat as much as we can get her to eat."

I stand up and feel Allister's hands wrap around my middle. I lean back into him and lay my head on his shoulder. "You saved our family. I'll live a thousand lifetimes and still be indebted to you for that," he says as he places a soft kiss on the top of my forehead, his hair brushing along my cheeks, tickling me.

I lift my head and spin in his arms, wrapping them around his neck. I pull his head down and plant a soft kiss on his lips. "They're my family too. I know you would have done the same. I just didn't give you the chance," I say as I wink up at him.

Ned clears his throat. "Ahem. Could you two not be all lovey dovey right now?"

Raven takes a breather from stuffing her face simply to say, "Aren't they infuriating?"

I turn in Allister's arms so I'm facing Raven and Ned. I glare down at her. "Just you wait. You'll be like this with Mylo here shortly." She huffs but continues silently eating.

"Why don't we leave her alone to eat." Ned moves his head indicating the back door to the barn. "Let's head outside? There's a table with some chairs back there."

Allister releases me and heads off with Ned. I stay behind and squat down in front of Raven. Petting her head I say, "I'm glad you're all right. I don't know what I would do without you." I plant a kiss on her head, she stops eating for a second, but only a second, before she resumes eating, making me chuckle as I stand.

I ease my way between Raven and Mylo. I stop next to him. "And Mylo." He breaks his gaze away from Raven only long enough so I know he hears me before fixing it back on her. "I want you to keep an eye on her, got it? If she needs anything you break down every door until you find me. You hear me?" Since he can't talk, his answer is a happy whinny, throwing his head up and down.

I make my way out to where the guys sit at a stone table with four wooden chairs around it. Ned and Allister sit opposite each other, simply sort of taking in the surroundings. I take one of the seats between them. I'm not sure why, but I'm still sort of shocked they can be this relaxed around each other now. "So, does Raven stay there all day?"

Ned leans back in his chair. "No, she sleeps in the closest stall at night. She's only been able to move around the past couple of days. The healer says it's best for her to move a little bit so we help her move from the stall to her spot in the morning and again at night." He chuckles and crosses his arms in front of his chest, "Mylo refuses to leave her side, but she's tolerating it well."

I lean forward and place my elbow on the table and lay

my head in my hand, "Well she did want a family" I shrug my shoulders but am secretly happy she found her mate. To think if we'd never gone to Sanctuary she never would have found Mylo. "Does she always hold court like that?" I feel Allister's stare hot on my face.

"Yes. She's become the popular one in the barn. Most of those animals haven't ever left the castle which means they want to hear all of her stories of the outside world."

"I'm surprised she indulges them."

"Indulges them? She eats it up. She exaggerates stories. I wouldn't be surprised if all those Fae animals think she beat the werewolf herself instead of you."

I lean back in my chair, a chortle escaping my lips. I sigh. "And what about you? How have you been? Were you hurt?" Concern plain in my voice.

Ned's brow furrows, the action confusing me. "Was I hurt? I didn't have a scratch on me!" He slams his hands down on the table in front of him, making me jump. "What the hell happened out there?" His hand shoots out toward the castle wall. I glance over to Allister for assistance, but he merely stares at Ned, eerily motionless. "You just take off half cocked and take on the werewolf by yourself? *You sacrificed yourself!*"

I stand up and stalk around the table, a sudden boost of confidence hitting me. "Yes, I did, and I would do it again for my family." I stop on the other side from where I was sitting. "Let's be honest, neither of you could have taken on that werewolf." Both of their heads spin to me, scowls on both their faces, but I ignore them and push on. "Raven was mortally wounded and Allister was wiped out from fighting the thing off as best he could." I stare down Ned, "I agree I should have had Allister stay with me and sent you on with the horses, but I knew you and

Allister, with your Fae strength, could drag Raven if you had to."

Ned cuts in and shouts, "I could have helped you! You could have sent Allister with the horses!"

I shake my head. "No. You would have gotten yourself killed." I take the few steps over to him. "You would have gotten yourself killed trying to save me." I lean down and wrap my arms around him, "I couldn't live with myself if you'd died on my account." I drag the chair next to him, sit in it, grab his hands from the table and hold them on my knees. "I'm sorry I worried you. I was only trying to protect my loved ones, you included. Yes, if I died Henrik would win, but if I lost any of you, I would be no use to anyone. Henrik would still win, and all of this would have been for nothing. What's the point of being a queen if I can't protect the one's I love?"

Tears well in his eyes as he yanks my hands forward and they land on his chest. "I love you too. Next time please rely on us more. You don't have to do *everything* on your own. We're here to help, ya know. I never want to suffer through the pain of watching you die ever again. Got that?"

I pull back and smile at him. Then out of nowhere Allister is next to me and wrapping us both in a hug. I chuckle. *Aren't we a strange lot?* I say into my mind and Allister and Ned both chuckle in return.

Allister is the one who answers, *Yes but I love our family and I wouldn't have it any other way.*

Then Ned says, *I love you guys too.*

Allister pulls back, puts his fisted hands on his hips, and puffs out his chest. "See, I told you he would eventually love me!" I hear Ned curse under his breath, but he doesn't argue, which makes me lean back in my chair, cackling.

I smack Allister against the leg with the back of my

hand. "Okay goofball, sit back down. We have things to talk about." He does as I ask, and I turn back to Ned.

"I have to tell you what happened. How I came back to life and what's happening with my Anima."

He scrunches his brow. "Anima?"

I lean forward and fold my arms on the table in front of me before I catch Ned up on what Anima are, how our conversation with Gerald went, and what's happened since I saw him last. I swear it feels like I only saw him yesterday, but *so* much has happened in the time I was asleep. Ned just quietly sits there while I talk, every once in awhile he grunts at my words, letting me know he's following along.

When I finish he stands and begins pacing with his hands laced behind his back. "I can't believe my ears. Henrik is more powerful than anyone knows?" He sarcastically adds, "Wonderful." Then he scoffs. "Well thank the gods your Anima were able to merge. It sounds like it saved your life." He stops and turns on his heel toward me. "Well, I think, given the circumstances, the best plan of action is to head down and interrogate that damn bird."

41

ATTINA

We make our way inside, down under the castle grounds, to the dungeon. "Wait, we're allowed to simply stroll down here? Isn't anyone worried we will release whoever is down here?"

I stare at Allister's back as he bobs down the stone steps in front of me. Ned walks quietly behind me, both of them holding lamps with candles lit in them, lighting the way. Allister answers, "I talked with Gerald before you woke up, he knows we don't want to release anyone down here." Interesting.

It seems like it takes forever, but we finally make it down to the dungeons. It's pitch black in here. I guess prisoners don't need to see to sit in a jail cell. Then the stale air, mixed with urine and feces, hits me. I'm almost bowled over by the smell before I compose myself.

With the boy's lights I can barely make out the layout around me. In front of us is a long hallway with what appears to be cells on each side. I can't see too far down the hallway though, so I'm not sure what's beyond. There are also cells to my left and I hear some skittering coming from that way. I lift my had to make a fireball to light the corners or the room, but Allister moves away from me and I decide to follow him instead.

Allister makes his way to our right where one lone cell sits. He opens the unlocked cell door and takes a step back, allowing me to pass in front of him. Inside is a cage about half my size and inside it stands Talon.

"Great, it's you bunch. How lucky for me."

I get on the floor in front of the cage and cross my legs under me. "How are you and Henrik connected?" I ask as I cock my head.

The hawk slices his brown head toward me."What did you say?"

I repeat as I cock my head the other way, hoping it gives me the same predatory appearance it gives Allister. "How are you and Henrik connected?"

He ruffles his feathers. "I don't know what you're talking about."

Before getting up off the ground I say, "That's too bad." I start pacing the small cell back and forth with my hands behind my back staring hard at the ground. "It's too bad because it means I'll have to kill you."

I hear the knock as Talon hits his head on the top of the cage and shrieks, "You what?"

"I'm going to have to kill you. You see there was no way Henrik could have known where we were. We spotted you the moment you spotted us. So I know you didn't have a chance to run back to Henrik to tell him our whereabouts."

"You won't kill me. You don't have the guts."

I stop my pacing and stand up straight, an evil smile cracking along my face. "Wow. Even with all your spying you seriously don't know me, do you?" I tilt my head back and let out a loud belly laugh. When I bring my head down

I notice Allister and Ned are both at the door grinning like fools, backing my play, like always. I can count on those two through thick and thin. "I hunted down birds like you daily for my hometown. You think you being able to talk means I'm not willing to kill you?" I roll my eyes and hope with his keen sight he can spot the movement. "You're awfully full of yourself if that's what you think. Hawk makes for some tasty eating, and I haven't had a hawk in *ages*. I have a hankering for some biscuits and gravy with hawk sausage right now."

He spits, "You wouldn't." But his voice waivers, like he's not completely sure.

I resume my pacing and flit one of my hands in the air in front of me. "Anyway, where was I? Oh yes!" I say as I lift a finger in the air before placing my hand behind my back again. "You couldn't have had time to tell Henrik where we were, which means there must be some other way Henrik can track you. If you won't tell us then I will simply have to kill you. Killing you will guarantee everyone in this castle is protected. The bonus is, I get to have hawk for dinner."

I bring my hands in front of me, rubbing them together greedily. I stop and turn to him, bend down, and reach for my dagger. It sings as I draw it, which seems to be the thing which breaks Talon.

I walk over to his cage with my hand out, about ready to open it. He viciously beats his wings against the sides of his cage. his feathers break from the impact, and he smacks his head against the top of it. He screams, "Wait wait wait!"

I stop in my tracks and squat down on my haunches. Sweetly, I say, "Oh? Do you have something to share with us now?"

He throws his head up and down. "Yes. I'll talk! It's not like Henrik has ever treated me well anyway. I've been with him my whole life, only been loyal to him, and he still treats me like trash."

I have to ignore the small pang in my heart and remind myself this bird has done evil things. He doesn't deserve my sympathy. I place the tip of the dagger on my pointer finger on the other hand and twist it as I say, "Hurry up and get on with it," forcing annoyance in my voice.

He hurriedly answers, "Henrik has a tracking spell on me. He can find me anywhere at any time."

I continue playing with the dagger in my hands, pointing at him with it, hoping to scare him some more. I'm glad to see him shiver a bit as I say, "If you're telling the truth, why hasn't come here and burned down the whole castle? You were out scouting for me when you were caught. He knows you're here, and I'm sure he assumes I'm here with you." I swing the dagger around in the air and gaze up at the ceiling. "See, it doesn't make sense. I still think it would just be easier to kill you."

I reach back down for the cage when he screams, "It's true! I swear to the Gods it's true! Please don't kill me."

I narrow my eyes at him. "Then why hasn't Henrik showed up?"

"That one is gone," he answers with a point of his beak at Allister.

I turn around and see Allister's widened eyes as he raises his hand to his chest. "Me? Why me?"

I turn back around to Talon as he droops his head. "He's the heart of the soldiers. While they will obey Henrik and head off to war on his command, they won't win without Allister."

"Why?" I push him.

"They see him as some sort of avenging spirit. If he's there, the men feel like they can't lose. They would fight against Allister if forced, but it would be a half-hearted fight."

I turn my head to stare at Allister. "Well, it seems like I'm not the only one to save us." He smiles but it doesn't reach to his eyes, something isn't right, but I can't allow Talon to see it.

I turn back to Talon and hurriedly answer, "Well, I guess that means you get to live." I rise from the floor and shake my head as I stare down at him. "It's too bad too. I was really looking forward to having hawk for dinner." I shrug, turn around, and walk out of the cell. Ned and Allister make room for me to pass through the door and I hear the door shut behind me.

But before I make it more than a few steps I hear a yell behind me. "Do you plan on keeping me in this cramped cage forever? I could help you ya know? I have information you could use, or I could even be your spy. But I have a condition."

His statement makes me turn around. I don't open the cell door again; I merely wrap my hands around the bars and lean against them. Not like I would trust him to leave this castle and be our spy, but his information could prove useful. "I'm listening."

"You can keep me locked in a cell but let me out of this cage. Take me outside of this horribly smelling place to see the sun and feel the wind on my wings again. You can tie me up if you must. And when you take down Henrik, let me be free to roam the land."

I glance between Ned and Allister who both nod. I think on it for a second before answering, "All right, I'll think about it and get back to you." I don't give the bird a chance to answer before I turn on my heel, my long hair flinging around my shoulders and make my way to the stairs leading up to the rest of the castle.

I watch as Allister and Ned turn to follow me. Ned is whispering something to Allister. Allister shakes and lowers his head. What in the world could they be talking about? When they make it over to me I cross my arms and push my hip out. "What is going on with you two? You're acting weird."

Ned quickly spits out, "Allister has something he wants to show you."

Allister turns and through the light of the lamps I see him glare at Ned but I try to ignore it. "Okay." I bounce on my feet and turn around to head up the stairs, "What do you want to show me?" I glance over my shoulder at Allister expecting him to be following me but he's not, he's staring at his boots.

I slowly spin back around, "Allister? What's happening?"

He clears his throat and stares at his hands. "I—um—well."

I lift my hands in the air, frustration radiating off me. "All right now you're freaking me out."

He doesn't say anything, he simply quietly peeks up at me with a downturned, sad face. I move down the few stairs I've climbed until I'm face to face with Allister. The light from the candle dancing across his face, like twirling shadows. I reach my hands up and cup his face. "Hey, whatever it is we can face it together." He closes his eyes and his shoulders droop as he silently nods his head once. "But you have to communicate with me. I need to know what's got you this freaked out." He opens his eyes, allowing me to peer into them, the blue is almost completely gone against the flame dancing in his eyes, making them more red than purple again. "You've never shut down like this with me. Tell me what's going on."

He doesn't answer me, he just grabs my hand. For a second I think he won't answer me, but then he steps around me and pulls me with him. We walk down the hallway of cells. They eventually open up to an area which is obviously meant for torturing out whatever information the Fae here would need. The open area has a few chairs thrown about. I notice one even has most of the bottom of it cut out. I *do not* want to know what that one is used for. Through the candle light I can barely see the walls on either side hold whips, chains, knives, and even some kind of strange metal contraption I can't quite make out.

We continue through the torture area and an adjoining hallway as more cells come into view. Allister is walking faster and by his walk I can tell he's surer of himself now. "When we got here, and I met with Gerald I was told they had recently acquired some new prisoners. Based on what Ned told us, I knew who they were, but there was a couple of strange things Gerald said which forced me to get down here and see for myself. Now, first I want you to know you'll be shocked."

Ned calls behind me, "But Allister and I are here. You can do this. We can get through this together."

I almost stumble as I turn around toward him, my brows knit in confusion. What are they talking about? I'd completely forgotten with everything else going on, but now since they're saying these things I remember James and Commander Demarco are prisoners here. Why would seeing them shock me? I mean I don't want to see either of them, but if Allister and Ned say I need to, I guess I need to.

Allister continues but his voice sounds heavy as he

squeezes my hand tightly. "Also, Gerald told me there are three prisoners down here, not two."

"O...kay? So they have someone else here. What's the big deal?"

Allister stops before an empty stall and turns toward me. I hadn't noticed while we were walking but now that we've stopped I distinctly smell wet dog somewhere around us. I turn and scan around but see nothing. Not like I could see much anyway, with only having candle light around us. Then I hear Commander Demarco's voice off in the distance. "Is anyone there?"

I peer up and around Allister, opening my mouth to say something, but Allister stops me by placing his hands on my shoulder. He dips down so he's staring directly into my eyes. "I need you to be strong. I'm right here with you. Forever."

I screw up my face. I don't think I've ever been more confused in my life. I pull back slightly, "Okay?" Then I place my hand on my hip. "Can we please get this over with? I really don't know why you two," I turn around and glare at Ned before turning my glare back on Allister, "are making me do this. We know James and the commander are down here."

Ned says, "Allister, let's just get this over with. We've prepared her as much as we can." Allister peeks up at him with determination, he sets his jaw, gives Ned a curt dip of his head, and peers back down at me. He silently grabs my hand, pulling me along.

We pass one more stall before I hear the growling snarl start. Is it coming from the next stall? I turn around and snatch the lamp out of Ned's awaiting hand, like he knew I would need it. I take a couple steps forward as the snarling gets louder and the snapping of jaws starts. I'm almost right up against the stall before a huge brown form slams into the bars. I jump away and fall on my butt, thankful for the ground catching my fall. I lift the lamp again and squint my eyes into the darkness until I see it. My eyes land on the huge paws, the black scraggly fur covering the legs, the pointed ears, the muddy brown eyes, and long muzzle.

A werewolf.

I get up and scramble back into Allister's strong, awaiting chest. His strong arms wrap around me protectively. "They caught one of those things?" I shriek.

He tightens his hold on me as I watch the werewolf weave back and forth in its stall, it swats its massive paw against the cell bars, making them creak. It's not nearly as gargantuan as the werewolf I just fought but it's still too big to actually turn around and move. It just stands there weaving back and forth, snarling. The creature growls and if I didn't know any better I would think it growled out the word 'mine'. I pull back and turn in Allister's arms forcing myself deeper into his chest, rubbing my face in it.

Then from out of nowhere the werewolf howls, but instead of a normal wolf howl, this one almost sounds pained. Is it hurt? I spin back around and hold out my hand, a fireball forming in it. "Let's put this thing out of its misery."

I lift my hand in the air, but Allister grabs it and spins me around. "Attina, as much as I'd love for you to kill him right here and now, I can't let you do it thinking it's only a werewolf. I pull my hand down out of his grip and onto his arm. Next to us Ned shouts "Attina wait!" My hand lands on Allister's toned, corded arms, the fire sputtering out.

Allister doesn't even flinch. He simply turns his head to Ned. "We're mates remember? Her magic can't hurt me but thank you for worrying." His head turns back to me, his eyes locking on mine. We don't say anything, we merely stand there staring at each other for a second. As the seconds tick by the werewolf behind me becomes more and more agitated. It growls and whines before I hear banging against the bars behind me as he strikes at them with his paw again.

I'm silently pulled back into Allister's arms and am guided a couple steps back. I gaze to the right of the stall we were just in front of and see Commander Demarco standing there, a little skinnier than before and in tattered, dirty sweats, but not much worse for wear. "Attina!" he shouts. "So it's true! James was right! You traitor! How could you!"

I ignore his screams and focus on the cell in front of me. Out of my peripherals I notice Ned walking around behind us, over to the commander's stall. I hear shouting but try to ignore it.

The shouting becomes too loud for us to talk over, but I hear Allister in my mind. *Do you see James in either of these stalls?*

Well no, but you said there were three prisoners down here. I turn to stare into his chiseled face, he simply shakes his head.

The other prisoner isn't James.

I pull away out of his arms, *Then where is he! You aren't telling me he's dead are you?*

No he's not dead.

I open my mouth to shout at him this is not a game. To demand to know where James is when realization floods over me and a feeling like my stomach dropping to the floor washes over me. I turn back to the cell. I lift the lamp in my hands high above my head as I take a tentative step forward. The werewolf instantly calms and takes a tiny step forward in return. I stare into those brown eyes. I was wrong earlier when I thought they were simply muddy brown ones. What stares back at me is the brown iridescent eyes I grew up gazing into, the eyes I thought I would know anywhere, but now I know that's not true. I didn't even notice them when I first saw him. The reaction this beast had makes more and more sense. When we walked up he was growling and snarling at the men around me, his sudden freak out when I was in Allister's arms, and the growl which sounded like it was saying, "Mine."

"James?" I ask the beast.

42

ATTINA

The werewolf lowers its head and takes a small step back. There's not much room in the cell so it's as far as he can get away from me. I watch as he tries to make himself into the smallest ball possible, but he's huge and so scrunched in the cell, there's nowhere for him to move. I slowly step forward and get on my knees before the cell. "James, is that you in there?" Any anger I had toward him instantly leaves me. Yes, he was *way* out of line, I will never trust him again, but now I understand him a bit more. He hates himself and this obsession over me is merely a way to prove to himself he's worthy. It makes me feel sorry for him, but in a he's pathetic kind of way.

He slowly nods as I hear the commander shout in the cell next to us. "Yes, it's James! The bastard tricked me too! Who would have thought a man could turn into such a hideous creature." In front of me, James flinches like the words have physically hit him.

Ned reaches through the bars of the Commander's cell, obviously trying to placate him, but he pulls his body back and verbally hisses at him. "You were obviously in on all of this, you bastard!"

That's it. I'm done with all of this shit. I put my finger up as I say to James, "Give me one second. I'll be back."

I get to my feet and walk the couple steps to the cell next to James. "Are you quite done?"

Commander Demarco throws his head back and a deep belly laugh falls out of his mouth. I glare at him as he tries to calm himself down. When he finally does it's instantaneous, like the laugh was a joke. His face becomes solemn, he crosses his hulking arms across his chest, something I thought he couldn't physically do, and stares down at me like a hunter staring at its prey. "I won't ever be done." His eyes move over to Ned before returning to me. "You nasty Fae infiltrated Sanctuary. You know our secrets. If I ever make it out of here, I will be sure to launch a full scale war against your kind."

"That would be suicide!" Ned shouts but I place my hand on his arm to calm him.

I cock my head like I did with Talon, and I train my body to go deathly still. I figure I can appear scary enough to intimidate a man like him. I simply stand there staring at him for an inhumanly long length of time and wait.

The seconds tick by slowly. He doesn't realize I don't care how long it takes me standing here staring at him to do it, I *will* crack him. I had a feeling he was a horrible person in Sanctuary, and this little interaction has confirmed it. I will show him who holds all the cards in this little power struggle, and it isn't him.

Commander Demarco stands there staring back down at me for a while, but eventually he shows the first signs of being uncomfortable. His eyes dart around, mostly toward

Ned. Then he moves back and forth on his feet a little. Finally, his arms fall to his sides and he shouts, "What are you staring at!"

I straighten my head, lift my chin, and ever so quietly say, "A man who will never see the light of day again."

It's like his whole body becomes limp as what I just said sinks in. "You can't. You're not in charge."

I cover my face demurely and chuckle just loud enough for him to hear. I turn my head and call to Allister. "Can you come here for a second love?"

I can't help but smile broadly as he swaggers over to my side. He leans down and places a sweet kiss atop my head. Again playing the part I need him to without question. From James, I hear the "mine" growl again, but I ignore him and turn my gaze back on the commander. I bob my head toward Allister as I ask, "See this guy?"

Commander Demarco stands there quietly for a few seconds, but I wait until he gives me a verbal answer. "Yes."

"This stunning specimen of a man—"

Allister cuts me off as he happily squeaks out, "Aww, kitten. You're too sweet." He leans down and places a kiss on my cheek this time.

A snapping sound comes from James's cell.

I push on. "He is my mate. Do you know what it means to be someone's mate?"

The commander doesn't waste time this time around as he shakes his head. "No."

Allister places his hand over my shoulders and pulls me in tight as he answers for me. "It means I'm hers and she's mine."

A "mine" growl releases louder than the last few times but Demarco ignores it, so we do the same. He throws his hands up in the air and shouts, "What the hell does that matter?"

I step forward, right up next to his bars and point behind me with my thumb. "He is the heir to the Eastern Fae throne." I smile as I tilt my head and lift my shoulder like I'm the epitome of sweetness and light. "So, yes dear. I do have the authority to keep you in this shit hole smelling your own piss and shit for the rest of your short miserable life."

The commander doesn't say a word. His head merely falls to his chest, and he stays there, staring at his boots. He eventually lifts his head and calmly makes his way over to me. We're standing mere inches apart.

He stares right into my eyes, his sharp green ones glittering back into mine. I know that shimmering anger, James showed it right before he hit me, but I don't care. The man still makes me feel all oily and like I'm covered in spiders, but I'm no longer intimidated by him on any level. I'm over having to deal with him.

In a flash, he slams his hands into the bars in front of me. I saw it coming though so I don't flinch. I felt the air move around him as he moved his hand. It wasn't a big move, but it was big enough for me to know what he was planning on doing. The men behind me both take a step forward, but I lift my hand, stopping them.

I glare defiantly into those anger filled eyes, "You don't intimidate me like you once did. You don't know who you're messing with—"

He cuts me off before I can finish, "Oh yeah little girl?"

I drop my head and silently chuckle. "Oh yeah," I say as I lift my hand, holding a ball of fire. He recoils, taking a step back. I call to the ground under him, his movement stops as the stone beneath him turns into liquid and wraps around his foot. He leans down and grabs onto his leg, pulling on it. Panic crosses his features as he pulls at his leg, like a rat caught in a trap. I smile as I think of him gnawing off his own leg to get free of the trap I've created. This man deserves every bit of torture I can dole out to him. I quietly and calmly inform him, "I am the heir to Henrik's throne and the mate to the heir of the Eastern throne. You will show me respect. And if you don't, I will just have to force it out of you." I breathe life into the fireball before me making it grow to twice its original size.

I hear Ned say from behind me, "Attina..." But I ignore him.

I call to the stone wrapped around the commander's leg, making it tighten down. I watch as his eyes grow big and his mouth drops open, letting out a guttural scream. The scream brings a warm sensation to my chest right before Allister's arms are wrap around me. He places a kiss atop my head but says into my mind, *Attina stop this! What the fuck are you doing?*

I bring my free hand up and rub his arms. *Showing him his place.*

Remember when we talked about you not turning into Henrik? I drop my hand holding the fireball and its sputters out, the fire disappearing into thin air as I listen to him. *This is too far, Attina. You need him. Remember the prophecy? Stop this.*

I let out a huff of air and wrap my hand around the bars in front of me, the fire sputtering out on the cold metal. I call to the stone, and it leaves the Commander's leg before hardening back up. It matches perfectly with the stones around it again. You'd never know it had moved and turned into a malleable liquid-like substance for me.

I say to him in the most bored voice I can muster up, "Remember your place. We will talk again, and I hope when that day comes you show me some respect." I scan his body from top to bottom and notice the front of his pants are wet. I didn't realize how much I scared him. I almost feel bad, but then I remember what a jerk he is, and the feeling quickly disappears.

I lift my head, turn, and move back to James's cell. He's pushed himself into the back of his cell as far as he can and he's shaking. I'm a little surprised because he wasn't this scared of me after I burned him. If he ever turns back into a human I'll have to remember to ask him why I spooked him so badly.

"I'll come check on you in a day or two. We have some things we need to discuss, and honestly I feel like you being in a jail cell is the best place for us to discuss them." He simply continues to shake so I walk off, back towards the stairs.

I move down the hallway past a few stalls before Allister calls to me, "Attina wait!" He sprints up to and around me, so he's facing me. "There's one more prisoner you must see."

I scrunch up my face and bring my hand up, pinching the bridge of my nose. "Why? It's not like I'll know who the person is. It's probably just someone who went against these people's rules or something."

Allister shakes his head and in his eyes I can see real fear there. The only other time I've seen fear like this in him was when he was holding me after I killed the werewolf. When I was dying in his arms.

I take a step back away from him, and another. "What's happening, Allister? You're freaking me out." I point behind him toward the stairs. "I'm about ready to run up those stairs, away from whatever has you this spooked."

From behind I feel a hand grasp mine. "Well then, let's get this over with before you run away." I'm tugged back by Ned, and I stumble backwards, barely catching myself before I fall to my knees.

"What the hell, Ned!" I complain, "Where are you taking me?"

He answers, "The last stall on the left." As if it explains everything. I don't have to see Allister to know he's following us.

We make it to the last cell, but it appears empty. I lift my lamp but it's not bright enough to reach all the way back into this one. The cells on the left must be a little longer than the ones on the right. I turn to Ned, "This is what you had to show me?"

Allister strides behind him, his hands laced behind his back, his head staring at the floor. He paces and for a second my gaze swings back and forth between the two men. "What the hell is going on guys? You freaked me out," I swing my hand out to the stall to the right of me, "and all you have to show me is an empty stall?"

Allister continues pacing. "Use your magic, kitten. Then tell me if the stall is empty."

I do as he asks, focus on my magic, and feel a person's lungs in there quickly moving the air in and out of their body, like they're upset. They must be sitting on the ground because I don't feel any movement. I call out, "Who's in there? Why won't you come out and show yourself?" I stand there for a second waiting, but the only thing which changes is the person's breathing. It hitches up. They must be hyperventilating now. "I won't hurt you." I try but nothing changes.

Allister stops pacing and takes a step forward so he's right behind me, his nervous presence leaches into me.

"Attina's waited an *extremely* long time for this. After every single thing she's been through this is the least you can give her. I know you're scared, but there's no hiding from this. Come out of the shadows and say hello to your daughter, Titania."

EPILOGUE
TALA

One week prior

I stride through the open doors of the throne room. *How strange, didn't Henrik have the throne room basically locked down?* I peer at my surroundings. Fire from the lit sconces bounces off the dead bodies scattered around the room. Foreboding washes over me as I search the room. The thrones are empty, and Henrik is nowhere to be seen.

"Sire? You summoned me?"

I hear a grunt from behind the dais as Henrik's hulking body stands. He moves like standing is hard for him which is new. I saw him about a month ago and he seemed so strong and spry then, how could his body deteriorate this quickly?

As he straightens and turns toward me, I notice his white tunic is stained red with blood. He runs one of his hands through his hair, somewhat taming his messy salt and pepper locks. He shuffles around the dais until he's standing in front of me.

When he was behind the dais he seemed weak but now that I'm face to face with him, I'm not sure how I ever came to that conclusion. His broad chest takes in a deep breath, his blood red eyes lock on mine, and I almost forget myself.

I hurriedly bow before my king. My fisted hand goes to my chest, and I hang my head in reverence.

"Have you heard the news, Tala?" His voice booms against the walls around us.

"No sire." It's a lie but I don't want him to think I'm a gossip who can't be trusted.

His voice is solemn, "Talon has been captured." I suck in a loud breath, loud enough for him to hear. "I killed everyone who could have had any sort of hand in it."

My eyes drift around the room at the bloodied, broken bodies and I smirk. "Will you send Allister after him? I know he's out on a mission, but this must supersede whatever mission he's on." I really just want to know where that bastard is. He's always been the king's favorite.

I should be the favorite. I am a much better warrior than him, but I've never been able to steal that position from him.

He shakes his head, "No, I don't have proof, but I know Allister has betrayed us. I threatened to kill his mother if he betrayed me, but I guess he's fine with forfeiting her life."

I drop my head again and pound my fist against my chest. "I would never betray you, my liege."

I watch Henrik's feet as he begins pacing in front of me. "I hope not, because if you do, your blood will be splashed across my floor like these other Fae's." His feet stop in front of me again. "You are my second best slayer," I wince at the words, "this is your chance to prove yourself to me."

I lift my head. "Yes, sire, anything. What do you need me to do?"

His blazing red eyes become hooded, and his skin starts to redden. "I need you to infiltrate enemy territory."

THE END

OTHER BOOKS BY CAITLIN DENMAN

She Awakens

She Rises

She Conquers

She Reigns (Coming Soon)

ABOUT THE AUTHOR

Caitlin lives and grew up in Southern California with her family and her three horses, three dogs, and a cat. She graduated from Cal Poly Pomona with a bachelor's in agribusiness.
Besides writing, she loves training and competing on horses. She has competed in barrel racing, breakaway roping, team roping, and mounted shooting. She has owned and ridden horses since she was twelve-years-old.

Caitlin would love to connect with each and every person who loves her books. You can find her on social media here: https://linktr.ee/caitlindenmanbooks

ACKNOWLEDGEMENT

First off, I would like to thank my fans for being the best fans around. You all have been so positive and supportive and I want to thank you for that. It means a lot to me to have people out in the world as invested in Attina's journey as I am.

Next, I would like to thank my parents. I will always thank my parents in all of my books, because without them, I wouldn't be here. Without their love, support, and guidance I wouldn't be able to weave these worlds and write these stories. And thank you for always telling me when it's time to get away from the computer and take a break. I'm terrible at remembering to take a break so that reminder is appreciated.

Finally, I would like to thank everyone else who makes these books happen. Paul Smith, thank you for helping me outline this story and for being there through every meltdown I had along the way. Belle Manuel, thank you for listening to all my dramatic complaints. To my sissy, Laura Trujillo, thank you for helping me traverse the confusing social media universe and for always having my back.

Morgan Kearley, thank you for being my continued reminder that people out there love my books, it really does help push me forward. Thank you to all my BETA readers (including my Nana and Barby), for reading through all my initial mistakes and not judging me for them. Finally, thank you to Amy Briggs for continuing to fix my grammar and for polishing my story.

Made in the USA
Columbia, SC
11 May 2022